Hamba Gashle

Ian Hassall

Published by eBookIt.com

ISBN-13: 978-1-4566-1445-4

Hamba Gashle is the inside story of white society in colonial Southern Africa during the 1950s and 1960s. Ian Hassall's edgy memoir provides a vivid and disturbing depiction of childhood and family life against a background of racial exploitation, political change and the disintegration of his white community. Written as a diary from childhood through to early adulthood, the deceptively simple style provides a sense of immediacy, building a vivid picture through apparently unconnected events. The child narrator arrives in Northern Rhodesia from England aged four. Soon after, his parents divorce and he is fostered for several years. His mother marries an anti British Afrikaaner who is a strong influence on the boy. As a teenager he becomes delinquent and fails at school. He moves with his father's family to Rhodesia as it is approaching UDI. The narrator has developed anti-racist views and joins the protest movement at university in South Africa. Finally he returns to London in 1970, alone, a stranger.

Ian Hassall produces a rich and informative picture of this period, honest, critical and unflattering, attacking its racism. The work is carefully researched so that key historical events are portrayed accurately and intimately. The youthful narrator's preoccupations, adventures, sexual encounters and daydreams contrast with more sober political observations, sometimes hilariously. This is also a study of childhood, and a celebration of youth which transcends time or location.

'Hamba Gashle' means both *chameleon* and *take it easy*, because of the animal's leisurely pace. The book's title reflects the author's admiration for this wonderful creature and its attributes, some of which he required to survive his upbringing.

Contents

Mufulira December 1957 1
England January 1951 1
Mufulira 1952 11
Mufulira 1953 16
Mufulira 1954 26
Mufulira 1955 29
Mufulira 1956 35
Mufulira 1957 54
Mufulira 1958 62
Mufulira 1959 73
Mufulira 1960 77
Ndola 1961 81
Ndola 1962 87
Ndola 1963 99
Ndola 1964 111
Ndola 1965 126
Salisbury 1966 154
South Africa 1967 175
South Africa 1968 191
South Africa 1969 210
South Africa 1970 215
Glossary 223
References 237
About the Author 239

Mufulira December 1957

Everyone knows that a three year old can't write a diary so I'm doing it now for the time when I was small.

England January 1951

Granddad pushes me to the market in my wheelchair. I'm eating an iced bun. Mummy's with us for a while. A veil hangs from her hat. A woman at an upstairs window bangs on the pane with one finger, "Oi!" Mummy shouts something back. At the market they're unloading pigs from a lorry. One squeals and runs back up the ramp, he wants to go home. Two men block him.

Anne holds my face with both hands and kisses my nose. "Little brother." Her breathing smells of sweets. She squeezes my lips into a bow. "Say book." "Bfwook." She watches carefully. "Say it again."

At a lady's house we watch Renfrew and Kelly, the Mounties on her new television. Kelly is standing on a bridge and has to shoot Renfrew in the stream below. "But Mummy, Renfrew is Kelly's friend!" "Kelly has to," says Mummy.

One bright winter morning a parcel arrives from Auntie Beth in Africa. She's Daddy's sister. It's full of shiny blue slabs of Cadbury's chocolate, lined up sideways. So many! You can riffle them and they click. Africa is hot and sunny, with lots of good thing to eat.

It's Christmas Eve. Anne and I are asleep in Nanna and Granddad's house in Bethnal Green. In the middle of the night I wake, and there standing in the doorway is Father Christmas! He's holding a lantern that lights his face, and his eyes are jolly and sad, like Granddad's. Anne's staring too. He smiles, then turns and goes downstairs.

On a train, a funny man sits down. Anne says, "Mummy, why's that man got a big black face?" Mummy goes red and says, "Shush!" and to the man, "Sorry!" He smiles and his teeth are all white.

We're going to live in Africa. That's where the Aunts are. Mummy gets us a book, Tintin in the Congo. African children have black skin, fuzzy black hair, big pink lips and don't wear shirts.

I pick up a woodslice, it waves its feelers at me and curls into a ball. Daddy says, "Put that down and wash your hands, you'll get tetanus." Mummy says, "No he won't!"

Anne's being naughty. Daddy tells her off. Nanna says, "Leter be, she ain't urtin no one." So he slaps Anne hard and she screams. Nanna shouts, "I spose you'rappy now! Lookow ee paider!"

Granddad shows us the sights of London before we leave. The pigeons at Trafalgar Square sit on your head. You can feel their feet gripping, tingles down my spine. Then at the Tower of London the beefeater says he'll lock me in and I'm scared, but everyone's laughing.

Sailing April 1951

At the docks the ship above us is big, big like a building. Nanna is crying. "I'll never see my daughter again, or my grand children, and it's your fault! I wish she'd never met you!" Daddy says nothing and Granddad looks away.

On the Windsor Castle, there's more food than you can eat, fruit we've never seen before. The waiter called Mike teases us, custard and jelly and a punch in your belly. He's a Cockney like Mummy, and they're always joking together. Daddy doesn't talk to him much.

Mummy looks different, with trousers like a man, and when you look up, her legs and tummy look big. "Slacks," she says, "it's the new thing." Daddy and Anne are seasick for a week but Mummy and I are fine. We have a porthole. "Close it," Ann says, "if the water comes in the boat will sink."

Las Palmas, hot sun. The taxi drives fast along the dockside, near the sharp edge. It might go over on to the boats below. It would smash right through them and then we'd be under water. Tonight's warm, with buzzing insects. The air feels soft and smells of fruit. Mummy's putting on perfume and saying they'll be just outside having a drink. Through the upstairs window we can see red, white and green lights in the trees. Below are tables with candles. Cats sit around on the dusty ground. I've got a red racing car nearly as big as me, soft and bendy, but it pops back again. Anne has a huge pink doll made of the same stuff. "Plastic," says Daddy.

The ship has stopped in the middle of the sea. The day is dark and grey, the water like iron, full of strong black fish swirling around. Two men throw orange peel into buckets, then lower them. The fish pile in. The men pull them up and empty them on to the deck. People stand in a circle, watching. The fish flap hard, making a drumming sound, then lie still, gasping, then flap again even harder, then stop, then flap again, then stop altogether. Their eyes stare up and go dull. After a while the men throw them back into the sea.

Our next stop is St Helena. It's sunny and warm. To visit the island you have to go by small boat. As you step off the ship's ladder there's a big gap of deep, deep blue water which seems very thin. If I fall into this I'll go down and down, to the bottom. A sailor helps me on to the boat. That night I dream I'm swimming deep in the soft warm water with the fish, and can breathe.

Across the equator in the southern seas the air is hot and mixes with the thin green water. Flying fish move between the two.

Africa April 1951

The train to Northern Rhodesia is brown and cream and we have our own sleeping compartment, with a washbasin. The train pulls in to a station. There's no platform, just yellowy sand far below. I get a shock, strange dark creatures running around shouting, smoking, all dressed in brown rags. "African children, picaninnies," Daddy says, but not like the children in Tintin. Now they're jumping up and down waving to us. "Throw them some of your liquorice allsorts." No, my sweets, but I throw a handful into the dust. The children dive on them, fighting and grabbing. But they mustn't eat them off the ground! "It's all right, they're used to it," says Daddy.

At night the seats turn into beds. The train goes tiggedy tig as we fall asleep and it feels good and safe. Next morning we wake with the sun big and yellow, level with the ground, shining on off, through the trees. It's cold. Some animals are standing in an open patch. "Deer," says Mummy from above. "Buck," says

Daddy. There's a knock on the door and the train man comes in. "Mora/morning," he says, "Coffee." He talks funny. It's sweet like caramel.

Later it gets hot but the air feels soft and fresh. I have a warm easy feeling all down my body. You can hear people talking and laughing along the corridor, bright and clear. I go through the carriage making friends. If you lean out of the window you can see the engine when the track curves, and hear it chuffing, but you get soot in your eyes. The trees have flat tops and the ground is red. Slowly, as the sun sets we cross the Victoria Falls, you can hear its roar. "The black North," says a man to Daddy.

Northern Rhodesia April 1951

It's late afternoon at the Aunts' house in Ndola. Auntie Mary rings a little bell and a black man, Thompson, comes from the kitchen with drinks. He's dressed in a white uniform with a red fez like the waiters on the train and he smiles a lot. Auntie Beth calls him the houseboy. The room is dark with white walls and wooden carvings. I'm scared of a face with real teeth. "It's a mask from the Belgian Congo," says Auntie Mary. That's Tintin's Congo in the middle of Africa, only ten miles away.

Daddy's working for Costains in Chingola, building houses and roads. He says, "We're carving a town right out of the bush." We live in a rondavel, the toilet is outside down a path. It has grass walls and is called the PK. Your poo drops far down and bugs eat it. For toilet roll we use newspaper cut into squares. We have hurricane lamps and candles. Everything smells of paraffin and tar and petrol.

I watch the bush being cleared. Some anthills are twice as big as our rondavel. They're hard red mud and need to be soaked before the bulldozers can break them down. You have to put in a hosepipe for more than a week because there are also underground tunnels. Yesterday I watched one being filled. Suddenly the African workers shouted "Nyoka!" A big black snake came out, and went straight at them, head steady, body zigzagging. They yelled and scattered and it disappeared into the bush, its tail flicking. "Black mamba," said the boss man. Then they bulldozed the anthill and there were all sorts of things like spiders and snake eggs and toads.

Daddy drives a Ford van with a long gear lever that wobbles in time to the engine. It smells of old leather. His boss is called Len Brand and he visits quite often in the evening. This morning he came for tea with us while Daddy was at work, and helped Mummy fix a shelf. We're moving to Mufulira. Daddy will work on the mine. Everybody says Muoff but Daddy says Muff like someone muffled up.

Mufulira October 1951

We're in a camp of rondavels, and the toilets and showers are in the latrine block. There's real toilet paper and electricity. In the evening hundreds of insects fly around the light at the corner. Two cats sit below steadily crunching their way through those that fall. Daddy stands nearby smoking, and talking to the other men, I sneak off with some children to play in the dark. Then we go to dinner in the mine mess over the road. In there it's bright and you can eat all you want. Natives are human beens but they're not europeens. We're europeens but not human beens or something like that. Everyone talks about the colour bar. The bar at the club is brown wood, but it's not that.

Ndola October 1951

Mummy and Daddy say there isn't enough room for Anne and me in the rondavel so we have to go to boarding school at the convent in Ndola, forty miles away. Why? Lots of children stay in the rondavels. When we get to the convent I cry and try to hide under the car seat but Daddy pulls me out by one leg. It hurts. I'm sure if I beg him properly he'll bring me home but he won't listen. He seems cross. I'm sick all over their parlour carpet.

Some nuns are nice. Sister Fortunata brings out a big wooden tray of toothpaste tubes and lets me choose my own. I feel important and take a yellow type we don't use at home. Everything else is new too, your own soap and face cloth, with their own smells. I tap my new soap against the wall and sniff it. I'm four, the youngest in the school. It's mainly a girls' school with only a few boys, the next one up is seven.

Breakfast is horrible, mealie meal porridge with lumps. I'm in the infants, ay be see dee ee ef gee, aich eye jay kay elo meno pee, the rest doesn't go. Halfway through the morning we have a lollipop and then a little sleep. In the afternoons I'm left on my own and wander round the grounds. I play with the canna seeds, like rosary beads, you get white ones and then they turn black and hard and click together. They say the lantana berries are poisonous but still I eat them. Now when I look at a lantana bush I feel sick. I sit playing with the ants and yesterday one bit me high on my leg. When I walk around I count my steps but try not to. And as the sun goes down I feel sad.

Some afternoons I sit in the grotto. There's a big statue of the Virgin Mary in a blue cloak and white dress, with a soft pink face. She looks kind and sad and a bit like she cares, and I feel better after a while.

By the dormitory wall the big boys have made stick garages in the sand for their dinks. This afternoon I walked past and kicked them all down. I liked the crunchy feel. A girl saw me from a window and then the boys were out to get me. I heard them shouting "Bloody monkey!" and thought of a grey one with a sad face and blood on its fur. The Garden Sister called me across and hid me behind the compost heap. It smells good. She's fat and kind and talks like a German. "Vy dit you do it my boy?" "I don't know," I said. I don't know. Tonight they're going to get me. Sister stops the boys hitting me and says she'll punish me herself. She whacks me on my bottom with the patch - patch. I don't cry so she hits me again.

We say prayers every night, holding our hands straight together, but the sisters fold their fingers and click their rosaries. We're all scared of ghosts. Anne said that last night, after lights out, they heard a tapping sound. It moved round their dorm from bed to bed. It stopped with Jane, then she felt a tug on her blanket and something heavy tried to slide in with her, she could feel its weight. The girls started screaming and the nuns came in. They told the girls to pray, it must be a poor soul lost in purgatory, looking for help and comfort. Now I put my head under the blankets when the lights go off. Sometimes, to cheer myself I think of Father Christmas. He's jolly and looks a bit like Granddad, surrounded by light and presents. But it's most spooky in the afternoon when sometimes I'm put down to sleep in the dorm all by myself. Yesterday when I woke, a mango had gone mushy in my pocket and I couldn't get my hand in. Sister was cross.

We're at the side of the building nearest the road. Anne's looking round the corner, nobody's there, she's going to run away. "Come with me, please, please!" she begs. I think I will, and then I won't, I want to be a good boy this time. She runs off.

She's back. I don't know how but she got to the Aunts' house and hid under Auntie Mary's bed. Thompson gave her milk and a biscuit but told Auntie Mary when she came home. Auntie Mary brought her back though she said she didn't want to. At assembly today a girl had to drink a whole glass of soapy water for lying. They say that's a venial sin. She stood in front of everybody and then was sick into a bucket a sister was holding. But Anne didn't have to because it wasn't a proper sin. She got the patch-patch. She wants to be a Catholic. She likes the holy medals and sticky pictures you get for good work.

Mummy and Daddy visit us every three weeks on a Sunday. They take us to the park and the Aunts. The Aunts don't visit us in between, I don't know why, because they're always pleased to see us. I feel happy in the morning but halfway through the afternoon I get sad, and then a kind of gripping feeling in my chest and stomach because I know we have to go back at four o'clock.

It's near Christmas, and we've all got to dress up and sing songs for when our parents come. Mine is "Twinkle twinkle little star" and I'm singing it for some sisters in the dorm after prayers. They're being nice, and say I have a good voice. Then they go off. One who I don't know stays a little longer. She pulls back the elastic of my pyjamas trousers and shines a torch on my thingy. We both see it in the yellow light. Then she lets go and walks off without looking at me.

Christmas day. Father Christmas has brought me a big blue cap gun. Mummy gives me a shoe box to keep it in, and Daddy lets me have a greasy cloth and a screwdriver to fix it. I keep all my spare caps in there, and even some used ones to give it the right smell. I put on my cowboy suit and go outside. Early morning, warm, silent, with heavy blue rain clouds, the ground's wet, the grass higher than my head and covered with dew. A dog barks far off and an echo hangs in the air. On the ground I notice eight tiny eggs, small as my smallest fingernail, white but just pinkish, joined in pairs, and all hatched. Then a ray of sun breaks through and lights up the bush above, and there in a glow I see the tiniest neatest baby chameleon, green, all in its own world. Then I see another, and, as the sun touches them, six altogether. I run inside to get a box for them. Dad comes out. He seems kind of sad though he's smiling, and puts his hand on my head. "Well look at that!" he says, "Let's just leave them as they are."

New Year's Eve. Anne and I are sleeping in Uncle Richard's flat just over the road from the mine club. The grown – ups are at the New Year's dance. I wake up late to the sound of pops and bangs like fireworks. Then Mummy and Daddy and lots of people arrive, all jolly and talking loud and smelling of party. Uncle Richard takes a long brown gun from a cupboard and gives a revolver to another man. We go outside and they start shooting in the air. Other men come out of their flats and do the same. The sound of guns echoes round the town.

Mufulira 1952

Mummy and Daddy have moved into a DK near the club but we still have to go to boarding school. In the holidays we play in the garden. I've built a mine with a rope and bucket going down. Julius the garden boy helped me. My fort was our packing case from England. The man next door has a shed built into the side of an anthill, with a door on it.

I play with Billy who's seven and Alfie who's five. They live over the road. Anne plays with their big sister Jenny. Mum says they're rough, straight out from England, and make their tea in the water they use to boil eggs. Their dad Mr Turner has a big face. He eats with his mouth open and was a soldier fighting the creans but was wounded. He never talks to us or even looks at us. We play attacking creans with our dink jet fighters. I want to play Germans but they don't. Sometimes their little brother Pookie goes mad, screaming and swearing at his mother. I think he hit her because she has a black eye. Yesterday we sneaked into a garden to eat some strawberries. Wow! So good!! A woman chased us away, shouting, "Little brats!"

Alfie and I built an elephant trap for the little girl next door, a hole covered with sticks and leaves and then guided her towards it. She fell in and cut her knee and started to cry. Mrs Turner came running out and started whacking Alfie, then told mummy and she hit me too, lots of times. Then she started hitting me all over again.

It's the holidays. We go where we like. One day we came to a castle with high wooden walls. We climbed in, there were furs and horns all around. They smell of dead animals but we took some home and hid them in my mine. The castle is full of cows. Yesterday we saw them killing one. They got it between two sloping metal gates and put a kind of gun to its head then shot it. It staggered around clanketty clank on the metal floor but didn't quite fall because of the gates. All the other cows started moving around and mooing with big eyes. Then the men saw us and chased us away.

Today we were playing cowboys and Indians in a vlei. We lit a fire like cowboys do, and were sitting round it when two old mfazis came along barefoot, with big white enamel bowls on their heads. They stopped. "Ahh, Ahh!" said one, looking cross or maybe surprised. "Eh, eh!" said the other, shaking her head, like we were naughty. They looked at us for a moment, then one knelt down and scooped the fire to one side with a hard black hand. She took some sweet potatoes from the bowl, put them onto the ashes, and pulled the fire back over them. "Puza !" she said, pretending to put something into her mouth. Then suddenly her face cracked into a big grin and she patted our heads in a rough way, and the two women walked off laughing and joking.

Some days we go to the mine club. It's big and exciting, you can get lost if you sneak down the back corridors. There's a bioscope, café, hairdresser, bottle store, badminton and lots of other things. Uncle Richard is the barman and gives us free cokes. We take them outside in the hot sun and shake them and put stones in so they froth over. The men who always sit outside the snooker room act in the Saturday afternoon cowboy films, I recognise the short one with the sad face. When I tell him they all roar with laughter and sometimes give us a susu for the shop.

Mummy is peeling me an apple in the lounge of the DK. She gets it all off in one springy ring which looks so good I eat it. "What's the point of me peeling it then?" "Don't know," I say. Then Zachariah brings in a letter. "We have a real house!" Mummy's kind of crying, "L84, it's up above town!"

Now we're going to leave the convent and live at home with Mummy and Daddy, and I'm going to Mary Moffatt school with real ladies teaching me, not nuns. They'll be just like Mummy's friends and won't shout at us. Anne's going to Muf Primary. We're all happy.

It's my first day at Mary Moffat. We sing "All things bright and beautiful, all teachers great and small." Then, "There is a green hill far away without a city wall." Why should it have one anyway? The teachers aren't as nice as I thought.

I've been to hospital because I cut my hand on some glass. Some big boys said they were going to lock up Anne and Jenny, they took them into a room and shut the door. I got upset and hit one of the windows. It broke and cut my hand. Mum tried to take me to hospital but I hid under the bed so Uncle Richard came and offered me a beer if I would go. After hospital we went to the club and he bought me my own bottle of Castle Lager, but I think he drank some of it.

Then yesterday I set the garden on fire and burned the grass all down one side. It was just after lunch and hot. The boys were in the kia and mum was lying on her bed reading like she always does. I felt lonely. I lit a little fire to heat a closed tin with water in, to see if it would explode. But the grass was dry brown and as high as my pants and soon the fire spread. I tried to stamp it out but it was eina on my feet so I went inside to get water, but by the time I came out the fire was all over the place. Julius the garden boy came running with a hosepipe and so did the lady next door. Mum came out and called me, but I knew I'd get smacked so I ran off and hid under a culvert. Then I wandered down town and got lost. In the evening a native brought me home on his shoulder, and mum was so upset she snatched me from him, and then felt bad all the next day because she hadn't thanked him or given him anything.

Now Mum's one of those horrible ladies with fat tummies and funny clothes who waddle around. I ask her if she could stop being like that. "Don't you know, it's because I'm having a baby?" she asks. "It's in my tummy, that's why I look fat." "How will you get it out?" "I'll have an operation." What? What about in cave-men times? I ask Dad. He says, "You know women are different from men between the legs?" "Yes," I say, but I don't like how he says it. "Well babies come out from there."

I don't like school much. I can't read or write. Miss Meggitt the headteacher came into our class to look at my writing. I tried to cover it up but she moved my hand and said "Write cat, dog." Everyone was watching. Then she took me by the top of my arm, and led me out to the dunces' class. Dad tries to teach me. We read the same page every day. I wish I was clever like Anne, she's always reading books and she writes all neat.

It's a play lesson. The teacher wouldn't let Anne Davies go to the toilet, so she's wet her pants. She sits with her head on the desk, a pool of yellow wee stretching across the floor. We boys fly over it in our plasticine planes talking into our hands with metal voices, "Roger, just crossing the Zambezi, over and out!"

Remembrance Sunday. We're at the service outside the club, opposite the bioscope. Everyone's standing to attention. Over there are 30 black soldiers with a white officer, and over here about 30 white police reservists, including Dad and Uncle Richard, trying not to look at us. It's funny to see Dad being ordered about. "They just about balance each other," says Mom. "Who do you mean?" asks Auntie Rene and giggles.

Christmas is coming. It's the rainy season and the dark skies give it that Christmassy feel. Nanna has sent me and Anne each a postal order for one pound. We go and change them at the post office for crisp green pound notes with the king's head. Straight away Anne starts working out what she should buy and worrying that she won't have enough. I feel rich like I can buy anything. She goes off on her own.

In Kingstons the bookshop the annuals gleam, shiny with Oor Wullie's smiling face, and on the Dandy Monster Comic, Korky the cat with all his toys. Then in Mclellands the big store on the corner I look at the dinks. It's so hard to choose, a chunky green Land Rover with a yellow driver and big white tyres for 5/-, a blue snouty nosed lorry, racing cars. The other big shop over the road, Thom Stores has the best silver dink planes like a Viking for 3/6 or a York Airliner. In the end I buy Mum a china alsatian for 2/6, and Dad some Vaseline hair oil for 5/- from Holdsworths the Chemist. I'll get my dinks after Christmas.

Christmas Day. The Aunts have came from Ndola, then Uncle Richard and two other men, and they're all sitting outside drinking and smoking and talking.

The garden is just cleared bush with tall African trees. Some blacks have just come up the drive, two boys and two picannins, singing and playing kaffir songs on guitars made of petrol cans and fishing line. They get a tickey from everyone except Auntie Mary who gives them a shilling, then they go to the next house. "You're too soft with them May," says Dad. "Ya man," says Uncle Oscar, "give them an inch and they'll take a bloody mile." Then Zachariah comes to the door and says, "Medem, de food is ready," and we go in for lunch. As the sun sets you can hear the drums playing in Kansuswa compound. "Gives me the creeps," says Mum.

Mufulira 1953

It's great being at home in a real house. Anne and I fight a bit but sometimes we play. The garden's full of big puddles. She uses the purple banana flowers as boats, and loads the yellow baby bananas as treasure. They sail off across the puddle, with matebele ants or beetles as passengers, sometimes a big chongololo trying to get out and swaying the boat. I have to play nicely with her, but after a while when she's bored she lets me bomb them from the air with clods of mud, using my dink planes.

Everyone's talking about the coronation. The king's dead and the princess is getting crowned. All the shops have red, white and blue decorations, and flags are everywhere. I have one and I'm allowed to iron it myself. Mum's Woman's Own has pictures of the Princess. She's pretty. When no one's looking I kiss her. Peter and Alfie have a rhyme

"Red, white and blue
The dirty Kangaroo
Sat behind the dustbin
Doing number two."

In Mclellands you can buy a gold toy coronation coach pulled by white horses. Mum buys it for me though I'd rather have the dink Landrover. I'm not meant to play with it outside but Alfie comes round and soon we're racing it through the mud. We put a praying mantis in the carriage and pretend it's the prince. One day we all line up in the drive at Mary Moffat and an important man gives us each a copper coloured medal with the new queen's head on.

Near our house is the echo tunnel. You can walk down it quite a few blocks, I can easily stand up, and sometimes you see bats and dead snakes. Cats go there to have their kittens. Lots of boys go down there. Dad says it's a storm drain. Once a big boy said Alfie had broken his paper watch and that he and his friends were going to hang us from one of the grills. They tied our hands and told us we were going to die. Then they said they'd let us off if we went to my house and got them some biscuits. When we got out I said "Why don't we go and tell my mom or just not go back?" But Alfie said it was onna and we had to.

Gleny's getting quite big now, and sits up. Yesterday he tugged a cord and pulled the wireless off the mantelpiece. It just missed him, and Mum was cross with Dad, I don't know why. Last night they were arguing in the kitchen while we were in bed. Mum was saying, "You just take me for granted." Anne put her hands over her ears and her face looked like something was sore.

Mum's gone to live with the Holmes at the top end of H Avenue and she's taken Gleny with her. I asked why we weren't going and she said the Holmes can't have us all. Dad's got to move into single quarters near the mine so we're going to live with some people called the Gearys in M86, just across the back lane. They've got a boy of eight called Chris, and girls of six and five called Jessie and Bertha.

The first night we sat down to dinner, Anne was telling the Gearys about her Enid Blyton books like the Faraway Tree. She thinks there's a magic circle and entrance to fairyland under a tree in L84 so she doesn't want to move. Uncle Oscar started teasing her and saying there's no such thing as fairies so she said, "Then Father Christmas isn't real either, how can he come all the way from England to Muf in one night?" So Bertha said, "Isn't he Daddy?" So Uncle Oscar told Anne to "Shut up!" about Father Christmas because there are small children around so Anne said, "Well you shut up about fairies!" and threw some rice at him from her plate. So now they won't have her and she's gone back to Ndola convent.

The Gearys are from South Africa. In the afternoons Auntie Elsie makes us a slice of bread and syrup, and we get one toffee every day. There's an ice box to keep food cool. Each morning the garden boy takes the wheel barrow to J Avenue to meet the ice lorry and brings back a big block to put in the top of the ice box. Dinner's at night instead of lunchtime like with Mum, and the food is a bit different, lots of sweet mashed pumpkin, and rice in a little pile like it's a normal vegetable. You have to wash your face and comb your hair before you come to table. It feels nice and cosy in the yellow light of the kitchen. Every Friday we get a Beecham pill to clean us out.

Uncle Oscar works underground, he's a ganger in charge of some blacks and blows up the rock with dynamite. He goes off to work with his choler box, and brings home cheesa sticks to start the fire in the kitchen. Chris and I pinch them. Yesterday we took the gunpowder out of one and stuffed it into a log and hit it with a hammer. It exploded so hard the hammer flew out of Chris's hand and his thumb is still sore. Uncle Oscar fights with us on the carpet, or makes us fight and gives instructions while he sits and drinks Lion lager. Today Auntie Elsie was cross because he and Chris sneaked into the kitchen and poured extra curry powder into the pot from the yellow tin, and nobody could eat it except him. When he eats curry the sweat pours off his bald head which he wipes with his grey handkerchief.

Uncle Oscar catches a fly on the window sill. It's something he's heard about at work. He takes Auntie Elsie's tweezers and holds it under water. Auntie Elsie says, "Don't use my tweezers!" Uncle Oscar's busy, breathing heavily while we crowd around him. The fly struggles and struggles, I hold my breath and feel its suffering but kept telling myself it's only a fly. After a long time it stops moving and Uncle Oscar takes it out, it lies there in a pool of water. Then he sprinkles salt over it and in a couple of seconds it starts twitching, then stands up, back to life!

Then Saturday afternoon is the big race! Uncle Oscar weighs over 220 pounds and there's this man, Mr Vrity, who's also quite short and even fatter. They don't like each other, and instead of a fight they agreed to a race, one hundred yards, with a five pound bet. The race is along the road outside the swimming pool. Hundreds of people are there, on both sides of the road, and a bookie is taking bets. I bet Mr Vrity's son 2/6 that Uncle Oscar will win. Both men are showing off, making muscles, bowing and fooling around. Then a man fires a gun and they're off. I can't believe it, Mr Vrity shoots ahead and wins easily! Uncle Oscar goes a funny colour and can't get his breath. He hasn't practised at all, and Dad said he shouldn't be running because most miners have dust in their lungs or even phthisis.

Most nights we go out in the Gearys' Vanguard to see friends. When it gets dark we play skop die blik in the garden. We smaak crawling around in the dark and sneaking up on the block. You feel like a spook or a wild animal. The girls won't, they're poep scared of snakes and spiders. Later Chris and I sneak off into other people's gardens and pinch fruit, or play tic toc, or roof rattle, or spy through their windows. But sooner or later we fall asleep behind the couch, wishing we could go home, but the grown ups go on and on drinking and smoking and talking.

Uncle Errol's got a space ship, which he flies to Venus. I say I've got one too, it flies to Mars. "Where's it then?" he asks. "In the bush," I say, I can see it there, gleaming silver. He says the creatures on Venus are like big spiders, he runs his fingers up my back and into my hair and I get a bit scared. Later that night I go outside and flash my torch at the sky in a signal. Chris says, "That's rubbish, you haven't got a spaceship." "Yes I have!" Then I think, "Have I?" I'm not sure any more. Oh, no I haven't.

Midday I sit on the Gearys' back step in the hot hot sun. The yard is dry sand and the dog's dish is covered in hundreds of flies. I whack them with the swatter that's always at the back door, you can't miss, and soon the red plastic is gooey with mashed bodies and blood. Then I wander round the yard, the sand burning my feet, paw paw trees full of green and yellow fruit, banana trees running along the back fence. The dog lies in the sand under the avocado tree, too lazy to move, and some fowls sit nearby, flicking sand under their wings. They're from next door and live in one of the neighbour's wrecked cars. In the evening huge fruit bats arrive.

Each day I catch the school bus from H Avenue, near where we lived. Yesterday I suddenly decided to go up and see Mom. Why not? I had to. There she'd just be, my own Mom! So I ran all the way, and she was just getting ready to go to work at the Co-op. She seemed kind of pleased but a bit shocked. She said I would be late for school and she was late for work and I mustn't do it again. Gleny was smiling and laughing and cuddling me. He started to scream and cry when I tried to go. They had to pull him off me.

Chris and I collect stompies from the ashtrays and empty the tobacco into a Marmite jar. Then we collect dry granadilla leaves from outside, and mix it all up and go into the echo tunnel to make newspaper cigarettes. It's the newspaper that hurts the back of your throat because ordinary cigarettes don't. Sometimes we get OK cigs, made for kaffirs, tickey for a packet of ten or three for a penny. Uncle Oscar says we mustn't smoke, "It stunts your growth, maybe that's why you're such a kafupi." He says, "Have a drag," then when you try, he puts his finger in the way, then he pokes your chest and says, "There's something on your shirt," and when you look down he taps your nose, not hard with his yellow stained tobacco smelling finger, sometimes I bite it, then he says, "Come on, fight me," and I punch him as hard as I can in the belly but it doesn't hurt him, then he throws me up on his shoulders..

Dad comes to see me nearly every day. He's got a big bike and cycles very slowly with me on the cross bar. He says four o'clock after work but he's always late. Auntie Elsie gets me clean then I sit on the swing by the bamboos, I mustn't get dirty so I just sit. We go to town or the pool or the club. Today a man asked, "How many kids you got?" "Just the two," Dad said, "The boy here, and a girl." "But Dad!" I said, "You've forgotten Gleny!" That night I wouldn't go back to the Gearys. Dad handed me over to Auntie Elsie and I was kicking and yelling, and gave her a big bruise on the leg.

Last night one of the Gearys' friends came round, his eyes all red. I've never seen a man cry before. His baby boy Johny who's about two has cerebral malaria. Tonight Johny died, he was fine the day before yesterday. Now we've got to be extra careful to spray our bedrooms ten minutes before we go to bed, but you don't usually get malaria in town. The mine boys come round all the time spraying puddles and everything with DDT. I've been in hospital twice with headaches and puking, last time they kept me in for a week and looked at my blood and poo. They thought it was malaria or sunstroke but couldn't find anything. Uncle Oscar says, "It's because you're still a bit of a soft soutie but you'll get used to our African bugs."

Dad's got a car, an old brown Morris Oxford. Now when I sit on the swing I can hear him coming as the engine kind of dies when he changes gear at the corner, then builds up again. A few days ago he said he wanted to pick somebody up on the way to the club and guess who, Miss Ackermann my teacher! I was so shocked I didn't know what to say. She was really nice to me, and seemed different from at school, like a real person, but I soon went outside to play. Then today in school I couldn't find my exercise book, so she opened my desk, and there it was under a few others. She was cross as usual and hit me round the head with it. When I told Dad he said, "Aha!" like he was surprised but not so surprised. Now, sometimes on Sunday mornings, we visit a lady called Eileen, a nurse with a pretty face. Usually other men are there too. As one left he sang, "Good night Eileen, goodnight Eileen, I'll see you in my dreams."

Some Sundays we go to Ndola to see the Aunts. As you leave Muf, the bush at the side of the road has been cut down, and charcoal is being made in ovens that look like native huts, but with mud all the way up. Natives buy it for cooking. There are also big piles of logs which are sold to us Europeans for our stoves. After that there's elephant grass higher than a man, tall trees and big dead snakes on the road. People say if you run over a live mamba it can get caught up under the car and bite you when you stop. Out of town Dad lets me stand and steer. Sometimes a tribe of baboons crosses the road. On the way back at night you can see the eyes of animals if the headlights shine into the bush. Dad says there are still leopards around. Anne was at the Aunts. I gave her a big hug. I miss her. She's got nowhere to go in the holidays because she can't stay in Dad's single quarters, so sometimes she stays with the Aunts, and sometimes with friends and sometimes at school for a bit.

Last Saturday Chris and I were walking down J Avenue when we saw a kaffir boy of about fifteen with a young grey monkey. It clutched his legs in fear when a car went past. We bought it for 17/6 and put it in the cage Chris had used for a mongoose. Auntie Elsie said it's cruel. But Uncle Oscar and the garden boy put up a tall pole in the yard with a little house on top, and then attached a long wire to the monkey's waist and to a ring round the pole, so it can run on the ground and climb to its house. We play with it. It stuffs extra food into cheek pouches, and looks like it's got mumps. If you squat and go up and down, raising your eyebrows and going, "Ugh, ugh, ugh," it gets cross, then does the same thing and tries to bite you. But if you sit with it quietly and put your head down it starts feeling around in your hair, picking bits of skin to put in its mouth and saying, "Tch, tch, tch, tch." It feels nice, I get goose pimples down my neck.

Lots of boys have animals, a few nights ago we were visiting the Engelbrechts and Jannie took us to his bedroom with the lights off. He switched on a torch and flashed it round. There clinging to one of the curtains was a nagapie, with huge eyes and long fingers. It started bouncing round the room, trying to hide and smashing into things. "Trouble is it shits all over the place, and the kaffir's getting the moerin and moaning to Ma. Pa says I got to get rid of it, so we're taking it to the bush tomorrow."

Mom's moved into J135 with Uncle Richard. He says I must just call him Richard now. Mom says Glen's crying for me. He goes to bed with my old jersey and cuddles it, and I must come to visit them, so Dad starts dropping me off . He and Mom sometimes talk but she always ends up crying. He never picks Glen up or takes him out, but he bought him a Christmas present, a grey plastic warship with wheels. "That's to keep *you* happy!" Mom says. But Glen left it out on the drive and Richard ran it over by mistake.

It's Sunday afternoon at the Gearys and we've just had lunch, the only time they have a big meal in the day time. Auntie Elsie and Uncle Oscar have gone for their Sunday snooze, they say it's 40 degrees, and we must rest, but we sneak out. It's moer of a hot. The tar on the road is soft, and we have to walk on the grass. If you go back inside it seems dark and you can't see anything for a minute. We go to the garden boy's kia where he and his friend are sitting on the step, cooking lunch. There's a big kaffir pot on a fire, with boiling water, and Jason is slowly pouring in more and more mealie meal, stirring it until it's thick and goes plob, plob. At the side is an enamel dish of hot relish. I ask, "Ini ena kuna lapa pakaati?" He says, "Lo ma tomati, futi lo," and points to a sack of dried black caterpillars. "Ena mushi?" asks Chris. "Ee, eh, mushi sterek, wena funa pusa bietchan?" "Ya," we say though we're not meant to eat kaffir food. You pick up a ball of mealie meal, make a dent in it with your thumb and then dip it in the relish. Yow! Only tastes good!

Anne can stay with Mom now in the holidays. But Richard keeps on getting cross with her so she can't come back and live in Muf for good. She says she wants to be a film star when she grows up, or maybe a trapeze artist.

Mom's sitting in the garden, and me and Len Maritz are playing around. Len dive tackles me and I go down. "Don't hurt him Lenny!" says Mom all cozy like I'm some kind of cripple thing, and "Lenny" her son, or the son she wants, then she hugs him when he goes. She doesn't understand, he's bigger than me but we fight like that all the time.

I walk around the garden flying one of my dink planes and holding a shuttlecock to my mouth saying "Roger, angels 30, diving!" I'm the test pilot in "Sound Barrier". When the jet dives to build up speed, it starts to shake and lose control. The pilot looks frightening in his mask with its dog's nose, his eyes strange as he tries to pull the plane out of the dive. He pulls and pulls and he's sweating with fear, but the plane crashes straight into the ground, making a big bang and a huge hole. I fall on the ground. His wife comes and stands looking in, crying. The pilot's friend comes up to her and puts his arm around her. She smiles at him through her tears and puts her head on his shoulder. The end

Today we had an important visitor at the school, the great – nephew of David Livingstone, Mary Moffat's husband. I was expecting a tall thin man with that famous cap, but he was just a short bald South African in ordinary clothes. He talked mainly about how David Livingstone had discovered the Victoria Falls, and had died of diseases in darkest Africa amongst savages he had tried to save. Yet here we are now, less than 75 years later, living where he had walked, in a modern civilised town, bright and healthy, with a great future.

Mufulira 1954

I've moved to the big school, Mufulira Primary, just next to Mary Moffat. It's all brown brick. I'm in 1C, the lowest class, Jessie's in 1A, Chris's two classes above, in 3C. Auntie Elsie asks Jessie to help him learn his homework because he's been getting bad marks. They practise a few times, "The camel is the ship of the desert," he says, like it's a fact. Some boys call him "Dozy arab", but they have to be careful. They can shove him a few times and he won't fight or say or do anything, but if they push him too far, a kind of switch goes on, and then he'll lay into them and nothing's gonna stop him, it'll take three or four boys to drag him off. But though he's twice as strong as I am he would never hurt me, like a big brother.

He's always toughening me up. Yesterday at the pool we were playing board touchers, whoever's "on" chases you onto the boards and you jump or dive off. I was scared to jump off the 3 metre board. "Don't be a baby it's only 9 foot," said Chris. "OK I'll give you a dink if you do it." So I jumped off, and after that I couldn't stop. Next week I'm going to get another dink if I jump off the high board, twenty-seven foot. School ends at 1.00 and most afternoons we go to the pool, by bike, just in shorts, no shirts, cozzies over our heads, towels round our necks. We used to play in the baby pool, sitting under the fountain or crawling around like crocodiles, but now it's the big pool, bombing each other, fighting on a tractor tyre, or seeing how long we can stay under water. Sometimes big water scorpions float at the deep end but we just stay away from them. The teenagers sit on the grass holding hands and get cross if you splash them. Uncle Oscar says we're so brown we look like a bunch of coolies, except I've got blue eyes.

Chris also thinks I'm soft with animals. The birds sit high in the tallest trees because the kaffirs hunt them, and we shoot up at them with catties. Yesterday morning I hit one and it came tumbling down, what a surprise, what a thrill! I picked it up, alive, so beautiful, red and black. It didn't move much, just looked at me. And then I saw a big bloody patch under its wing. "It's suffering, it's suffering!" I cried. "So?" said Chris, "What did you expect?" He took it from me, and suddenly pulled its head off. "There," he said, "now it's not suffering." We also shoot at blue-skops sitting half way up the trees, and if you hit them their derms all come out, so now I miss on purpose, but I don't say.

A few days ago I went to play with James who lives in L Avenue. His younger sister was there, and one of the Swanepoel girls who's in our year and lives near Mom. We started playing hide and seek in the house, the girls had to hide. I easily found the Swanepoel girl under the kitchen table. "You have to come to the block in Estelle's room," I said. She didn't want to but I pulled her by the arm because that was the rule. When we arrived I got a shock, Estelle had no clothes on and was rubbing herself up against James. She made the Swanepoel girl take all her clothes off and lie on the bed. James took her ankles and started moving her legs apart and together. He had his glasses on and looked kind of like a doctor as he examined her. She started saying "No, stop!" Then they said to me, "Your turn." "Don't," she said, "or I'll tell my mom and she'll tell your mom." A shock of cold fear went through me. "Let's stop," I said and James agreed. I was scared for a few days but nothing happened so I've cheered up. Today on the bus I asked him, "Why don't we play that game again, just with your sister?" But he looked worried and said, "No, better not."

A dog's just bitten me. My leg's bandaged but my foot's purple and the bite is eina seer! I was in the road with Lassie, the Gearys' collie when a whole pack of dogs came round and started to climb on her. They had their thingies hanging out, big and red. So I started kicking them and trying to get them off her and they started growling and then one snarled with its teeth all showing, and they went for me. I fell over and one snapped at my throat, but then the garden boy and some other blacks came and chased them off. I thought I was alright but then saw some big holes in my leg. Auntie Elsie took me to the hospital, and the doctor gave me a tetanus injection, and said I'd have the scars for life. The garden boy said it was one of the Bergers' ridgebacks so I won't need rabies injections because it's been vaccinated. That's good, you get them in your stomach, lots of them, ow! I'm off school, so Auntie Elsie went to town and got me some sweets, a Captain Marvel comic and some of those old fashioned marbles that you can't see through, with swirly patterns. Then she put her arm round me and kissed my head, and I felt good. Nobody else cuddles me, not even Mom. Mr Berger came round with a big 2/6 slab of chocolate. He teaches boxing and said I can have some free lessons when I'm better.

I saw her today, smiling from the back of her school bus, and when I see her I get this warm feeling and everything seems different. She has dark eyes and black hair and soft brown arms, and when she smiles my chest and throat go tight and I know I couldn't talk to her. I can hardly say what she looks like because she's at the centre of a kind of glow, but I'm happy when she's near. I think she's in the year above and she probably hasn't noticed me, and if she did she'd see me as just a little kid. But I daydream about her, rescuing her from snakes, or from a pit in the bush, and sometimes when I'm in bed, when the rain is rattling on the tin roof, and the thunder crashes, I hold the pillow and imagine cuddling and protecting her and whispering in her ear.

Mufulira 1955

Buildings are going up everywhere, with the smell of new cement, and Chris and I like playing in them, climbing up to the ceilings and walking across the planks. At first the kaffir watchmen chase us away but some gradually stop bothering. Yesterday evening when Auntie Elsie threw away a vanilla essence bottle we filled it with Uncle Oscar's brandy and took to it an old native guarding some new buildings by the Buffalo Hall. He was cooking cane rats, hunted with his bow and arrows and a skinny kaffir dog. The arrow tips are from ordinary nails, hammered flat into fantastic shapes, some with three barbs. We got his bow, with a buckskin string, and three arrows, for the brandy and 2/6. He said he'd make another one for me for the same price. Kaffirs aren't allowed to buy hard drinks like whisky and brandy in case it sends them mad, so they always want it.

In assembly we sing hymns, "My father for another night of quiet sleep and rest," and I think how happy I am when sometimes Dad lets me stay the night in his single quarters, EF7 on a Friday or Saturday night. It's so close to the mine you can hear it humming, and it's good to lie in bed listening to it. The single quarters are in rows off the road, you just drive up to your door across the open ground. Dad's houseboy is called Make, and he works for a few other men too. Mr Cloete says, "Ya, he must make my bed, make tea, make my lunch, so we call him Make." Make's always asking about England. He says he wants to go and live there, but doesn't seem to understand the distance, or what sea is. "You go by boat, to cross the big water, lo makulu manze." I don't know the word for sea, if there *is* one. "Yes like the Kafue," says Make. "No, no it's not a river, it's like a swimming pool, or a puddle but bigger than from here to Ndola, to Lusaka, to Johannesburg." I draw it in the sand. "Eh, eh, no, you cannot have so much water, you are joking." "Wena cluma munga."

Last Saturday morning when Dad had gone off somewhere, the houseboys were sitting around talking, when a pygmy from the Congo turned up looking for work. He was about as tall as a ten year old boy, wearing European shorts but some skins over his shoulders. His front teeth were filed to points, and he had muti marks in a kind of rope shape on his face and more on his chest. The local boys looked scared and moved away. "Witches," said Make, "Funica lo tokolosh," and said his friend had seen two in the Kafue, deep under the water, sitting on a rock chatting, then walking on the river's sandy bed. They can make you ill or kill you. Sometimes they turn into animals like cats or bats and visit you in the night. When he looked straight at me his eyes were yellow and I got a skrik. I hope he doesn't come and spook me.

This morning Mrs Walker came running up the drive, crying, her hair tangled, hand over her mouth, and told Auntie Elsie that her daughter Maisie has polio and is in an iron lung. It must be like a big coffin. We're in quarantine and can't leave the garden because we visited them on Thursday. It's good being off school, but a bit scarey, if you don't die you can end up with one of those short thin legs. A boy in the high school, Danny, has one fat leg and a short skinny one covered in long ginger hair. The girls don't like him and the boys mock him and call him hopalong. He's always on his own and rides a Velo Solex. Mrs Walker was crying that she doesn't want her beautiful daughter to die or end up like Danny. Some blacks have two skinny legs and go along the ground on a tray with little wheels, like spiders. Jessie's the worst, she goes round feeling her own head all day to see if she has a temperature. I heard Dad say to Auntie Elsie, "It can just get you like this in days," and he grabbed his throat.

Chris says we must spend the time working on our skills. Everyone plays marbles for keeps so we start on that. You draw a den in the sand, a rectangle about nine inches long and each put in one or two maalis.

Then you walk about four big steps away and draw a line. You shoot from there with your ghoen. If you hit one out you get another shot til you miss. Then the other oke goes and he can aim for the den or your ghoen. If he gets your ghoen, you're sommer dead and your maalis are his. You can have up to about five okes in a game, some use big ghoens because they can knock out more maalis and bulldoze through the sand, but then they're a bigger target. Everyone says that if you get your exact right size ghoen you can't miss, and some have stories about how they once did and won hundreds of marbles, but now they've lost the ghoen. "Jiss," says Chris, "some okes only praat kak."

Then we practise throwing with our sheath knives. You stand about two steps apart and throw the knife by the blade to within a knife length of the other boy's foot. If it sticks in the ground he has to move his foot to where it was and then he throws. The first person to stretch so far he falls over is the loser. Auntie Elsie tells us to wear shoes when we play this. No! We also practise pegging into trees with one or two spins of the knife.

Then we practise with the bows. I got into trouble for sitting in the avocado tree and shooting a box of Surf in the houseboy's hand as he walked across the garden. He went and told on me.

Ya then also we must practise with our catties. We buy them from the kaffir kids in the backlane for a susu each. "Hey, how's this quarantine?" I ask, "Our polio will be all around the compound by tonight." "Maybe not," says Chris, "maybe there's a kaffir kind and a white kind." As soon as we have the catties in our hands we turn them on the kaffir kids, not really, just at their feet or maybe their legs. They're ready for this and run off with their susus. The catties are really lekker, red or black, the main rubber from car inner tubes, the rubber binding it to the stick from bike tubes, the leather beautiful and soft, all perfectly balanced, easy to pull, not like those rubbish catties from England. We practise and practise until we can easily hit a tin off a post at ten paces. Most boys have a catty around their necks when they're not at school.

By the time our quarantine is ended there's polio everywhere. The swimming pool and bioscope are closed, then the schools, and a few of our friends have got it, but not us. But I'm more scared of rabies. It gets spread by the kaffir dogs or wild animals. We often have tie ups and then you can't even stroke a cat and everyone's poep scared of their own dog, even if it's been vaccinated. This Jehovah's Witness girl died because her parents wouldn't let her get injections. Uncle Oscar said it's the worst death, and the parents should have been shot.

It's good to be free. We go off to play in the slimes dam at the bottom of M Avenue. It's a stream running over rocks, making pools at the side, with white sand and green slime. It smells like rotting but we like it. Uncle Oscar says, "Sis man, you shouldn't play there, that's where the water comes out from the sewage farm. The kaffir shit goes in there also. You'll catch something bad." But we still go. We've built a little pond with cement pinched from a building site and put in the tadpoles and small barbel we find there.

Just near the abattoir there's a piece of open ground where we have catty fights with the kaffir kids. They turn up soon after we arrive, and then we start shooting at each other. We don't speak to them much because most can't talk fanigalo, but there's a kind of rule you don't aim for the head, though you can get hit really hard on the body. We got a shock the first time, we thought they'd be useless or too scared to shoot back. They were at first, but then they kind of warmed up, shooting really well and forcing us back. One side could easily arrange to outnumber the other but it doesn't work like that, when one side wants to go you just raise your hand and the other side does the same and off you go. It's like we want to find out about each other.

Every Saturday afternoon we go to the matinee at the bioscope. From the outside you go up some steps to the main entrance, with the ticket office and pictures of film stars. It costs a tickey. Inside children are sitting, talking, and walking around. Some have piles of old comics and are selling them or swopping them for marbles or dinks. It's like a market. Then the lights begin to dim and everyone cheers and claps and the films start. First we have a cartoon, then a feature film, then if we're lucky a weekly serial, then it's interval. We all cheer or boo everything, sometimes you get a horrible feature film like classical music, and the audience moans and groans all the way through. At interval we go out the side door to the club shop and buy a cooldrink or some chips for 6d, or a sucker for a tickey. The little kids buy lucky packets and swop the charms. Then you can go and buy a new comic from a kaffir who has them all laid out on the grass round by the badminton courts. I get 1/6 pocket money a week so I have to be careful. A few months ago we discovered condensed milk in town, tickey a small tin and 6d a big one, it tastes lekker and is much cheaper than sweets. So now if you look towards the screen you see lots of arms in the air, children leaning back, sucking from a tin.

After interval the big film starts. Usually it's a cowboy in black and white, but if it's in colour, or there are red indians, we all cheer. If we get soft films like Gene Autry the singing cowboy we boo. Sometimes it's something really smart, like Tarzan.

"Tarzan swings, Tarzan falls, Tarzan hurts his monkey balls."

"Down in the valley where the green grass grows, there lies Jane without any clothes. Down comes Tarzan, bold as a brick, down with his costume, out with his prick."

But usually it's cowboys and crooks, and we follow every movement, "Watch out stupid, he's behind you! Shoot now, shoot now!" We sit behind the best girls and, just as somebody's about to shoot, burst our chip packets in their ear. They tell us to bugger off, or grow up. Then we get out our fly catties, made from the elastic inside a golf ball, and shoot chewed up paper at people's heads. By the end of the film a few fights have started and these carry on outside. Some okes really think they're the cowboys and some like being the crooks. Last week Billy didn't seem like Billy, he was a crook, and gave me a bloody nose because I was the main cowboy. I couldn't get him to stop.

Mufulira 1956

We're off on holiday to St Michaels, fifty miles South of Durban, the sea! That's 2000 miles away, four days journey, so we're going for six weeks. The Morris packed in, blue smoke everywhere, so we have another car, a Ford Consul, green, long and modern. I've £2.15/- holiday pocket money, and Anne £3 but she's already worrying that it's not enough. We were to leave at 9 o'clock this morning, but now it's one in the afternoon and Dad's still packing and fiddling with the car. We set off at two and pick up Auntie Mary in Ndola an hour later.

You have to do 55 or more on the dirt road to get a smooth ride over the corrugations. It's August, the dry season, and you keep your distance from the car in front or you're choked by dust. We pass Kapiri Mposhi where the road goes off to Tanganyika, and then Broken Hill. As the sun sets, big and soft and red, we drive through Lusaka, and then on into the dark. Suddenly, by the side of the road, there's a hotel, all bright, with tables outside and coloured lights between the trees. Dad goes in and comes out. "It's fine, they've got rooms," he says. The main building has an entrance African style, thatch roof and red polished floor, big wooden animals and masks, old chairs strung with strips of animal hide. The bedrooms are outside, in a square with a veranda running round, in the centre of which there's a garden and pond, all brightly lit. There frogs croak non stop, throats ballooning like plastic toys, joining the hiss of the crickets, like a magical scene from Walt Disney. I share a room with Dad, mosquito nets over the bed, a musty smell which I like. The boy who carries our suitcases brings a jug of hot water and places it in the bowl on the wash stand.

In the dining room, there are eight tables, most full. The menu starts with fish cakes and tomato sauce. Five big grass mats hang straight down from the ceiling, moving side to side, cooling us. "How do they move?" I ask the waiter. "Lo picannin ena donsa," he says pointing to where ropes disappear though the wall. After dinner people start moving to the tables outside, ordering drinks. I sneak round the back, where, sitting against the dining room wall, two picannins about eight and ten are taking turns to pull the rope, and sharing a cigarette. I sit down with them. "Wena funa pemba?" asks one, passing me the cigarette. I take a drag. "Wena funa donsa?" I reach out and start pulling the rope. It's not so hard if you pull at just the right time. We sit and chat and smoke. Suddenly Dad appears. "Come here at once!" he says. "Makulu indaba!" mutters the older boy. "What're you doing with those picannins?" "What's wrong?" I ask. "Don't be funny, and don't embarrass me, what if the owner had seen you? Now go and wash your hands!" Dad goes back to join the other grown-ups. By now they're all sitting in one large circle, four tables in the middle, talking, laughing, drinking, smoking, and teasing the waiters. They sit late into the night, in a pool of light, surrounded by the darkness.

Next morning we set off on a tar road. After a while it winds down some steep hills which Dad calls the escarpment, into the Zambesi valley. Here it's really hot and I feel all good and relaxed like I've been drinking Uncle Oscar's beer. I lean out the window watching the view, then we hit a flat section with dry red soil and big baobab trees. We stop as a herd of about fifteen elephants slowly cross the road. A huge male stops and turns his head towards us but then turns away. A few miles on we pull off the road for lunch. Outside everything seems stunned by the heat and the deafening buzz of crickets. A big hawk sits on a branch nearby. Auntie Mary and I make a little fire and boil the kettle. She opens a big Quality Street tin full of food from the hotel. I throw away a chewed chicken leg, and as it hits the baked ground three silver lizards pounce on it from nowhere. I sit playing with a couple of beetles then wander off to look around, you never know what you'll find under a rock. Dad calls me back, I don't think he likes it here.

We cross the Zambesi at Chirundu, Dad says it's a suspension bridge, the only one in the world apart from America. That night we sleep at the Great Zimbabwe Ruins Hotel. After dinner the grown ups are sitting round outside discussing the ruins. We saw parts of them in the late afternoon, huge walls like the Tower of London. "Of course, nobody knows who built them," says a man with an important voice, "but most now believe it was the Phoenicians or Romans." "The Romans?" asks Auntie Mary, "What on earth were they doing down here? Wasn't it the local Africans?" The man looks at her like she's stupid. "The local black builds in wood and straw, this kind of building would be completely, beyond him." "Mmm," says Auntie Mary.

This morning we're up early. Our shoes, left outside the door have been polished. Yellow weaver birds fly in and out of nests in a big tree by the dining room. Grey monkeys sit on the roof watching the scene. Breakfast is fantastic, jungle oats, kippers, steak, kidneys, all sorts of things. Two men are joking with Dad. "So you're from the black North! Do you all live in huts up there? Jiss man, British Colonial rule! But the English are only Kaffir lovers eh? You'd better pasop!" We set out, I feel excited, it's different from around Muf. The trees are smaller, acacia thorn but big baobabs once in a while. Everything's dryer. The road is dead straight, and has two strips of tar with soft white sand in the middle and on the sides. When two cars pass they each leave one wheel on the tar and one on the sand, Dad skids a few times until he gets used to it. Every few miles natives are selling curios laid out on the ground, giraffes as tall as a man, drums and other things. We pull into a small village just off the road, only a few huts. Blacks crowd around us, skinny, smelling of wood smoke, eyes wide, trying to get us to buy this one instead of that. Anne buys a small zebra made of real stuffed zebra skin, but most of the animals aren't very good. "Just villagers doing their best," says Auntie Mary. A thin old man comes up to Dad, "Plis Sah, we are verr houngree, no rain, no food." We end up giving them all the food in the tin, and our biscuits and some money. Next time Dad won't stop.

We cross the Limpopo into South Africa. There's hardly any river, just pools, then on through Pietersburg, and Potgietersrus. South Africa seems old fashioned, blacks on donkey carts, big red petrol pumps worked by hand, old jalopies. In Nylstroom the shop lady talks to us in Afrikaans. Auntie Mary says all polite, "Do you speak English?" like she's in France or something. The lady gives her a look, "Ya coss I cn tok nglsh!" That night we stop in the middle of Johannesburg at the Victoria Hotel. Auntie Mary says it's scruffy. This is a big city like you see in the films, a funny petrol smell in the air, trolley buses and tall buildings, some more than five storeys.

I lie in bed at the Hotel Metropole, Shelly Beach, listening to the waves crashing. Exciting! Today Anne and I were standing heads out the window to get the first sight of the sea as we came down through the mountains of Natal, all bright green with small African kraals. Then we saw it through a gap, deep blue against the sky! As soon as the car stopped at the hotel we rushed down to the beach without even asking. Then Anne drew a square around her and said "This is mine, you can't come on it." I was shocked, the beach was empty.

It's six in the morning and I'm on the beach before breakfast all by myself. It's cold cold on my feet, it goes right through your head. The smell of the sea! I run along the edge of the big waves, and as they go back you can hear shells tinkling. I find all sorts of things, shells, cuttle fish bones, and then a whole dead baby shark about two foot long! I pick it up.

"No sah you cannot bring de shak into de dining room, you musty put it outside!" says the waiter of the children's dining room. There are about ten other kids. I order five eggs from different waiters, maybe showing off a bit. A lady, quite young, comes in to check on her two little girls, one about seven the other four. They're fussy eaters. "Come on darling, eat your bacon!" "Don't like it, tastes fishy, and my egg's too squidgy! Mummy that little boy ate five eggs and he said a bad word and he made a face at me!" The lady looks at me like I'm an insect. "Don't worry darling, I'll talk to his father."

Every day sun and sea! I start fishing before breakfast and go on into the morning. Some young men show me how to improve. We fish from a rock. Sometimes I catch a proper fish but usually it's a toby, horrible, poisonous puffer fish with green eyes and teeth like bugs bunny. People get the moerin and kick them around like footballs. The young men dive for crayfish, or if the wind is off the land, fish for shark by hanging the hook from a kite and releasing it when far out to sea. Today they caught a five foot shark, with razor teeth, that took over an hour to die. There was a small crowd around it. By midday it's so hot you're dizzy, we float in huge warm rock pools full of small fish, or splash around in the sea at low tide. Monkeys live in the bushes between the hotel and sea. To the right of the sandy path there's dark forest where, any time, you can see two or three bright green boomslang hanging from the trees. I'm not allowed in there. In the evening at high tide we sit on the wall of the beach swimming pool, letting the waves wash us in.

After dinner we're allowed into the lounge for half an hour to have our cooldrinks. Auntie Mary's cross, which is unusual for her, "Why shouldn't I be allowed in the bar, these rules are ridiculous, the hotel's almost empty!" "Well my dear," the manager says, "I'm sure you'll prefer the lounge which is more comfortable, and more suitable for ladies." "Don't patronise me," says Auntie Mary, "I'm not a child."

Back in Muf, Uncle Oscar's at home all day, on strike. He says to Dad, "They're giving white jobs to kaffirs, now we even got kaffir pipe-layers, and every day they're getting more cheeky. The Mine Workers Union has caved in, we've been sold down the river, the place is going to the dogs." The Gearys are moving to Luanshya, I have to go and live with Mom in J. Avenue. I'm sad. Uncle Oscar gets me in a headlock. "Heh, kafupi, don't be so sad, you must come stay every holidays or I'll pono no you."

At one o'clock when I come back from school we have a big cooked lunch, then Glen sleeps and Mom lies on her bed reading and eating Cadbury's chocolate. I wander round the yard feeling full and dozy and lonely, all my friends are near Chris's place. At half past three Mom has a bath and comes out smelling perfumy, then Richard comes back from work at four. We have tea outside on the lawn, commenting as the cars go by from the day shift. "It's amazing how many drivers are picking their noses," says Mom. Then usually we go to town where they do some shopping and chat in the quiet street, the sun low, just a few shoppers about. Then we go to the club which is busy by five. Richard, who's the club manager, raises one finger and the waiters come running, and snap to attention. "Yes Bwana Richard, yes Sah!" He orders "One cold Castle, a Tio Pepe for the dona, a coke, and a cream soda." After a few drinks we go home for a light supper like avocado on toast and Richard goes back to the club.

Saturday and Sunday nights are sundowners, you arrive at about six. Tables and chairs are laid out round the dance floor and in two outer areas. First there's a rock and roll band and all the teenagers start jiving. The older people sit around and comment, "Just look at Eddy Jackson, he's grown so tall, but my God he loves himself." "Mavis, hasn't Hilda Geldenhuys got lovely legs!" "Ya, I'd like to feel them all the way to the top!" "Shut up George, who asked you? You're old enough to be her grandfather!" Then the grown-up band comes on and the old people get up to dance. Mom comes halfway up Richard who's six foot two. Later the lights go low and a ball with little glass mirrors sends out rays of silvery light, all smoochy.

We kids go outside in the dark and usually start by playing Bulawayo fighting, smaller boys on bigger boys' backs try to pull other pairs down, but soon the fights start. Last week John Stevens from England hit me as I pulled him off George's back. I got him down in a headlock, then he put two fingers in the side of my mouth right up between my teeth and cheek and pulled. I was going to punch him in the face but someone said, "You can't hit an ou on the ground!" so I didn't and with the pain of his sharp nails he easily pulled me over, then, on the ground, thumped me twice in the face before he was stopped. Later when I went inside there was still blood on my shirt. Richard said, "Christ, what a sneaky limey way of fighting, next time don't listen to what they say, just hit him first. And if anyone tries to stop you, hit them too."

Sometimes on a Sunday we go to Mokambo in the Congo, only ten miles from town. Everything's different, Simba beer, and matchsticks with red tips. Mom says the men like visiting the hotel at the weekend and Richard laughs. A man says Elizabethville is just like a small Paris, fresh fancy food flown out from Belgium every morning for the restaurants.

There's a State of Emergency! The blacks are on strike and the mine's hardly working. Now we mustn't go into town on our own. Yesterday an armoured car was parked on the road outside Mclellands, and about thirty black soldiers with white officers marched up J Avenue, guns over their shoulders. We kids, black and white all followed them.

Dad keeps going down to South Africa, to see that woman with the two girls from our holiday. Her name's Catherine. She lives in Joburg, and she's divorced. When he gets back the car's always messed up and dented, last time he fell asleep and rolled it, and spent three days in Bulawayo hospital. He reminds me of one of those panting dogs that followed Lassie. He usually brings me a present, last time a big pick-up truck. Now he says he's going to marry her and the next thing she turns up. She's staying with the Morrisons in F Avenue.

Anne's back for the holidays, at Mom's place. Dad says, "We have a nice new house at the top of J Avenue near the Ndola road, I'm sure we'll all be happy there." He takes us to see it, long and narrow, new style, with a green roof, on an acre. The houses in this part of town are all the same but set at different angles to their plots, and the tin roofs go red, green, red. Over the road there's solid bush, Dad says, "That goes all the way into the Congo, for maybe a couple of thousand miles." Just then a red Vauxhall Velox pulls up and two women step out, one of them Catherine. She looks different from how I remember her, taller, kind of strict, in charge, and high class. She's quite friendly but says, "God George, this is the back of beyond!" I think, "No it's not, it's just the top end of Muf." In the house she says, "This place is filthy, we'll need to scrub it out with caustic soda." I get that sinking feeling like going back to boarding school.

We've moved into the new house, the two girls are still in Joburg with their Dad. They're Catholics and are going to the convent in M Avenue. I'm going to a new school at the top end of camp called Ross Avenue, and Anne's going to Muf High. Catherine dishes us out some ice cream and jelly. We both watch. "Stop comparing who's got the most," she says, "My girls aren't used to that and I don't want them to pick up bad habits. Ian, wipe that milk off your lip!" I look at Anne, "We weren't!" "Don't be cheeky!" she says, "and do you have to talk like a jaapie skaap from Benoni?" I go off to play with Billy and Alfie. When I get back I'm in trouble for not asking. That night I hear her in the kitchen saying, "How can you let him play with those horrible rough children? They're not coming anywhere near my girls. That boy's out of control, no wonder he's failing at school!"

We go to pick up the girls from Ndola aerodrome. On the way Catherine is all worried that the plane will crash. I love the aerodrome, the green Nissan hut airport building, the special pink bubble gum that you can't get in Muf. Soon we hear the plane and then the big Viking lands and comes right up to the fence, its nose in the air, propellers turning. Catherine runs along the fence as the girls walk to the building, "Hallo darling, hallo my darling!" As soon as the big girl sees me her eyes go wide with shock and she says,

"Mummy it's that horrible boy from the hotel, you didn't tell me!" Then she has a tantrum right in front of everyone, rolling on the floor shouting, "I don't want to live with them, I want Daddy, leave me alone!" and has to be dragged out of the airport. The little girl, Janet is holding a doll and watching all this. Then she looks at us and smiles, she's got two front teeth missing and she's sweet.

I have to stay in the garden with the girls every afternoon unless they go out. Catherine says one of her cousins or friends was raped by blacks in Joburg, or something, and they were all hanged, she says, so she doesn't trust blacks with her girls. The older one, Phillipa has a plastic Jesus in her room that lights up with a glowing heart when you switch it on. She's deadly serious about everything. If any of my friends teases her they can't come round again. Anne's gone back to boarding school in Bulawayo because she and Phillipa are always fighting.

Our new houseboy Patrick is a mdala, because that's meant to be safer for the girls. He comes in every morning at six to light the wood stove and cook porridge for us, real oats. He's like a Dad, he doesn't call me baas Ian, he says, "Ian, come here, naughty boy," and straightens my school tie or collar, then pats me on the head. He fought in the war against the Japs in Burma. He said they were poep scared of blacks. We also have a new garden boy called John, who's quite old, maybe thirty, and about six foot. He gets my njinga out the garage. I'm meant to check the tyres and pump them myself, but usually he does it for me. Then I cycle off to my new school. I'm in 2b. Soon I make plenty of friends, and lots of them live near us. In the evening Dad tells John what to do in the garden, but I have to translate into Fanigalo. John calls me "Lo intapreta." Dad says he's bright for a black.

But I feel bad about Mom's houseboy George. One Sunday Mom told me his mother had died so he was going back to his village for the funeral. But lots of people say that kaffirs make up this kind of thing just to get a few days off. So I said to him, "Your mother's not really dead is she, you just want to go home." He looked at me like I'd just hit him, then tears started pouring down his cheeks, then he started crying. Mom came running in and he said he didn't want to work here any more and was leaving for good. Richard came in and said "George, please stay, we are very sorry, he's just a stupid child." I tried to explain but Richard said, "Don't talk shit!" In the end George promised to come back after the funeral, and he did, but it wasn't the same, and he left two weeks later. I keep thinking about it. Malanga the garden boy is the new houseboy.

Yesterday one of those sale boys came round to the house to buy old clothes to sell in the compound. We have a basket of them and I bargained with him and settled a price. Then I had to write a note listing them in case he's stopped by the police. He showed me his situpa so I could get his name right, made me feel important.

At the bioscope one of the serials is about Jungle Jim. He's running along a bush path chased by three kaffirs with spears. Suddenly he stops and crouches, and all the kaffirs trip over him, then he stands up and knocks them out with a couple of punches. "Jiss man, he's strong eh, we must practise that," says James de Long. He says, "Do you reckon a white man can beat a kaffir in a fight?" Pieter Maritz thinks about it and then says "A South African could, but not an Englishman." "Ya," says James "the English are too soft and white and they got these long shorts like skirts, ya and have you seen Wendel's dad, he wears sandals with socks! Ghut man and they talk funny, why do they say wa-a for water?" "Don't know," says Pieter.

The next week we watch a Pathe news film about the Mau Mau in Kenya. They've hacked the back leg muscles of some cattle so they're crawling around on their knees, mooing. They show a white family, a mom, dad, and boy about my age, lying in a row, all killed by pangas. Then they show dead blacks who've refused to join the Mau Mau. They've had their hands and feet cut off and been suffocated by having their heads rammed into anthills. They show ceremonies where they chant and drink blood and call up spirits. All these savages are spooky, like red Indians with their shamans, or that film where Tarzan was going to have his eyes burned out by these crazy kaffir witch doctors, but broke away at the last moment and stuck the red hot iron through the savage's chest. I tell Richard about the Mau Mau and the torture. He laughs, all sarcastic, "Don't worry, from what I hear, your soetie police are doing a lekker job on them too. Ya, they're busy torturing them, cutting off their balls, kicking their heads in, and killing them left right and centre. They're even raping their women! The wonderful English who lecture us about 'African Advancement and Partnership' and all that kak, but as soon as the blacks turn on them, they kick the shit out of them. Fucking hypocrites!" "I'm not a soetie," I say. There's a few okes from Kenya in Muf, come down since the Mau Mau. They can't stop talking about it and they really hate the munts.

At the Vic Falls for a week with Auntie Janice, wife of one of Dad's friends, and her son John, who's seven.

We leave on the sleeper train in late afternoon. After sorting out our beds we go to the dining car. Everything's all smart and each plate has 'Rhodesia Railways' stamped on it. All the staff are white men, and they're nice and friendly, one even invites Auntie Janice for a drink later. We're at a rest camp on the NR side of the river above the Falls, at night you can hear its roar and in the day you can see the spray from miles away. We stay in African thatched huts, with mosquito nets. I never think, "I'm living in Africa", but here you can't help it. Auntie Mary once told me how when she first came to NR in 1947 she flew from England in a wartime flying boat, maybe a Sunderland, done up to take twelve passengers. The trip took five days and ended at the Falls. I try to imagine what it must have felt like, landing as the sun set on the great Zambezi, full of hippos and crocs, and the green bush turning black around you.

That night we walk along the river to the restaurant, by the water's edge and sit outside under heavy old trees, strung with bright coloured lights. You can feel the strong flow of the black river nearby. John orders a fish with the head on. He pokes at its eyes. But I order something more exciting, crocodile tail. The next morning we're woken by a small dog yapping. Outside, it's bright sunlight much hotter than Muf. There bouncing up and down on a large bush are two vervet monkeys, staying just out of reach of a terrier, which is going mad. You'd swear they are deliberately teasing it. A few minutes later we're sitting on our beds eating cornflakes when this monkey appears at the door. It looks at us, then at the fruit bowl, back at us, measuring distances, then dashes right across the room, grabs a banana, and out again.

Later we walk along the river to the Falls. This area is completely wild, the only thing keeping lions and hyenas from our huts is their fear. Animal tracks run down to the water. It's the hot, dead time at midday, and I think of dozy animals resting in the palm thickets. I say to John, "I bet I can find an animal in three minutes," and dive into one of them. Immediately I hear a heavy rustling, and jump out, heart thumping. So does a large male warthog with huge tusks. It stands and faces me for an instant and then, faster than you can think, whips round, and trots off. We arrive at the edge of the Falls, so much bigger than I had expected, easily twice the size of Niagara. Auntie Janice is crying because they're so beautiful. Africans are selling curios laid out on the ground, exciting things like wooden animals, tokoloshes, bows and arrows. I spend 2/6 on a half size sjambok, real Rhino hide, smooth butter colour with a round stone handle. I'm walking along swinging it when we notice a baboon as big as an Alsatian following us. Then it singles me out and suddenly I'm all on my own staring into its yellow eyes. I feel hypnotised, as I back away, my skin cold goose pimples, terror. I throw down the sjambok, which must have upset it. But still it comes on, now a foot away, crouching, ready to spring, its pupils shrinking. I hear my own voice crying, "Mama!" Even then I'm shocked and ashamed. Auntie Janice yells, "Ian, the chocolate, your top pocket!" I throw down the slab. The baboon stops, picks it up, sits and starts to unwrap it, all delicate. Auntie Janice's face is white. "Look where you are!" she says, "Two steps more and you would have been over the edge." Yes, and all alone.

I've started having nightmares. I hate them more than anything, and when I go to bed I pray they won't come. They start with a steady thumping like a beating heart, then I'm in a field of flowers. I try to pick one up but it's too heavy, like lead, then the sound builds. Everything's heavy. My legs are glued to the ground, the air like treacle so I can hardly move. Sometimes in these dreams I wander into Dad and Catherine's room and ask strange questions which have nothing to do with the dream. Last time they woke me because I was standing there yelling, "The kaffirs are coming!"

It's nearly November and the rains are near. It hasn't rained since April and the ground is bone dry, the bush dead and brown. For a week or two we have dry electric storms. NR has the most in the world. The fork lightning stands in the sky, then there's the thunder. You count distance, "One crocodile, two crocodile," six for a mile, but sometimes in less than a second it's crash, straight overhead. During these storms we have to wear shoes and mustn't have a bath in case we're electrocuted. When the first drops fall you can smell the dust, then it rains harder and harder, excited we run out, yelling and dancing, and are soaked. In minutes the garden is flooded, the ditches along the roads are small rivers. This is my favourite season, fireworks, Christmas, mangos. It's fresh and cool, then the sun comes out and the water on the roads turns to steam, rainbows everywhere. Just before the rains, green grass shoots appear as if they know. Now the world comes to life. Flying ants pour from the ground, and somehow get into the house covering floors in inches of wings. We have plagues of different things, last year red and black caterpillars, now small black round toads, oozing milk from their smooth skin. I threw one into the chicken run thinking the fowls wouldn't touch it but they gobbled it up in seconds. Matebele ants an inch long march in ten foot columns. If you disturb the leaders, the column runs round confused, hissing, and if one stings you it's worse than a wasp. In the evenings we sit on the stoep, looking across the road to the bush. Sometimes you can hear hyenas laughing. I wouldn't go in there at night.

Most white miners are on strike. Early afternoon me and Johny Oosthuizen, dressed as clowns, go from house to house singing, "Guy Fawkes Guy stick him in the eye," begging firework money. A man in underpants comes out blinded by the heat, blinking and rubbing his eyes. "Bugger off!" he yells, "I've got no money for my own kids, why should I give to you?" At church they're collecting food for the strikers, yes for whites. Dad's a member of the Mine Workers' Union, in England he was in the labour Party and a shop steward. He says, "One of the things the strikers are pushing for is equal pay for each job, whether you're white or black." I'm surprised they're being so nice. "So there's blacks in the union too?" "No, they've their own union, the African Mine Workers' Union and they don't want equal pay." "Why not?" "Because the mines are trying to let blacks do white jobs on lower wages, sometimes less than a quarter, to make a bigger profit. But the white unions know that if the Company has to pay the same wages they may as well employ whites to avoid trouble." "Who's winning?" "The blacks, by steadily taking over white jobs or parts of white jobs. Back in 1951 average white wages were sixteen times more than blacks, now it's down to twelve and falling fast."

It's the Christmas holidays, about six of us hang around together, moving between our houses, or the swimming pool, making go-carts, having pellet gun fights, playing football or cricket, exploring the bush. There's a railway track about 200 yards in, and they say that once you cross it you're in the Congo, and you might come across gorillas or chimps. Hennie says he's seen some but that's rubbish. Sally our labrador has already been lost twice in the bush, she came back last time after three weeks, skinny and covered in ticks with a wire noose cutting her neck, which she must have chewed through. The kaffirs set them to trap buck. We chat to blacks we meet on the sunny bush paths, some of which are broad and sandy. They say they run between villages and have been there for ever, the Congo border means nothing. They show us what fruit we can eat, pundus which smell rotten but taste OK, and msukus, with three little pips, which are sour and make your teeth raw, but stop you being thirsty. Yesterday we shot three wood pigeons with our pellet guns, and cooked them over a fire. An old mdala who was passing showed us how to pluck and clean them, then he stayed to eat some with the bread we'd brought. He smelt of wood smoke and had interesting things like a knife made of sheet metal, with a wooden handle nailed on. He smoked in this heavy way, drawing in a third of a cigarette in one pull, blowing out through his nose. Then he took some snuff with a deep sniff up each nostril, going "Eh heh" from deep in his chest when he had finished. Then he turned away and had a good cough and a snot. He says it cleans everything out and is good muti. The pigeons were lekker but not much meat.

Usually when we go by bike we use the roads but you've got to pasop for dogs. Most are trained to go for blacks, but sometimes they also attack us, and some of the gardens have no fences at the front. When we're walking we mostly use the back sanitory lanes, which are safer from dogs because the gardens always have back fences. They aren't tarred so they don't burn your feet, and they run parallel to the roads right into town. The kaffir kias are at the backs of gardens so the sanitory lanes are like main roads for the blacks who also use them to visit others' kias or just to stand around and chat. That's why they're also called kaffir lanes. You almost never see a white grown-up there.

Today we were sitting on a culvert over a storm ditch which crosses our back lane. We'd dammed it with a three foot mud wall and now, after a small shower, water was right up to the top, where we'd parked some dinks. We were about to blow it with penny flash bombs, which are so powerful they can blow the lid off a dustbin, or split a petrol can, and they say they're banned in England. Hennie arrived with an orange necklace, the heads of white ant soldiers. You get them to bite you with their big nippers, then they won't let go, and you break the bodies off. We lit four flash bombs stuck into the wall, at first it gave way slowly, then the whole thing went, washing our dinks downstream. As we jumped down to find them there was a heavy rustling and a big green snake coiled to strike. "Nyoka!" someone yelled and we jumped out fast. Hennie picked up a stick, and as the snake finished its strike, rammed its head into the mud and held it there until it stopped moving. "Green mamba," said Douglas. "Maybe just a grass snake," I said, picking it up by the tail. Hennie yelled, "Put it down, it's not dead!" "Of course it's dead," I said. "Maybe, but not properly, a snake can only die when the sun goes down, my garden boy says that's when its spirit leaves." I thought of it dying all alone in the evening and got that sad Ndola feeling.

Hennie's in trouble. On Monday we were sitting on his back step and decided to go swimming. He called the garden boy, who's about twenty, "Heh, Garden, buisha lo njinga kamina." The bike was against a tree no more than ten feet away. "Shit man, just get it yourself," I said. The garden boy had come all the way from the front and was cross, he said, "Eh, ine indaba! Wena tata, wena dooze sterek!" and walked off. Hennie yelled at him to come back, and when he wouldn't, called him a bloody macaque. Now that was a big mistake, everyone knows you don't do that. The garden boy stopped and turned, you could see he'd lost his temper. He came towards us saying, "Do noty colla me macaque, you are stupeed, mena asi chaiya wena." The houseboy came out and grabbed his arm, calming him, but Hennie had run into the house and came out with his pellet gun, loading it as he reached the door. Without pausing he shot the garden boy. The pellet hit his bare chest bone, ran under the skin for about half an inch, and came out again. He wasn't seriously hurt but he looked shocked. By now the neighbour's houseboy was at the fence. He disappeared into the house and within five minutes an African constable arrived on a bike. "You musty give me the gun," he said. Hennie held it tighter. "No. You can't make me, you're just a kaffir cop," but he looked scared. "He was going to hit us." The constable looked like he didn't know what to do and started talking to the houseboy in Bemba. Then a car drove up and a white policeman got out. That night Dad asked, "*Was* he going to hit you?" "No of course not. What should I say?" "You just tell the truth, the exact truth." said Catherine, "That pellet could easily have hit him in the throat or the eye."

Mufulira 1957

Well here we are back in the present, 1957, modern times! The date even looks modern, the 7 goes with the fins on the new Chev Belair at Goldring Motors. Been put into 3A because I've started reading and writing, and came first in the B stream. I think it's because I have to stay at home every afternoon with the girls. Sometimes there's nothing better to do, so I read. I started on the Beano and Dandy, then on to American comics like Superman, or British ones like Battler Britton who can knock out three Germans with one punch, then Dell Comics, then Dell Classics which tell stories like A Tale of Two Cities. Some boys just look at the pictures, some read the bubbles but I started reading the thick writing below. Now I'm going on to books, like The Famous Five and Zane Grey, Call of the Canyon.

At school we do Roman Britain in History, and England in Geography. There's a roller that you ink and roll out to get a map of Britain. Then you have to mark where steel or textiles are produced and that kind of thing, I get all mixed up and it's *boring*, who cares anyway? "Sir, why can't we do our own history and geography?" I ask. "Well," says Mr Booker, "that's the syllabus from the Government, and we have to follow it. Anyway there isn't really much history, Europeans have only been here about thirty years, and we don't know much about what went on before that. And there's not much geography, it's all just bush." Lots of hands go up, "Sir, what about the sunken lake? They've never found the bottom." "Sir, in the holidays we went to Lake Banguela." "Sir, we went to the Zambezi valley and there was this tribe called the Tonga who still wear skins and have fantastic spears and don't talk Bemba. My ma bought a lekker mask from them. How many Kaffir languages are there?" "I really don't know," says Mr Booker, "and don't say Kaffir, say African." "How come they're African and we're not?" asks Christos, "I was born here too." "You're just a bloody Greek," says Hennie. "Don't use that language," says Mr Booker.

Christos' Dad runs Mike's Café at the bottom end of town. We used to cheek him before we knew who he was. It's like there's a ladder of who you can cheek, first kaffirs of course, then coolies, then Greeks and people like Mr Chenian who's Armenian and then proper white men. It's not just how good their English is because we don't cheek Walter Carlitz' dad, he's German and fought against us in the war. Maybe it's if you think they'd thump you or tell on you, and your dad would listen to them. But even with some coolies, we wouldn't cheek Solanki, he's a big trader from Kitwe who visits Mom once a year to take her order for things like furniture, and she gets a present from him every Christmas. Last year it was a revolving ashtray on a stand. She even sits with him and has tea, so you'd have to call him an Indian rather than a coolie. Anyway we got a shock when we went round to Christos' place to swop toys and stamps and there was his dad at home, just like a normal dad, so we said sorry, and we don't cheek him any more.

Mom and Richard live halfway down J Avenue so I pass their house when I ride into town or to the pool. Whenever I stay with them they start criticising Dad and Catherine. Mom says Dad should go back to England because he thinks he's smart and doesn't fit in here. Then they get cross when I don't say anything. I feel they're kind of criticising me too for being Dad's son, and Richard sometimes calls me professor because I've started reading a lot. I feel bad like they think I'm not quite right, so I avoid going now. On Sunday, coming back from church I rode past without stopping, but Mom and Richard ran on to the road and told me off. They complained to Catherine and she took me on one side saying, "You must go and see your mother at least once a week, and you mustn't ever pass her house without going in. She's your mother and it's not fair on her." But it didn't feel right, I can't explain why. Catherine won't actually criticise Mom, but you can still feel what she thinks. Everything Mom does, Catherine does different, even like how we crack our boiled eggs, and what toothpaste we use.

I get mixed up, yesterday Catherine told me to take my library books back. I asked couldn't I do it another day because Len was coming round, and she said "Right don't then!" so I thought, "Good, that's alright then." When Dad came home she told him I'd refused to take them back, and he took me into the spare kia to give me a good hiding. I thought that when we got in there, he'd pretend to hit me, and give me a talking to, but he just bent me over his knee and whacked me over and over again. Then he walked out saying, "Behave yourself in future." "But..." I said, "Don't say but," he said. He doesn't speak to me much on my own any more. Often when I get home from a weekend at Mom's and I'm in bed on Sunday night, I think the voices in the kitchen are Mom and Richard until I remember where I am. Sometimes as I drop off to sleep I think I see Dad's face by the door of my room, come specially to say goodnight, then his head seems to shrink down to a point, and I realise it's just clothes hanging on the back of the door.

When I'm at Mom's place we play with the Swanepoel kids who live down the road. Mrs Swanepoel's big and fat, and Mr Swanepoel is small and thin and must be about half her weight. He talks and sounds like a coloured. The family have a reputation for being rough, there's almost no furniture even though everyone in this part of town earns about the same. Richard says, "Jiss, but look how they live eh? Sis man, it all goes on bloody drink." "Look who's talking!" says Mom. The Swanepoel girl, Liezl, who we played with at James' house has hair under her arms. I ask her why, it doesn't look nice. "Everybody gets it, stupid, it's when you grow up." Willem, who's about my age says she also bleeds from you know where every month. "Is she sick?" "No, all girls do." He has lots of teenage cousins, and tells me all about them. "Louis was in his bedroom with this girl. We were spying at the window." He goes on to say what they were doing, it's so dirty I mustn't write it down. He tells me this poem

Dirty Dick had a six foot prick
And he showed it to the girl next door.
She thought it was a snake
And hit it with a rake,
And now it's only five foot four.

His other cousin Johannes is visiting from Pretoria. He's thirteen and knows all about dirty things. We ask him, "Why do girls bleed?" He says, "It's when an ou squeezes her tits, the blood comes out." "So if she squeezes her own tits she also bleeds?" "No it's got to be an ou, so she's excited." So Liezl must be doing dirty things with an ou. Johannes is always playing with his prick. He says, "You okies will find out, when you my age you must pull your wire every week. If you don't the spunk dries up and you sommer die."

Mr Swanepoel's dead. Mom told me about it. She said the small Swanepoel boy, James came running across shouting, "My Dad's fallen down and he's gone purple, please come help!" But Mom said, "I'm not a doctor," and wouldn't go across. But when he started crying and screaming she went to the neighbour, and he called an ambulance. Just then James came in with Glen. "My Dad's dead," he said smiling, like he was proud of it.

Mom's been given permission from the Bishop of Northern Rhodesia to take communion, though she's divorced and remarried, so now we all go to church together. Richard's Dutch Reform, he drops us at the Church of England and goes to the club. Mom goes up to the communion rail and comes back smelling of wine. She kneels humbly, with a holy suffering look on her face.

Cycling to school, I move my legs up and down pedalling, then pause, then decide to pedal again. Funny how I can control my body, look, I'm going to lift my right hand from the handle bar, like that, see how it does what I want, now my left hand, no I won't, yes I will, but how to decide what to decide, hell I'm going round in circles. I don't know where these stupid thoughts come from, sometimes I think I'm different from everybody else, see the world differently, almost like I've invented it. When I got back from holiday I was surprised to find that marble still on the floor, rather than back on the table where I remembered it. Then I think but how come I'm just like everyone else, I like HP sauce, and chocolate, like I'm just ordinary, so maybe everyone else, say even Chris, also feels they're special. Is that possible? What about kaffirs? Do they think? Yes, but do they think like us or do they just kind of copy what they think we want them to do, like those robots in the comics, or like a trained ape? Some people say kaffirs go mad when they hear drums or drink a lot, like they don't have real minds, something just switches on inside them and controls them, that's why people are scared of them. But what if each of them also feels just like I do, at the centre of everything? Say that picannin over there, could he feel just like me? Would that make him as important as me? Then what do they think of us? I look at him, and he looks back.

Dad comes into my bedroom on Saturday morning. "I think we need to have the talk which all fathers have with their sons." Oh no! I set my face all still so I won't look embarrassed. "Do you know how babies are made?" I say I'm not sure. I have been wondering, not very seriously, why children look like their fathers, maybe spit or something passes to their wives through kissing? But then people who aren't married kiss too, yes but they do sometimes get pregnant. "Well," he says, "the man puts his penis inside the woman, and his sperm comes out into her." I'm shocked, that's exactly what those dirty teenagers were doing! That's disgusting, I think of Dad lying on top of Mom, surely not? I say, "I'd never do a thing like that!" He says with a slight smile, "Yes you will!" Later, I'm cycling past the Church of England when I think, "The Queen and Prince Philip must have done it," so it must be all right.

Anne's back for Christmas. She's a teenager now. She's got some rock n' roll records and plays them for me, Elvis, *Heartbreak Hotel* and *Blue Suede Shoes*, Little Richard, *Lucille, Tutti Frutti*. I get goose pimples down my back and all over, I've never heard anything so exciting! She says she loves Elvis and shows me her Elvis magazines. She jives round the lounge and tries to teach me. When Catherine comes home Phillipa says, "Mummy, Anne's been playing that horrible music and doing that funny jiggly dancing again." "Let her if she wants to," says Catherine, "though I can't see why, it sounds just like kaffir music." I think, no, it doesn't, but who cares, some kaffir music's quite mush, but I don't say so. Anne plasters her wall with pictures of all the singers and film stars, Elvis, Eddie Cochrane, Debbie Reynolds, Little Richard, Fats Domino, Richard Burton, Elizabeth Taylor. Hennie comes across and we sneak into her room. "Eksclaim, why she got pictures of kaffirs?" "They're not kaffirs, they're American negroes, they talk English." "Same thing, a kaffir's a kaffir," says Hennie.

I've come second in the A stream and won the prizes for English and History, and the progress prize, all books. I don't mind being beaten by Elizabeth Macauley, she's so mooi and gentle and quiet. I never see my girl from Muf Primary, so after a lot of thought, I've decided to drop her and love Elizabeth instead. Last Saturday night I was sleeping at Johnny Oosthuizen's house and we were telling secrets before we went to sleep. He kept asking who I loved so in the end I told him after he swore he'd keep it to himself. By Monday break time the whole class knew. I could hardly believe it, what kind of friend is that? But it worked out well because next time I looked across she gave me a smile! It was like her whole face lit up. But I don't know what to say to her.

Mom's had another baby called Grant. They do baby talk to him and are all lovey dovey. Richard blows farty noises on his tum and calls him Grant Moodie butterball.

Dad and Catherine gave me this big book, *A London Anthology*, for Christmas. It has some letters written in the middle ages. There's one from the fourteenth century saying, "If a man committeth murther he should be hanged, but if a woman committeth adultery she should be cooked alive in boiling lead." Richard says he's got so much secret information on Auntie Gail, he could have her any time he likes. I'm a bit shocked, I thought it was all about love and people wanting to. Mom was talking about this book *Peyton Place*. She says it's got nothing on Muf.

Mufulira 1958

It's Sunday morning at Mom's after church and we're sitting in the front garden drinking tea. Two black youths, about eighteen, climb on our fence to pinch the neighbour's mangos. "Hey!" shouts Mom, "Get off our fence!" "Get out of our country!" replies one of the youths. "Go on voetsek jou bliksem!" yells Richard standing up. "Fuck off ma boere!" shouts the same youth. "Malanga!" yells Richard. Malanga comes running round and they both go outside the fence to take on the youths. I expect them to run off, but this time it's different. Richard's fighting the leader, then I can't believe it, he goes down and the youth's sitting on his chest, punching his face. Blood spurts from Richard's nose, then the youth kind of hesitates, maybe thinking he's gone too far. In that instant Richard hits him from below, pushes him off, stands up, and drops from his full height, his knee landing on the youth's neck. The youth chokes and coughs while Richard twists his arm behind his back and drags him up the garden. Malanga does the same with his guy. Mom's phoned the police and soon a van arrives with a white cop and three black constables. They throw the youths into the van. The leader youth's complaining that he's lost one of his tackies, so one of the black cops goes to look for it. The white policeman settles down for a cup of tea. "Well, as you say, you struck the first blow, outside your yard, so I wouldn't press charges if I were you," he says. "We'll sort them out a bit at the police station and then we'll have to let them go. Things aren't like they used to be." He goes on to say that if you ever shoot a black on your property at night you should drag him into the house, because that would look like burglary and self defence.

Richard has four guns, a Lee Enfield 303, a German Luger, a Colt 45, like a cowboy gun, and a .25 automatic which he says is for Mom. The 303 stands in their bedroom cupboard, the magazine empty, and Glen and I practise cocking and aiming it. Richard doesn't mind, but we must keep it in the room. Sometimes he takes me to the shack, off the Muf - Kitwe road. Mom stays at home, she doesn't like the bush. You turn left just at the Muf side of the Kafue bridge and drive along the river for a mile or two on a rough track. The shack is wooden, green, no bigger than a garage, with a little kitchen, a bedroom with one bed, and a veranda. There's no water or electricity. I sleep on a camp bed in the kitchen. A short way from the shack, on higher ground, is a little kraal, and the headman, a mdala, looks after our place for 10/- a month. Usually we arrive early afternoon, and Mdala soon appears, bowing and clapping, and discusses any business with Richard. Then he makes a fire on the baked ground outside and leaves plenty of wood. Richard settles down on a chair, puts a kaffir pot of water on the fire, and starts preparing the evening stew by throwing in anything he can think of. He switches on the battery radio, puts on loud kaffir music, and opens his first Castle.

I go off fishing with the Kaffir kids, led by a couple of teenage boys. The rods are bamboo with fishing line attached to the end, no reels. We've brought them some line and hooks as a present. You put a little ball of mealie meal on the tip of the hook, the float is a little stick. The fish bite all the time, and the mealie meal is lost in half a minute, the trick is to strike just right. We keep the first few to braii with our dinner, then the kaffirs have the rest. Using very small hooks we also catch a couple of tiny fish, kapenta, as bait for night fishing, and put them in a tin with water. When dinner's ready Richard fires the 303 to call me back. Afterwards he puts the tops back on the Castle bottles and throws them into the river, and we take turns shooting at them as they float downstream. He's teaching me how I hold the gun. Later the mdala comes down for a drink. First he has a beer, then he and Richard drink brandy and coke. They talk in Fanigalo about old times, when there was more game and fewer cars or white people. Last time I was surprised, he brought a young girl with him, maybe sixteen, and she was also drinking, which also really surprised me, but she didn't talk, except once or twice, all shy, through the old man in Bemba. Usually women and girls are kept well out of the way.

We wee in the bush, Richard calls it draining his lizard. For shitting there's a long drop toilet a few yards away with a thatched roof. Last time I tried to go in the middle of the night I heard a heavy movement in the thatch above, "Nyoka," I thought, and gave up til morning. Before bed we put the night lines out, hooking the kapenta sideways through the spine and leaving them to swim around. By morning there's usually a big bream on the end. Sometimes we use a piece of meat and sink it to catch a barbel.

It's my birthday, eleven today. I got a fishing reel from Dad and Catherine that I'd seen in Shorty Halliday's sport shop, red plastic and silver metal with the reel running sideways, price fourteen shillings. It wasn't wrapped up or anything because Dad said he was busy, and it's what I asked for, but I felt disappointed, like nobody had bothered. I think Dad and Catherine are short of money, I saw Dad's pay slip one day, £68-6-8d per month, which is low, everyone says underground men get over £100. Catherine also works, as a book keeper. When we go to the club which isn't often we have to share a king size coke between two. But I don't understand because Mom and Richard throw money around like water, even though Mom doesn't work. I can have as many cokes as I want, and crisps and sweets. Richard also works on the mine now, in the refinery.

We're on holiday in South Africa, on the way to Illovo beech, staying with Catherine's brother, Uncle Alan in Craighall Park, Johannesburg. Their house is small and old, from before the Boer War, with moulded ceiling patterns, but they have six children, so there are three to a room, with bunk beds. The night we arrived, Ronald, who's eight, was sick and vomited from his bunk. Auntie Andrea was cross and made him clean it up. We met Catherine's Granny, who's over eighty, she stared at me, her gums moving, and I got a bit of a skrik. Catherine said "Well come to think of it you don't see any old people on the Copperbelt, not even natives." The whole place is spooky. Auntie Andrea says that one afternoon, when she was alone, she heard a rushing sound and saw a little boy in old fashioned clothes walking away from her down the corridor. At the end he turned left into the store cupboard and disappeared. That night I was sleeping on the lounge carpet and needed a piss. I felt nervous, but finally started to get up when suddenly there was a rumbling noise, and a child's face appeared in the doorway. I stuck my head under the blanket my heart thumping, expecting something to touch me any moment. Finally after about an hour I fell asleep. In the morning I discovered that the face was Ronald off to honk outside, and the noise was the old fridge which cranks itself up once in a while.

That day we went to visit some of Catherine's relatives called the McKays. Old Mr McKay who's about eighty-five was sitting on a kitchen chair in the garden, feeding rice to turtle doves. He had a Scottish accent. "Aye," he said, "I fought the British in the Boer War. I was farming near here and all my neighbours were Afrikaans so it seemed the natural thing. And you've got to defend your land. But sometimes I think it was wrong to fight my own kith and kin. What do you think?" I didn't know what to say. His family just see it as one of those things. Catherine is English South African, very loyal to the Commonwealth. One of her brothers died fighting the Germans in North Africa during the last war and another came back not quite right in the head. She said, "My brothers respected the Tommy," they told me, 'He doesn't wash much but he knows how to fight!'"

Mom, Richard and the boys are also down here, staying with Richard's parents on their farm in Muldersdrift. Catherine drives Anne and me across. Oupa is standing at the bottom of the drive. He's tall and good looking but old, and talks to Catherine in Afrikaans. Then he leads us off, "Kom," he says and walks ahead without talking. There's a bit of a problem at the plaas. Oupa and Ouma can't or won't speak English, and Mom can't and won't try to speak Afrikaans. Oupa fought the British in the Boer War, and Ouma, as a teenager, was interned in a British concentration camp at Krugersdorp. Thousands of women and children were dying in the camps. They thought the Engels were trying to poison them, and combed every tiny bit of their food for ground glass. So the old folks are not so pleased that Richard has left his nice Afrikaans vrou for this bad English woman who's been married before. Richard's name is really Theunis Marius but he changed it to help him fit in, up in NR. The farm house is small and old, two bedrooms, and there are only a couple of fields. The farm covered most of Muldersdrift when Oupa's grandfather had it, but was divided between sons, and then grandsons, which is the Afrikaans way. Richard said that even when he was small they only farmed for their own food and a little money for things they couldn't grow or make. He had to run back from school to help with the farm, and if he was late his Dad hit him. When he was nine he used to take an ox-wagon full of vegetables into Joburg, leaving at midday the day before, arriving in the evening, sleeping under the wagon, and selling the next day. He had a kaffir and a picannin with him but was in charge. He left school aged twelve, the end of primary, because his family couldn't afford to keep him in education.

Ouma gives us lunch, mutton, sweet pumpkin mash, spinach mixed with something, and rice. For pudding there's wonderful creamy melktert. Then Mom and Richard and us kids go to the Muldersdrift Hotel for a drink. "This is where Richard was working before he went up to Muf in 46," says Mom, all proud. "He was only twenty, but he was the barman, well, really running the hotel, and the Muf club manager happened to be passing through and thought he was good." "What did you do during the war?" I ask, thinking of Catherine's brothers, "Did you fight?" "Ya you could say that," says Richard grinning, "but not for the English." "Shut up Richard," says Mom. Richard suddenly goes quiet like I haven't seen him before, tears in his eyes, a muscle quivering in his cheek, like he's going to hit someone, or cry. He says quietly, "Don't you tell me to shut up in my own country, I did what was right for my people OK?" "All right Richard," says Mom. Richard's quiet for a long time after that.

Afterwards we go to the family cemetery. It's overgrown, tombstones down, black squatters living right there, fowls scratching between the graves, mealies growing up against the graves. Richard's shocked. He talks to a couple of the blacks, you don't get the feeling they're trying to destroy the graveyard, it's as if they haven't really noticed it, or just don't care. He arranges that they'll look after the graves for fifteen shillings per month. We go into Krugersdorp to buy spades and things for them, and to fix it up with his cousin Dannie. I notice that some graves go back to about 1840. "Ya," says Richard, "our people came up from the Cape with the Great Trek, to get away from you English, but you keep following us around."

That night I ask Catherine about it. Her family were on the British side, but some of her relatives are half Afrikaans and she's upset about how they were treated. She says the British burned Boer farms, killed their livestock, deliberately poisoning wells and ruining the land. Over half of all Boer children died in the concentration camps, and if a Boer soldier went on fighting, his family was starved in the camp. After the war, thousands flooded into the towns, with no education and no jobs. "My father remembers them sleeping on the platform of Johannesburg station, barefoot and hungry, real poor whites. Even when I was a child the Afrikaner hadn't recovered from the war, he was only one up from the native, and had to compete with him for work. No wonder they don't trust anyone. That's why they want a republic, to make sure it never happens again."

Back in Muf, Chris has come across for the holidays. We're going fishing. As we set off he notices a dead lizard in the back lane. He puts a hook through it on the end of a line. "Let's try it on those fowls," he says pointing to a run near our house. I go along with it. I have this picture of a chicken peck pecking in its careful way, gradually finishing the lizard, leaving a shiny clean hook. He puts it through the wire, the fowls come running up clucking, and in half a second there's a horrible squawking and a brown hen's flapping at the end of the hook. We run off to hide under a culvert, but the garden boy's spotted us and comes running up. Gently he takes our arms, "Plis sa, you musty come weeth me, thee boss, he is verr cross." We go back, by which time an old man is holding the hen, the hook sticking out of the top of its beak. It doesn't look too upset, but then I don't suppose a chicken's face can. The man seems more sad than cross, and says, " Boys, how could you do such a thing? Now I'm going to have to kill her," and asks where we live. That night Dad and Catherine don't make a big fuss about it, and seem to accept my explanation, but this makes me feel worse, do they think I'm cruel?

Dear Kasuhiko or is it Dear Ozawa? He has the same problem, last time calling me Dear Hassall. Anyway here is part of a letter to my Japanese pen friend who I swap stamps with. Dad said we have to move on although they did some terrible things in the war. Dad and I sometimes talk about things like that. I ask why somebody should want to invade someone else's country, like the Japs did to the Chinese, or the Germans did to the French, what's the point, and why are they so cruel when they get there? I can't believe all Germans and Japanese are bad people, but Catherine says a lot of Germans were Nazis or knew what was happening to the Jews, and nobody could forgive them for that. I ask Dad why he called Jo Jackson the Auctioneer a Jewboy, and he looks embarrassed and says that's just what people say, and that was what everyone in London called them before the war. He's got nothing against Jews, in fact Auntie Mary went out with a rich Jew in London and nearly married him. There are quite a few Germans in Muf, and

Douglas says Dieter Barsch's Dad was a Nazi or a Communist or something during the war.

"Dear Kazuhiko, you asked me to tell you a bit about Mufulira my home town, and I've looked a few things up in a book. To me Muf is the best place in the world. Last year our school cricket team won the Copperbelt trophy and we are on the way to doing the same this year. Muf is a copper mining town and the Copperbelt is a seam of copper that stretches hundreds of miles, through Mufulira, Kitwe, Luanshya and Chingola, and Katanga in the Belgian Congo. Muf mine started in about 1924 but only really got going in the 1930s and is one of the biggest copper mines in the world. We have about 6,000 whites, with two primary schools not counting the convent, and a high school. The town started near the mine, and all the oldest houses are down there. Each house has about an acre of ground, with a kia (house) for the black servant, and you can move to a bigger or better house if you get promoted or have lots of children. The town is full of big trees like in the bush, so you can hardly see the houses from a plane. Most of the main things like the club, hospital, Boma, swimming pool, and town centre, are at the bottom end of the camp. Our house is in the top end which is newer. The shops are mostly in one main street and start with two banks, like castles, one on each side of the road, Standard and Barclays. This end of town is for whites, so blacks aren't allowed into the big department stores, if they need to pick up their madam's groceries they get served from a hatch. They mainly stay off the pavements, and it's quiet round here. As you get to the bottom of the street, it's still the white section, but some blacks go into shops like the bakery, and Werner's butchery right at the corner. If you turn left you're in the African shopping area, which is much more crowded, and closes on a Tuesday afternoon instead of Wednesday like ours. The market's down there too. My friends and I like going into the African shops because they have all sorts of interesting things. I don't suppose you have blacks in Japan. Sometimes we get Zanzibar stamps and here are a few for you."

I didn't tell Kazuhiko but last Sunday Auntie Mary was saying. "Would you like to queue up at a hatch to be served? It's not treating people with dignity, it's inhuman. And this 'boys' meat' they sell, it's worse than dogs' meat" But Bennie Rousseau said it's only practical because they would swamp our shops while we couldn't swamp theirs, and also they carry diseases and feed their babies in public and that kind of thing. Benny says, "Sis man, I don't go into their shops and bioscopes, why do they always want to come into ours? You don't get us whites protesting because we can't go into black beer halls do you?" "I think," says Auntie Mary, "you're missing the point. The ANC is boycotting European shops, particularly butchers until people are treated properly, it's hurting trade, and some shops are giving in now." "Ya," says Benny, "but at the same time they're trying to get served in our hotels and cafes. They should make up their minds, but they're too bloody thick, pardon my French." Auntie Mary looks at him and says nothing.

It's Christmas day at Mom's house. Auntie Rene and Uncle Led are visiting for morning drinks. Uncle Led works for the Housing Department. If anything needs to be done, like a leaky tap or broken window, he turns up with a gang of three boys and they fix it. Usually the boys know what to do, so Uncle Led goes inside for a cup of tea, while they do the job. Today, he's sitting on the veranda with Glen and me, shooting at a target with a toy bow and suction arrows. Every time we beat him he gives us five shillings, and so far we've won five pounds because he's so drunk, he can hardly fit the arrow on to the string. Mom tells us to give it all back but he won't take it.

By midday a little party's going on the lawn, with about ten visitors, mainly from the police and flying club, all well on their way. I'm the barman because Richard's busy talking, and Mom's mainly doing the lunch because Malanga arrived drunk, staggering up the drive, and isn't much use. I have a little swig of this and that to check the taste. There's a man I don't recognise, straight out from England, with one of those accents, and he's getting a bit pushy and saying he can drink Richard or any South African under the table. So every time I pour Richard a whisky and ginger ale I pour him a treble. When they all start leaving at lunchtime he gets into his car and reverses straight into the gatepost. We all piss ourselves. "Ghut man," says Richard looking pleased, "these English can't hold their drink." I say nothing.

We go in for dinner. But Richard's bad tempered because of the drink, and by the pudding I think he's sick of wearing funny hats and talking to women and kids. So he says, "I'll check on the garden, and take Malanga something to drink." "All right Richard, off you go," says Mom with her martyr's face. He takes a whisky bottle with about three fingers left, pours in some brandy, gin, sherry and bits from a few other bottles and tops it all up with beer. Then he gets some Castles and goes outside. When we look out the window, there he is sitting on the ground under a mango tree with Malanga, both with bottle in hand, chatting away.

Mufulira 1959

I'm staying with Chris in Luanshya for the holidays. This is when we have a lekker time. Some days we hitch around the Copperbelt. Towns are about forty miles apart. Last night we were stuck in Ndola as it got dark, so we went to the Aunts for the night, and they agreed not to tell Dad and Catherine. Other days we take Uncle Oscar's 303 to the quarry and shoot at 44 gallon drums and things. One oke stays at the target end to put the drums back up and you hope the other guy shoots straight. We also do a lot of fishing but Auntie Elsie tells us to be careful because Chris's just had bilharzia and the treatment nearly kills you.

But Chris and his friends talk mainly about girls and sex. They're all fourteen or fifteen and can't talk about anything else. They've got a young woman maths teacher with short dresses and big tits, and last term three of them sat in a row at the back of the class wanking while she wrote on the board. Farney was leading, and he'd say "Tits," and they'd all concentrate on her tits, then "legs," and so on. They all think she smaaks them, and dream of having her on a desert island and things like that. "She likes all of you?" I ask. "No just me," they each say, and then each gives a reason like, "She smiled at me in a special way." Farney has a story about how this older woman, about twenty-five, a nymphomaniac, invited him into her house and started undressing him, and he screwed her, but Chris says he's making it all up. I say what about girls your age? But they say you can kiss them in the bioscope but that's all they'll let you do. The worst is Peter Duke, just out from England who says girls there are easy, and has lots of stories. He's so frustrated he's always wanking, even once when they went out fishing on a boat. Chris says last time Duke came to his house he sat down on his bed and started immediately. Chris told him to stop because his sisters were around, and when he didn't, hit his prick hard with the narrow side of a ruler, and Duke was rolling round on the floor crying. Now he's got to the stage where he's plotting to screw a kaffir girl who sometimes visits her father down the lane, he's going to offer her ten bob. They're not interested in kaffir girls but nobody says anything, they know he's not being a kaffir boetie, it's just need.

On Saturdays I don't go to the matinee any more, people my age go to the morning show, then when you get to about fifteen its the five o'clock show. Everyone turns up early and wanders around talking to their friends and showing off their clothes. You wear either shorts with coloured long socks, say red or green, or jeans rolled up at the bottom, and velskoens. Mom bought me some moccasins which lots of the okes wear now, and Anne got me an Elvis tie, one of those with two strings like they wear in Alabama, but Catherine said I couldn't wear them. She said I should wear sandals! Sandals to bioscope! So I change at Mom's on the way, and then again on the way back. The films are different, more grown up, the girls go mad any time a guy with a ducktail comes on. A few weeks ago, for a few seconds they thought it was Elvis, then realised it was Eddie Cochrane, but they still screamed. A few boys sit with girls but mainly we sit separate. After bioscope we go to the pool or Mike's cafe. Last Saturday two new boys turned up, one my age, one older, from Liverpool in England. They were dressed all in black leather, jackets and trousers, which I've never seen before, and had black hair combed back Elvis style. Straight away there was a crowd round them, and they were showing off all their English stuff, like flick knives, and English cigarettes called woodbines.

Mom's just come back from England, seeing Nanna and Granddad. She calls it going home. I can't quite get what England's like, is it old fashioned and dull, like the black and white films, or maybe more like the Christmas cards, bright and snowy? Mom says "I've got something for you." She opens a little box and pulls out two bright reddy purple cherries, joined by stalks. I recognise them from books. "I bought them yesterday afternoon in London." I picture a London street, like out of Oliver Twist but with black London taxis. I play with the cherries for a long time, so shiny, there yesterday, here now, before eating them. Mom tells me about England, how Nanna and Granddad live in Old Ford Road. They bath once a week in a tin tub in the kitchen, or go to Bethnal Green baths near the tube station. Their toilet is outside, through Mrs Smallwood's kitchen, and they have gas lights. Granddad who was born in 1885 still works as a furrier, making sheepskin slippers, and Granny works in a factory opening up cardboard boxes which have arrived flat. "When I was a little girl I didn't have a bed," Mom says, "I just slept on two kitchen chairs." Richard has come in, "Ya, and now you know the bishop of Northern Rhodesia and talk to the wives of the big shots." "Give it a rest Richard," says Mom. "Jislaaik, some of these soeties straight out from England, you can tell how they used to live, they smell like they haven't changed their shirts for a week, and they offer cigarettes to the kaffirs like they're pals. But after a couple of weeks they're yelling at the kaffirs, and acting like they're bloody king of the castle." Mom says, "Yes it's true, I cannot tell a lie, but at first you don't know how to treat them. When we arrived in Chingola I invited the garden boy in for breakfast, he was straight from the bush, and when George found out he told me to stop it because the boy would get the wrong idea. And he was right, he kept staring at me, couldn't take his eyes off my legs, always stood too close, and in the end we had to sack him."

It's the Christmas holidays, I'm at Mom's house quite a lot. Malanga plays football with us in the garden and he's as good as Glen and me and Willem together. Mom calls him a mampara. Last time Richard ran out of whisky he opened one of the miniatures that run round the lounge pelmet, took a swig and spat it out. It was tea. So he tried a few more and they were the same. Malanga was called in and finally admitted he'd drunk the lot and refilled them. "I'll bloody kill you Malanga," said Richard but did nothing, and you got the idea he kind of admired his cheek, because he started telling the story to his friends.

Mom and Malanga are always arguing or something. Malanga polishes the red stone floor the usual way by standing on two big flat brushes with straps for your feet, and then sliding around. "Put de music, Dona." "Don't be ridiculous," says Mom, and then puts on a record. Malanga dances around, overdoing it, pretending to lose his balance, grinning and making faces, and we all laugh. "Silly arse!" says Mom. A few mornings ago he was ironing in the kitchen and somehow carrying on a conversation with the garden boy at least fifty yards away near the gate. "Hey chongo!" says Mom. "Ahh Medem!" says Malanga as if telling her off for being unreasonable. "Don't talk to me in that tone of voice Malanga, now be quiet!" Malanga goes "Tchlll," a real long juicy one as only a black can do. Mom says, "Right that's it, you're fired! I'm sick of your cheek! Take your things and go. The boss will see you at four o'clock and sort out your money." "Ahh Medem!" says Malanga and goes off to the garden boy's kia. He sits in the doorway complaining loudly in Bemba. Mom's already made their morning tea, a huge pile of "mixed fruit" jam sandwiches, and tea in two family sized jam tins. She comes to the door again, "And Malanga, just look at this ironing, this shirt is still creased, what's the matter with you? You'll have to do these three again." "But Medem, I am sacked!" "Don't be silly," says Mom, "and come and get your tea before it goes cold." Glen says, "She sacked him last week too."

It's either raining or hot. We sit on Johny Oosthuizen's veranda, sweating, playing records, *He's got the whole world in his hands*, Laurie London, Elvis the King, Jerry Lee Lewis, *Great Balls of Fire*, Little Richard, Johny sings

"Short fat fanny she's my heart's desire
She took me to bed and she pulled my wire."

The needles on Johny's big old radiogram wear out quickly so sometimes we use the Christ thorns growing along his drive, but you've got to keep changing them. We talk of girls, and sometimes play football or cricket, or go to the pool. It's high school next year and everything will be different. I've won most of the prizes this year, including the dux ludorum. Nobody said much about that at home, as if it doesn't quite fit me, and that's how I feel too.

Mufulira 1960

At first Muf High is a bit scary, it's easy to get lost, or not know what lesson you have next, and then you get that panicky feeling. But there's also the excitement and smell of everything new, uniform, maths tin, books, people. There are some clever pupils from

Muf Primary, and some from other places, but I'm still in the top five. We've started Latin and French. History is my favourite subject.

Last night there was a big fight at the Buffalo Hall. I was staying with Mom for the weekend and she let me go to a dance there with Anne and her boyfriend Wally. He's an apprentice with a Ford Popular painted in stripes of different colours. Anne says I'm a baby teenager now so I must learn to dance and chat up girls. Anyway with a little help from her I was actually jiving with Marlene when someone shouted that the Kitwe boys had arrived. About twenty of them drove up in five cars, marched in and started fighting with the older boys. They were led by a big oke called Eddy who was looking for Gerald Anderson and his friends because of something they'd done in Kitwe last week. I tried to join in but one of them said, "Fuck off peepi joller," and hit me hard across the face with the back of his hand. I was dizzy and my nose was bleeding, but he was hardly trying, just getting me out of the way. Soon the hall was wrecked with flying bottles and chairs and then the police arrived. Eddy and some of his friends were arrested because they'd come in a stolen car, pinched just for a joy ride. When we got home Anne said, "I love Eddy. Isn't he fabulous? They say he's the biggest JD on the Copperbelt." Funny how a year ago I couldn't understand how boys could act like that, what would their mom and dad think? Now, I don't care, I want to be like Eddy.

There's big trouble in the Congo. The army's mutinied, gone mad, killing whites, raping nuns and everything. On Sunday we went down to the club and it was chocabloc with Belgians everywhere, in the main lounges, the mess, even the bioscope. The car park was full of Congo cars, dirty and dented. Just then a green VW with Congo plates rolled up, full of bullet holes, with a man, woman and two kids. The man kind of fell out, collapsing to his knees, then got up and stumbled round to the passenger door. The woman was covered in blood, not moving, her face grey. Some men helped her out, then an ambulance arrived and took her off.

I bought 2/6 worth of sweets and went round giving them to Belgian kids, trying out my French. The boys wear short shorts, like swimming costumes. Now people all over the camp are putting up Belgians in their homes, just like we did for the Kenyans after the Mau Mau. "God help us if the blacks get independence here," said Dad. You can't go into the Congo now. "Heart of Darkness," says Auntie Beth.

On Sunday we went to the pleasure resort, me and Marlene, Anne and Wally, and Robert and Janet. I don't really smaak Marlene, a bit fat, but so what, a girl's a girl. Wally's car's got a record player, balanced by gyroscopes, that plays 45s, and he put on Ricky Nelson then switched to Chuck Berry. I felt excited, ya this is it, in with the in crowd. We stopped at the garage for petrol. The two petrol boys, about eighteen, were sitting in the shade chatting, in no hurry to serve us. Wally said, "Eh, ewe, isa kuna, checha!" The one boy said in snooty English "Do noty coly mi uwe, coly mi by my name." Wally said, "How can I call you by your name when I don't know what it is?" So the boy said, with a clever look on his face, "Theny coly mi meester hoom." We all packed out laughing. "Call me mister whom! What kind of English is that?" The boy looked confused, then embarrassed, this hadn't gone as he'd expected, and for some reason, maybe because I was concentrating on him, he suddenly looked a bit like a normal oke, in a way like Hennie, only darker. "Better than your Bemba," I said, without thinking. Wally looked at me shocked "What? Fucking little kaffir boetie!" Anne put her arm round me, "Don't be horrible to my little brother, he's not a kaffir boetie." But he kept looking at me funny after that.

We got to the pleasure resort at midday, it was baking hot. There's soft sand like a beach and we played a game where Robert and I sat on the car bonnet while Wally raced up and then jammed on the brakes and we'd go flying off. Anne said it was dangerous and we should stop. Then we had a swim, "Bugger bilharzia," said Wally. Then we sat in the sun with another group, drinking Castle and smoking Life cigarettes, singing the radio advert,

Life is great
And it's fun
Life is great for everyone
You'll enjoy, we can bet
A king size filter cigarette.

But I don't like filter cigarettes, and gradually began to feel sick, then I went into the bush to puke, and came out feeling like a fool.

This is the worst thing I've ever had to write about, Dad has told us we're leaving Muf to live in Ndola. I have to admit I was crying when he told me, why do we have to move? I don't know why but he doesn't like the mine and he wants to start a business. But everyone else's dad likes the mine, why doesn't Dad? It's not fair. This is where I belong. Ndola's a big dump, nobody on the Copperbelt likes it. It's got no mine, and it's full of English government type people. Anne was crying too, but the girls seemed happy. "You'll mix with children from a better background there," said Catherine, "and you'll be away from certain influences."

This morning I stood on the pavement outside Bata, looking up towards Barclays Bank and then down towards Mclellands, then across the road at the post office thinking I'm going to fix this picture in my head forever.

These exams I've dropped from 5th place in class to 26th. The headmaster's written to Dad saying I'm not working. Dad thinks it'll all come right when we get to Ndola.

Ndola 1961

Agreed with the girls that we wouldn't say anything about our parents being divorced because it's so embarrassing, just act like we're real brothers and sisters, a new start. Anne's living with us again. I still have to stay with the girls when Anne's not around, though nobody has to stay with her. But Anne and Phillipa have already started fighting. When Catherine comes in Phillipa bursts into tears and makes up a load of rubbish, and Anne gets the blame. Last time when I tried to protect Anne by saying what happened, and refusing to talk to Phillipa, Catherine climbed into me and whacked me all the way round the garden. But there was something in the way she did it and the things she said that make me think she genuinely believes she's right, and that Anne is just a trouble maker, a bad influence on me. Janet never causes any trouble, and never tells on me, she's a sweet kid. Anne's gone to live with Mom in Muf.

Ndola's not as bad as I thought, no it's great. We live in Kenmere Avenue at the Kansenji end and I've started at Llewellyn High. I'm in the A stream but the teacher says I'm on trial. I've fallen big time for this girl called Emma Farmer in the year below. I never talk to her, but I make detours just to walk past her class, and I ride past her house in the hope of seeing her in the garden, and, how can I explain it, even the house seems special. It's got so I feel excited when I get up in the morning for school. I'm making lots of new friends, and have a new best friend called Barry Jones, which is good because you can't just turn up at bioscope or other places on your own.

Saturdays are the best, first we go to Barry's to listen to Lyons Maid Hits of the Week from 9.00 to 9.30, then to town to check out the babes. We all sit in the Golden Ray café nursing one coke at a time, then a burger for lunch, the freedom of not going home, then Broadway Cinema for the afternoon matinee. Last Saturday at bioscope I got my first kiss. I heard that this girl Jenni likes me. She was sitting up behind us, so I sent Barry up to see if she wanted to come sit with me. He came down saying yes, and a minute later a girl came down to kind of negotiate the arrangements. Three boys sitting next to me had to shift to the back, then Jenni came down with two friends and sat next to me, staring straight ahead, chewing steadily with her mouth open. I didn't know what to say so I said nothing but decided to put my arm round her when the lights went down, but chickened out. I managed it halfway through Pathe News. She didn't respond at all, like her shoulders were stiff, but I thought, "I'll snog her as the news ends." I chickened out again and finally decided, at the end of the cartoon, "It's now or never." I thought if I don't get things going now, she won't come back after interval. So I leaned across but she moved at just the wrong moment and I got her on the chin. I was kissing a big salty chaub. I thought, "I've got to get this right," so I pulled her head towards me and kissed her properly, but it was like kissing a dummy, she didn't kiss back.

Then I remembered something Barry had said, so I whispered, "Jenni, you're the most beautiful thing in the world." Somehow everything changed, "Really?" she said, and turned and gave me a big fat smooch. It nearly blew my head off. After that we were at it all afternoon, I can't really remember the film, and at the end had sore balls though all we did was kiss. "Lovers' balls!" shouted Barry and all the okes laughed. How do they know all this stuff? Now we're officially hitched, except I still really want Emma.

One of the big problems is cash. I get 17/6 pocket money per month, bioscope costs 1/- and a beer is 1/3 so if I'm not careful I can run out in a few days. I can make a bit helping Dad, he's got this printing business which he learned in England. He does things like leaflets, and is trying to get into doing school books and things like that. John our garden boy from Muf, who's really smart, has come with us and now works Dad's printing machine. Dad's also got these girls stacking pages and so on. They're coloured, between black and white, which you don't see in Muf, the okes call them goffles. Well, one of them, Janet, is about seventeen and she's the sexiest thing you can imagine, soft brown legs, and a beautiful gentle face with freckles on her nose. I'd love to kiss them and a lot more too. Who would I like on a desert island, her or Emma or Jenni? Well Emma of course, but Janet's the one I imagine most at night when, you know what. I told a couple of the okes but they looked shocked. "Jesus, dirty bloody goffles, I wouldn't touch one with a bargepole, what's the matter with you?" So now I keep my mouth shut.

Once a week we do ballroom dancing at school. It's a load of rubbish but that's where I meet Jenni, and we sneak off down the corridors for a snog. I'm making a bit of progress and last night managed to get my hands under her bra. Tits are so soft! There's something about doing this at school, knowing how good you'll feel when you walk past the spot next day. Cycling home, three of us stopped at the garage as usual for a coke out of the drinks box. We usually pay for three and then when the garage boy isn't looking pinch another one each. This time he came up to us, an old guy, maybe forty. "Please my boys, do not steal thee drinks, I see you before." Of course we denied it. Then he said, "I have to pay for each one from my wages, you know how much I make? Six pounds ten shillings per month, you are stealing nearly half my day's wages. I have three children." Shit, I hadn't seen it that way, I didn't think anyone would find out. So we apologised and gave him the money for the cokes and a bit more.

Got caned today. Four of us were following short, fat Mrs Thompson along the corridor, imitating her waddly walk, like four ducklings in a row. Mr Loubser the Deputy Head was watching from across the quadrangle, and as we spotted him he raised one finger and signalled to us to come across, in such a way that Mrs Thompson didn't notice. "Well boys," he said, with a half smile, "we can't have this disrespect towards staff, and Mrs Thompson would have been hurt if she'd seen you, so I think that's worth two don't you?" The pain of the whack goes straight into the back of your head. When I looked at my bum in the mirror that night the lines started blue at the edge, working up to purple in the middle.

One thing that's good about Ndola is being near the Aunts. I often go round for tea at four. They always have these fancy little cakes covered in icing, I can have as many as I want, and sugar cubes you pick up with tongs, I've never seen that before. Then Auntie Mary and I take her daschund bitch for a walk in the park. We talk about all sorts of interesting things, and she lets me smoke. She's the only person I know who treats kaffirs like whites, and thinks they should run the country. She calls them 'men and women' so the milkboy is the 'milkman' like in England. Dad says she gives all her money to blacks who make up sob stories and don't pay her back. She never actually argues, if you say something she doesn't agree with, she looks surprised and says, "Really? Ohhh." At most she might ask a question, "But don't you think?" and that's it. Years ago when the Elvis hit "*All Shook Up*" came out and he was causing a big stir she asked, all innocent, "Shouldn't it be 'all shaken up'?" and I thought she was being stupid but that's how she makes her points.

Auntie Mary and Beth are always going to the theatre and to parties with the local theatre crowd. On Thursday afternoons they go to tea at the Savoy wearing smart dresses and white gloves. They play bridge, and on special occasions smoke coloured cigarettes. Mrs Collins, Auntie Mary's best friend, is the queen of this group and holds cocktail evenings in her big English style house. The fifteen acre garden has been left mainly wild, with huge African trees, and sometimes in the evening you still see monkeys and buck. The house slopes up a hill, the entrance hall panelled Tudor style, then dark wooden stairs up into the light of a stone courtyard also at ground level, half open to the sky, with green polished floors and a fish pond full of frogs. Many doors lead off, to the garden, the kitchen, more stairs, and to a huge lounge with the largest picture window you've ever seen, looking out over the bush-garden below. People sit drinking Pimms and other fancy drinks watching the sun set, some talking in actor voices, and throwing their hands around. At Christmas there's a wonderful party, with a huge tree and expensive presents, and although it's for adults, they play games like charades, or run round the house posting slips of paper into boxes labelled Moscow, Berlin. I'm the only boy there, but usually there's a pretty girl, I think deliberately arranged by Mrs Collins, and somehow, in this situation, it feels romantic. Next year they're putting on *Under the Sycamore Tree*. The brochure says it'll be part of an NR drama festival including *A Streetcar Named Desire, The Seven Year Itch, Waiting for Godot, and Twelfth Night.* Boring!

Visited the Gearys last week, Uncle Oscar was sitting with his hand in plaster, broken climbing into the swimming pool grounds on Christmas Eve, with a load of friends, after a night of drink. "When will you grow up?" asked Auntie Elsie. But he's proud of Chris and started telling Dad how this Australian was in the club bar boasting about how they were better than South Africans, but mainly mocking the Afrikaaners, saying how some Australian shit called Breaker Morant had massacred some in the Boer war. "Maybe he thought he could talk like that because we're English speaking but we're all South Africans, and when he said that I just got the moerin. Who the hell did they think they were coming to our country and killing our people? And then he was praating about their wonderful dangerous outback, shit man, pardon my language, what have they got, nothing, no real bush and no real animals except, what's its name, kangaroos, like big bloody rabbits. Anyway I couldn't take him on because of my hand so I sneaked off and phoned Chris. He came along and just climbed into the bloke without a word, laid him out cold. That's my boy, not even seventeen." Chris sat there looking ahead, expressionless, like a sphinx.

Ndola 1962

Ndola's so good! Shit I love going to school just to be with my friends and see the girls. I cycle up through a bit of bush and join a path Emma has to take, and by careful timing I see her about one day in three. But gradually I've got to know her brother Jimmy who's in my class and in my crowd, and he's invited me to his house tomorrow afternoon. I can hardly believe my luck! When we get to school our crowd sits at the far corner of the rugby field, so we can see anyone coming. We sit cross-legged on the grass smoking and blowing into the ground. We do the same at break. We hide the cigs in all sorts of clever places, up our ties, in pens, but if necessary the girls put them down their bras. Sometimes the prefects run at the group to catch us out. The usual rule, but you can never be quite sure, is that if you hand over the cigs, they just take them, and that's it, but if you hide them and get caught you have the choice of eating them or going to the headmaster for six. Yesterday afternoon in the snooker hall I had my own cig offered back to me by a prefect from his 30 box of Life, stashed with a range of confiscated brands. Sometimes Finch, the PT teacher, stands at the corner of the quad with binoculars trying to identify smokers.

Jimmy's house after school, his houseboy makes us a polony sandwich, and we sit in his room. It smells just like him, only stronger. It's funny how you get to know the smell of your friends, each one different, sweat and stale hair oil, farts stinking out your blazer, we flap them before putting them on. Jimmy has his hair combed back at the sides, Elvis style, like mine, but with a crew cut on top. He seems to get girls quite easily but might do even better if he had fewer greasy zits. He reads all these books I've never heard of, some by a bloke called Mickey Spillane, about a detective called Mike Hammer. There's lots of sex in them, he reads me a few paragraphs. He's also got one about a woman called Beebo Brinker who smaaks other women, she's called a lesbian, like a female moffie. He keeps his Lucky Strikes hidden in a fat book about commandos, with a square cut out of the middle. He gets 10/- a week pocket money, more than twice as much as me, has better clothes, and knows all the main JDs in town. "Come, let's get a Coke," he says, and we go through the lounge to the kitchen, my heart thumping. There sitting on the couch is Emma, still in her school uniform but no shoes, her dress up to her thighs, their big alsatian on her lap. She sits the dog up in a silly human-like pose, "Say hello to Rinty," she says, and waves his paw at us. Now I can see all the way up to her pants, her legs brown and sturdy but also soft and dimpled, and in the heat there's a glow of sweat on them. I hear myself say, "Let me lick that off for you," but it's in my head. She puts the dog back on her lap. "Lucky Rinty," I think. It's funny, I usually have two different kinds of girls, those I'm in love with, and want to kiss and protect, because they're beautiful and gentle, and those I just want to mess around with in a sexy way, but today, with Emma, the two are the same.

Got caned four today. Mr Price the maths teacher was writing on the board so for a laugh I threw a rubber at him. It had just left my hand when he turned and saw me half standing with my arm out as the thing whizzed past his ear. They cane you at break. If it's four or six, news gets round and everyone gathers in the quad outside Mr Loubser's office, including all the girls you like and have ever liked. It reminds me of a hanging in a cowboy film. Finally the caned person comes out, usually with a sickly grin on his face, and moist, newly wiped eyes. This time Mr Loubser wasn't smiling. I couldn't believe the pain, I had to grip my hands tight together to prevent them swinging back to protect my bum. At the end I said, "Thank you sir, sorry about that sir, won't do it again sir," and anything else to buy time before going out. "Yes, yes, off you go," he said, so I stepped out, having decided to keep a completely straight face because the grin never works. That night right in the middle of each purple line was a strip of blood. Last time Mr Loubser had been taking it easy.

In Muf for the holidays, Jimmy's come for the weekend. It's great at Mom's because she lets us do just about anything we like, and we can booze at home, just help ourselves. Now I live in Ndola, I'm beginning to think we're better than the Muf okes, like we know more and have done more and have better babes. On Friday night we were sitting at the club, drinking ginger ale to save money, and pretending it had whisky in it. Then up comes that bastard John Stevens from England who I fought years ago and he and his oppo start mocking our drinks. So we agree to go outside, and while we're standing on the driveway arguing he punches me straight in the face, out of the blue. Then before I know it, he and his friend are holding identical studded belts, and each has a big sharp copper knuckle duster going right round all four fingers. Just then two men come from the direction of the bar. One says to Stevens, "Too chicken to fight normally? You're getting too big for your boots you little bastards. Put your toys down or I'll kick your fucking heads in." He turns to Jimmy and me, "I'll give you each 2/6 if you donner them." "Me too," says the other. Anyway Jimmy and I laid into them, and they were useless, maybe because of the men, and we got five bob each.

On Saturday morning Jimmy and I hitch across to the Kitwe agricultural show and get there at about eleven. It's June so it starts off a bit cold, but by mid morning the sun's beating down and everything's covered in red dust. We wander from pavilion to pavilion, looking at things, picking up free samples, ten cigs from BAT, ten from Peter Stuyvesant, a free coke, miniature brandy bottles. "Come on boys, you're too young, oh OK just one each," and then off to the next stall for the same, pinch a few here and there. By mid afternoon, we're full of food, semi pissed, and seriously trying to pick up girls. We're bolder than usual because it's not our town. Everything feels good in a hot, hazy way. "Heh baby, come and walk around with us." We have some success, but it doesn't seem to last, it's hard to find a pair who each likes one of us and then hold the right girl's hand. At one point we try to switch partners, and they both go off in a huff. But then at about six, as the sun is setting, our luck changes. We see these two girls looking at us and giggling in a friendly way, and we just drift over to them like it's the natural thing to do, and the girls seem to choose which one of us they want in a natural kind of way too. Being a kafupi I have the small one and Jimmy the taller one. We wander over to the braai area, the smell of meat cooking, and that romantic feel of the evening ahead. We buy some boerries in a roll with Mrs Ball's chutney, then go to the Lunar Park, on the octopus. You have to hang backwards high up at quite an angle while they're loading the seats below, which makes her nervous, and that's my opportunity to cuddle her and act comforting, and kiss her sweet face and soft black hair, all alone above the fair. After that we wander around with candy floss, playing some of the games, and then go behind the animal stalls and settle down on some hay for a snog. I start squeezing her tits, she won't let me go any further but that's OK. I feel in love with her and don't want to push too hard, I just enjoy having a girl to myself, looking at her face in the moonlight, and kissing her as much as I want. Then she pushes me over on my back and lies on me and runs her tongue over my lips and teeth and I feel a thrill going right through me, like an electric shock. Suddenly she looks at her watch and says "Oh no, no, I'm late, gotta go, my Dad's waiting at the gate!" She calls the other girl and they rush off shouting, "Come to bioscope next Saturday!" Jimmy comes across looking pleased with himself, "How'd you do?" he asks. I tell him. I'm feeling a bit lost and sad now she's gone. "Get a load of this," he says and sticks his finger under my nose. Lucky for her she doesn't live in Ndola, the whole school would know by Monday.

We wander round the grounds which are emptying. It's not worth trying to hitch home now, so we sneak into the animal sheds and settle down on a pile of hay. Later it gets cold so we climb further into it. Next morning we're up at seven because of the cold and hunger. Then I hear that egg –laying cluck cluck from the fowl section so we take eggs from their cages, make a hole in each end like Richard showed me, and suck the middle out, a bit slimy but OK. We hitch back to Muf at midday, dozy and comfortable in the hot sun, feeling pleased with ourselves.

Jimmy's been on holiday to Greece and he's brought back three flick knives, for him, me and Charlie. They aren't so good, they open sideways instead of straight out, and look more like a penknife than a dagger. But still. I sit in the Golden Ray flicking it open and cleaning it to show off. Gerald Anderson who's left school says, "Would you use that on anybody?" "No," I say. "What about a kaffir?" "No." "Well then don't bloody carry it around, you stupid little prick, or some one'll use it on you, you're just a big bloody act." He's right, I act like a skate, but I still rescue insects from the bog and things like that. Hamba gashle.

We've moved to a fantastic place in Kansenji, with a nine acre garden. The house has a huge central hall, with all the rooms leading off. The rent's cheap because it's owned by an old guy who believes he's descended from the last dauphin of France, and is going to Europe to stake his claim. Dad says Mr Nichols does look like a Bourbon. The store house is full of old books on the revolution, and furniture which the guy says belonged to Marie Antoinette. He ran the place as a market garden. There's a dark, sunken celery garden, crisscrossed by water channels, fed by a bubbling spring. The water leaves the garden through a deep dark pool, full of leeches and river crabs, then appears in full sunlight, running down the side of a wide, dry vlei, to a stream below. This is where I go in the hot afternoons, to the cool shade, to enjoy the scent of celery and trickling water, and daydream about making a fortune from the garden, or bringing pretty girls to my new den.

Mom has given me back my bantams from Muf, and John helps me build them a run and house. I let them out all day to peck where they like, and get to know their secret laying places, doing the rounds to collect eggs before school. I've never lost the thrill of finding a hidden egg, the yolks deep orange from an insect diet. I sell spare cocks to the blacks for 2/6 each, but insist they kill them one scaat with an axe, because once I saw Chris's houseboy killing one by sawing casually at its neck while chatting to his friend. The place is so big there's a kraal at one end with three huts where the old garden boy Kilikanka lives with his family. He looks about 70 and has always been there. Last night when we came home from the bioscope, there he was, standing to attention at the front door, a panga upright in one hand and a full length spear in the other. We can't really afford enough labour so the garden is getting wild in parts and is infested with spiders and snakes. Mom and Richard call it "The wilderness".

Joined the school cadets a few months ago. It used to be compulsory, a company of about two hundred boys, but with black rule coming there's no point in training up whites, so the whole thing folded. But Mr Muldoon has started it up again, just for fun, and I volunteered, also just for fun. We've just one platoon of about thirty boys, all in my year, and a huge amount of equipment from the compulsory days. Apart from the parading and the drag of getting your uniform ready it's great, we have Lee Enfield 303s and can fire as much ammo as we like on the rifle range. Some weekends and in the holidays we go on camps and basically play Germans and English or cowboys and indians like we did as kids, except with real rifles and blanks. Last time we had to attack a bren gun which was firing blanks, blue tipped wood to hold the gasses and force back the action. Sneaking up a ditch some idiot fired his rifle by my ear and I was semi deaf for three days. A couple of guys also got a bit of blank cardboard in the eye. Some of my skate friends wonder what I'm doing in this uniform, and sometimes so do I.

Mr Muldoon's the lieutenant, Bloomberg the sergeant, and recently I've been made the lance corporal! Sometimes I get to parade the platoon when Bloomberg's away, but I feel a bit uncomfortable. One of the biggest guys, Geldenhuys, doesn't like a kafupi like me ordering him around. Last week, marching in the ranks I was diagonally behind him and he kept swinging his arm out so our fists clashed as my arm went forward. I told him to fuck off so he challenged me to a fight. After cadets we went to the Big Tree where most of the fights are held, and just about the whole of the platoon came too, so high stakes. I was lucky, got him down with the head lock I've practised since my days with the Gearys, a running jump, feet off the ground, all my weight in his neck, then on the ground thumped his nose. I couldn't bring myself to do it twice, so let him go and stood up before he could use his strength. He got up groggy, "I'm gonna fucking kill you, you little bastard!" and ran at me head down, making it easy to step back and punch his nose again. After that he couldn't really fight and gave up. But he's big and getting bigger so I reckon I'll pay the price one day.

Shit man, things are going too far, now the kaffirs can come into the bioscope! I think they can come into the cafés too but so far they haven't tried the Golden Ray because there are too many of us. Also they're scared of being overcharged. I heard that in Chingola a group of cheeky smart political kaffirs demanded to be served in a café, expecting to be thrown out. "Come in gentlemen, please sit down," says the owner, then charges them £5 each for a cup of tea! Anyway, on Saturday a big gang of them, maybe fifty, turned up at bioscope. They came early and by the time we arrived they were already in, sitting at the front, which was a mistake because we were above and behind them. We were the moerin, partly because some of our friends couldn't get in, they hung around outside, in the entrance hall, on the pavement, and in the café, some just helping themselves to sweets and cigs. Inside we started throwing bits of rubbish from the back, and soon there were fights in the aisles. Then the police turned up, white officers and black constables, with their truncheons out. It was helluva tense, the cop officers acting all reasonable because they knew that if a kaffir cop hit a white boy all hell would break loose, and we easily outnumbered them. Anyway in the end we all went home, no film, should be interesting next week.

But this kaffir business is getting big. They seem to be more interested in fighting each other than us. Sometimes when we see a group we give the UNIP sign, the open - hand shaky wave. If they're UNIP they start grinning and waving back, then we change it to the ANC thumbs up, and they lose their grin, look confused, then angry, and then sometimes if there's plenty of them, they come towards us saying, "Eh, uwe, I shall beat you," or something like that. They're only half serious, and we can usually get away by backing off, but I think things are getting worse. They say the whole of the Eastern province is out of control, or rather, controlled by UNIP and now KK is stirring things up much better on the Copperbelt too. Muf is an ANC town but UNIP is much stronger in Ndola. At the Aunts' house Gert Rousseau says, "Have you heard about Nchanga? Last night seven ANC boys were hacked to death with spears and pangas, and over a hundred injured. I'm getting out if things go on like this, I got to think of my family. Look what happened to Mrs Burton and her kids." "Yes," says Auntie Beth, "horrible, I'm glad they caught some of those savages, and I hope they hang them." But Auntie Mary says, "I think that terrible crime was a one-off. I don't think white people are generally in danger, even though government forces have killed quite a few Africans. I can't think of any other cases, can you? For example the Eastern Province is full of isolated white settlements, and so far no white person has been harmed." Auntie Beth says, "I think you're being terribly naïve May, what about Kenya and the Congo?"

It's the Christmas holidays, one of our jobs is to make mango chutney. We've a grove of seventy two mango trees in the garden so there's no shortage. Dad's addicted to it and uses a jar every few days, even on his Christmas dinner. We kids have a big production line, peeling, cutting, mincing the half green mangos, mixing ingredients in a big brown bowl, cooking, bottling. The rain's been solid for four days, pelting down on the tin roof, and inside you get that cosy feeling of Christmas coming, and tradition going back hundreds of years to Europe, except that here it's mid summer.

When the rain lifts, Jimmy and I decide to cycle out to Bwana Mkubwa, about eight miles from town. It was an open cast copper mine in the old days when whites first came to this country, around 1900, with a huge crater, about two miles across, but now it's mined out, dead. There's something about those days, when there were only a few whites around, the tribes still in control. Like there's a huge old steam tractor in Ndola Park, which they say came down from the Congo in 1896 before the countries were separate, but how did it get from Europe in the first place? We're a thousand miles from the sea in any direction. And even in Muf there's the old town, near the mine, before the town centre moved to where it is now. Richard showed me a hut, which was the old post office. There's a picture of it in Muf magazine, taken in the 1920s, men outside with those big moustaches, and blacks in uniform, fez, barefoot, standing to attention. Then there are the old boys, like Chirupula Stevenson, who lived in the bush with a few black wives, but nobody blamed him because that was how it was in those days. There were gun fights in the Selbourne

Hotel in Ndola, and a lion walked into a butcher shop in Luanshya, and was whacked by the butcher with his meat cleaver.

Anyway, to get back to the story, it started pissing down a couple of miles out of town so we stopped at a little kaffir shop on the side of the road. They're great, a small room smelling of woodsmoke, sweat, and stored goods like mealie meal. Mfazis and kids with snotty noses sit around on the veranda. There's a cosy feeling being out of the rain. Inside, the walls are covered with things like pots and pans, bicycle parts, hoes, and shelves with tins of food. Below the glass counter is a shelf with matches, razors, soap and other smaller goods. We bought a packet of Marie biscuits and a bag of toffees, and were soon surrounded by picannins. So we handed them all out and bought some more, then set off.

At Bwana Mkubwa we rode through the deserted township, old colonial style houses with rusty corrugated iron roofs and open verandas, the whitewash splashed with years of red mud. I imagined what it must have been like in the old days, this tiny white community, people passing in the street, pausing to chat in the sunshine, perhaps a small club or bar, dinner invitations. Spooky. Then a face appeared on one of the verandas, then another, and we realised they were occupied, by blacks. The crater, a mile further on, is huge, much more than a hundred feet deep and as far as the eye can see. We're not supposed to be here because they say it's full of leopards which prey on the baboons. I started to climb down, but it was still drizzling and the sides were really just pebbly red mud which broke off as you grabbed it. Suddenly a piece gave way, and I slid down ten feet, landing on a flat section about a foot wide, carved out by running water. I had to lean in close to avoid falling. Below was a hundred foot drop, and I could feel the ground kind of giving under my weight. I got this panicky feeling. Jimmy tried to pull me up using a branch but it was too short. "Hold on I'll get help!" he shouted and disappeared. After what seemed ages three heads peered over the top, two blacks and Jimmy. One of the blacks stood up and threw down a rope saying "Bopa funica so," and tied it around his waist, then untied it and did it again. It was hard to do without falling backwards, but in the end I managed. Then I grabbed the rope above my head and they pulled me up. I stood there shivering, my teeth chattering. One of the blacks, about forty, was watching me, "Wena makasa sterek," he said, "Buya lapa kia katina." We followed him back to the old township and into one of the houses. A black family seemed to be living in each room. We sat on beer crates in what had been the lounge and a mfazi came in and signalled us to take off our shirts. "She will dry them," said the younger man and pointed to the wood fire on the veranda. Then he put a blanket round my shoulders, it smelled of wood smoke but soon warmed me up. He went out and came back with two enamel mugs of tea. Whites don't usually drink from the same cups as kaffirs because they're meant to have diseases but I didn't care and the tea was good and sweet. When we were ready to go Jimmy and I got together 2/6 which was all we had and offered it to the older man. He shook his head and said, "Wena mzungu, maali zonke skaat!" The younger man laughed and held the back of my hand, like you would a child, and said, "No, my brother we do not want your money, we are happy you did not fall."

Ndola 1963

Dad's business isn't going so well, and he's got a second job now as a bailiff, five bob for each job, but I don't think it suits him, he's not hard enough. I was moaning about my pocket money the other day, still 17/6 per month, when Catherine suddenly said, "Look don't you realise we're broke?" something I'd never thought of. Anyway we had a talk and now I get £4 per month but have to buy all my non-school clothes. Fat chance of actually buying any. It's funny, lots of blacks think that banks have a pool of money for whites, all we have to do is sign a cheque and we can take out as much as we like.

On Saturday we went to the Ndola agricultural show. Jimmy and I turned up on his Garelli motor bike. It's not fair, he gets everything. You could feel the excitement and tension, Sir Roy appeared on a big open air stage with Moise Tshombe, who until a few months ago was President of Katanga. He was shown as an example of a good kaffir, someone we can work with. Strange this good kaffir business, Mom loves Sonny Sonda, a trumpet player, who's chubby and cuddly, and likes whites. He was given a trumpet by Louis Armstrong when he visited in 1960, I suppose it's a bit like a pet dog. Anyway, Sir Roy, still looking tough but a bit fat was giving a speech, "**Civilised rule, responsible government, western democracy, partnership, UNIP intimidation, murder, communism, you have been warned, British double dealing.**" Many more blacks were around than last year, youths showing off in UNIP T shirts, a few with mfazis dressed up like white girls. As the sun was setting there was a bit of a fight between a white oke and a kaffir. Three kaffir cops arrived and did the usual thing of arresting the kaffir. But then some official looking kaffirs turned up dressed all in black, with full length leather coats. "UNIP," said someone, "Must be fucking hot in those coats!" They started lecturing the police in Bemba, wagging their fingers. The police removed the prisoner's handcuffs and let him go. The whites started yelling, and one guy, about forty, went up and started arguing. He was promptly hit over the head with a baton and went down like rag doll. Then all hell broke out. There were fights all over the place. You could call it a riot. Suddenly I felt my arms pinned to my sides, two blacks had grabbed me. A big guy, about thirty stood in front. "Fucking sheet!" he said, his mouth twisted with hate, as if it was all my fault, then hit me across the face with the back of his hand. They let me go and I staggered around, dizzy, blood streaming from my nose but otherwise OK. Jimmy was standing there looking useless saying, "You're lucky, they were just messing around with you."

We went off to the Lunar Park. It was all barricaded with caravans and fencing and they were charging an entrance fee of 5/-, except if you're white. The Lunar Park's from South Africa and some of the okes who work there seem to hate kaffirs like it's a religion. Four munts started to climb in over the fence. The white workers were on them even before they were properly in, pulling them over the fence, then laying into them with an anger I'd never seen before, kicking the shit out of them once they were on the ground. It seemed they'd had a lot of practice. An older man came up and dragged them off, shouting, "Don't be fucking stupid, do you want to be arrested in a shithole like this?" Then he led the blacks back to the fence.

A little later we saw Anne and Eddy who'd come across from Muf. Eddy had blood and goo running from the back of his head, he'd been hit with a brick.

He looked a bit stunned. "Christ," I said, "Aren't you going to hospital?" "Fuck that," he said, "we're going off to jive at La Cantina." This is a dance hall in the show grounds with large curved windows nearly down to the ground, Spanish style. We went along but the entry charge was 5/- to keep the kaffirs out so we wandered round a bit and then went home.

Next day, everyone was talking about it. Later that night the blacks had started stoning La Cantina, quickly smashing the windows, and it was difficult to dodge stones and flying glass because the building was more windows than walls. People were getting injured, girls screaming, and the police nowhere. The okes were worried about what was going to happen next. They had a powow and then about thirty of them ran out the front door together, each pulling up one of the eighteen inch metal posts that protect the flower beds along the path. They went straight for the stone throwers who turned and ran, but one tripped and fell. The okes were on to him in a second, whacking him with the bars and kicking him, and they say he's dead. I spent Sunday in a kind of daze, though Dad said there's nothing about it in the paper. When on Monday morning I went to sit with the smokers at the edge of the rugby field I was expecting them to be discussing it in a shocked way, but instead they were laughing and joking! "Ya," said Titchy Smith, "Dobsy was jumping on his head, boing boing," like it was some cartoon scene. I felt lonely as we went into class.

School is more and more like a party, plenty of girls, lots of fun, and not much work. The teaching seems to be falling apart. Some classes are fine but in others the teacher doesn't always turn up, or they just chat to us. Mr Townsend fools around and flirts with the girls. He says the teachers are unhappy because next year the school will be taking blacks, pupils and teachers, and they don't know if they'll have a job. Many are leaving at the end of term. Mr Martins says, "Most of you think life's a big joke, but can't you see what's happening? I'm concerned about you. We'll have African rule next year, and they'll be competing with you for jobs on at least equal terms. Unless you get really good GCEs you could end up with no hope of employment in a country where you're a minority. How many of you know what you'll be doing next year?" Only a couple raise their hands.

Freeda's Dad says the school's not up to much anyway. He went to ask Mr Crawford if she'd be able to do this exam from England called A level. But Mr Crawford said nobody in the school would be capable of it except maybe Douglas D'Arcy who's the school swot and even in the afternoons goes around with his shirt top button and sleeves done up. Freeda's Dad says these English kids must be really clever, or we're all bloody stupid.

Every day the newspapers talk about bloodshed and violence, mainly the struggle between ANC and UNIP. UNIP says not enough blacks are allowed to vote, and is threatening strikes and riots if that's not changed.

On Fridays we go to youth club from seven til ten. We started at the Church of England one but the priest tries to do activities all the time, like ballroom dancing and it's boring! You feel trapped. A few weeks ago we sneaked off to the scout hut nearby and chucked a few flash bombs through the door. There were yells and screams and then the scoutmaster appeared in the doorway. "Who threw those, identify yourselves!" "Yoohoo!" we replied. "If you don't leave the area right away, my scouts will sort you out!" "That's lekker, send them out!" shouted Easty. After a few moments Patrick Mercer appeared in the doorway with a few boys behind him. He looked completely different in his uniform and silly hat. "Hey Patricia, come and sort us out!" yelled Jimmy. Patrick backed away from the door looking nervous and spoke to the scoutmaster who came to the door, "Now I know exactly who you are, and I'm going to report you to the headmaster unless you clear off right away!" "See you in school on Monday, Patrick!" yelled Easty, but we cleared off because we'd be caned if reported to Mr Crawford. We wondered off to the public toilets and flushed a few flash bombs down. Once fizzing they don't go out under water, and blow up five seconds later. If you time it right you can blow the clay outlet pipe

The Catholic youth club is much better and everyone's moved there including all the best girls. The priest lets you smoke and do what you like unless things get out of hand. He did stop us playing a dare game where you put your head against the dart board and the other okes throw darts round your head. There's ping pong and music and we just sit around and talk. The first day I arrived Emma Farmer was there. My heart almost stopped. She said something to me as I passed and I paused to reply, I don't know what I said, my mind was blank. My friend Beverley said, "You like her don't you?" "How do you know?" I asked. "It's obvious by the way you were acting," she said. How do girls know these things, how was I acting? I asked her to check with Emma next week, not now, whether she likes me. I could hardly sleep while I waited for the reply. Now I've found out she doesn't, only as a friend. I was really upset for a while but now I'm getting over it and feel kind of free.

Anyway, the convent where I went as a kid is just over the road, and they've started to let the boarders come to the club. What a thrill, all those soft, deprived, innocent girls, including a mooi one I've eyed out before at Janet's prize giving. There she was, so beautiful, and by the end of the evening I was chatting her up, her name's Jean. The following Monday at school she told Janet she loves me. Woo! Anyway, the next Friday I persuaded her to sneak out with me. We walked down to the park at the end of the road, through some trees, and sat on a bench at the edge of a clearing. A full moon shone just like in the films, but her face was half in shadow as I kissed her, which made it more romantic. You could tell this was her first time so I didn't want to frighten her off, I just frayed her lightly from the outside, and thought I'd have more of a go next time. After a while she said she'd better get back because it was nearly ten, so we wandered out of the park, arms around each other. Just then a car pulled up, "What time do you have to be home, young lady?" asked the priest, all disapproving. "Oh no, I'm a boarder," she says, idiot! "What? Go straight back inside, I'll see you in a minute!" he says. Now the boarders are banned from youth club, all because of me, and now, on club night, they've started flashing torches from their upstairs dorms and that kind of thing. One or two of the older boys are talking about climbing the drainpipes to screw them.

I can hardly believe it, Dad's decided to move again, this time to Southern Rhodesia! This is too much, Ndola's the best place in the world, and all my friends are here. And also I'll be far from Muf and Mom. "Look at the Congo," says Catherine, "I'm not letting that happen to my girls." "Everyone's leaving," says Dad, "Jobs are being Africanised. The Gearys are going to South Africa." Dad's going to Salisbury straight away to set up a printing business, I'm going to live with the Aunts, and Catherine and the girls will live in a flat. We'll all move down at Christmas.

So here I am staying with the Aunts. Their house sits across the vlei from our last place, on a dirt road, in a dry dusty garden, with a dried up stream running across the brown, dead lawn. School's out at one, and I have lunch with the Aunts, Ryvita, celery and cheese, until, when I start stealing the dog's steak they realise I'm being starved, and buy bread and other food for teenagers.

After lunch Auntie Mary goes back to her lawyer's office and Auntie Beth has a sleep until four. I wander round the hot, dead garden, infested with huge blue-skops which jump round to face you if surprised. Gives you a skrik. It's September, the sun's heat increasing daily, so usually I end up on my bed, feeling sleepy and randy. Just two houses down there's this second year girl, only fourteen but well developed, slim but not thin, forbidden fruit. My thoughts slip to her, probably on her own bed, not two hundred yards away, and I daydream of sneaking her back to my room and undressing her, and all that.

Last week, as I was sitting out front, this car came screaming round the corner too fast, you could see the panic on the driver's face, then it rolled into the vlei. I rushed out and by the time I arrived, a small group had gathered and pulled the man out unhurt. Standing there, barefoot was the girl, motionless like a Greek statue, in a short white skirt, her legs athletic, soft and brown. Then slowly she turned and looked at me, expressionless, like a child looking at something new. In the mornings I wake fresh and excited with anticipation, feeling just so good. At this time the air is warm and dry, like crystal, a drug, alive, zinging, you can almost hear it. Sometimes I wait til she cycles past and then ride behind her, admiring the way the skin stretches over the back of her legs. In Latin we're doing the Roman goddess Diana, and I sit, in a dream, seeing this girl as the goddess, running long-legged, bow in hand. But the other day, I heard she smaaks me, then at the school gate she gave me a sudden big smile. It changed her whole face, kind of split it, making her jaw and nose look big, made her seem ordinary, and somehow spoiled everything. Anyway, Janet says she's horrible and bitchy.

Living with the Aunts I get to see them more clearly. Auntie Beth hates blacks, no that's not right, she hates the political ones. She says the old boys are alright and just want a peaceful life but the young political ones are **thugs** and gangsters who get others to do what they want by **intimidation and violence**, and take advantage of the African's **primitive** belief in **witchcraft**. They use spirit mediums to denounce their enemies as witches, who are then killed. We want the best for the African but we must recognise his **stage of development**, and move forward slowly, **evolution** not revolution, maintaining **civilised standards.** These thugs like Kaunda are influenced by **irresponsible** Pan African ideas, which have led to the Mau Mau, and all the raping and killing across Africa, and don't realise they're being **manipulated** by the **communists** including the **Chinese (yellow peril).** We believe in **democracy and western civilisation** and the **rule of law.** Kaunda is the **devil**, and now there's a Stop UNIP movement which even the ANC has joined. When she goes on like this, all Auntie Mary says is, "Do you really think so Beth? Mmmm." This drives Auntie Beth mad and maybe pushes her to more extreme statements, in fact she's getting so bad that if a plant dies in the garden you expect her to say Kaunda himself has sneaked in and pissed on it. Last night it came to a head, Auntie Beth said, "Look May, stop humouring me, I won't sit down to dinner until we've had this out." Well, after some more vague talk, and because the food was getting cold, Auntie Mary says, "Mr Kaunda seems a reasonable man, I think he's misunderstood, I'm sure things will settle down once we have democracy. You do believe in democracy Beth?" Auntie Beth repeats the points I've underlined above, and Auntie Mary says, "That's all very well, but don't you think that's just an excuse to deny black people their basic rights? Isn't it a disgrace that under British rule we have all this racial discrimination? We break the rule of law whenever it suits us, now the police can arrest anyone without charge. **Civilised standards**, cutting off hands in the Congo to force more rubber production, **superstition**, are our religious beliefs any more rational than theirs?" And so on.

I'm in the shit with Catherine. Last night when I got back from youth club, she was waiting for me at the Aunts' house. It was nearly midnight and I was meant to be back by ten. "Where have you been since then?" she asked. "Er, at Charlie's house," I said. Actually I had been drinking with Gerald Fourie and some other guys in the gardens of the Selbourne hotel. Gerald's seventeen and is so well off that I can go through a month's pocket money in one evening, just to keep up with him. But he has a car, he's part of the in-crowd, and you get respect from girls if you hang around with him. "Rubbish!" she said, "I phoned his house and you weren't there. You're completely out of control, and it's not fair on your aunts." While she was going on like this I suddenly puked right in front of her, and a nice pong of beer wafted up. "Er, ate too much cake," I said.

I've just failed my GCEs. Well I got three, English B, French D, History E, and the rest F. How was I meant to know Science was in the morning? Jimmy said it was the afternoon. And every time I tried to swot I felt sleepy, or started to think about girls. But I'm not the only one, lots have failed including Jimmy, who's going back to Scotland. He says he's going to be a ton-up boy, a rocker, with a big bike. Sometimes cold fear runs down my spine, what am I going to do next year and for ever? Perhaps I could get an apprenticeship on the mine but I'd be useless, and the idea of living in Muf seems flat now, lonely. Auntie Mary was talking about me becoming an articled clerk in her solicitors' office, but not with three bad GCEs, and anyway, now they're sucking up to the new government and thinking of taking on black clerks. Plenty of smart kaffirs around these days, with glasses and briefcases.

Back in Muf for Christmas, seems wilder than usual. I hang around with some apprentices my age and up to about nineteen. They've plenty of money, and spend their spare time at work souping up their cars. Abe has fitted a new cam to his Zephir Six and reckons it can do 130. We took it along the Kitwe road and at about 120 the front started going up and down like a ship's bow and I thought it would hit the road. "Ya, must strengthen the suspension," he said. The other night we started in the club bar, drinking hards with mixers, like brandy and coke, vodka and lemonade, doubles, swallowing them straight down, one after the other. With the sweet cooldrink you hardly notice the alcohol. One moment you're cold sober, the next you're in another world, all bright and wonderful. "Let's fuck off to Kitwe!" shouts Abe, so four of us pile into his Zephir, me in front, followed by two more cars. It's about forty miles away and there's meant to be a party. Out on the road we pick up speed and start racing each other. I think, "I could die here, but who cares." We pull out to pass the car ahead and I see lights coming straight at us. "Look-out!" I shout. "Fuck him," says Abe and drives straight at the oncoming car. At the last second it swings off and slides into the bush. We all piss ourselves laughing. "Chicken, baaak bk bk!" yells Abe, and that's the game we play all the way. I've heard NR has the highest death rate per car in the world, plenty of okes from Muf have died. Anyway we arrive at the party but there are only about three girls free, so we spend the whole time competing for them. They say people with daughters are leaving NR fast, or maybe these parties are getting too wild so they're not allowed to come. There's plenty of booze and I can't remember anything else til I wake up in a different car in Ndola with some guys I don't know. The driver's saying, "Come on, get out quick!" It turns out we pinched it in Kitwe, and a cop car has just driven past twice. So we walk to the main road out of Ndola and they start hitching for Kitwe while I go on to the Muf turnoff and hitch from there. A Muf mine lorry stops, full of blacks. They let me sit in the cab because I'm white. "Ee Ee, you have drunk too much my friend," says the driver, putting his hand to his nose, "I can smell it." "I'll sit in the back," I say, "so you can breathe." The driver shouts something and all the blacks cheer and laugh and clap as they pull me onto the open back, like I'm a hero. "Wena puza too much, bad boy!" says one as he passes me a cigarette and pats me on the back. I feel good and comfortable.

Christmas Eve is like the end of something, a big party. Town is full of people I've known since I was a kid, the older okes in ridiculous little cardboard top hats or English bobby helmets from Mclellands, some actually crawling across the main road to the Flamingo bar. There's a boozy circuit from the club to the golf course bar, the little theatre, and town. Of course we all end up at the club that night where there's a big dance. At the end everyone congas through the lounges, the leaders in huge sombreros from a holiday in Mozambique. Finally to the Catholic church in J Avenue for midnight mass, never mind your denomination, even Irish protestants, because it's the only thing on.

Then home to H Avenue where Mom and Richard are sneaking presents into the boys' bedrooms while having a big fight. At eight, Richard was just popping out to the mine to check things over, but came home hours later drunk. Worse, he's finished all the Christmas and New Year booze, except for one bottle of gin. "Christ I can't stand your mother's moaning, let's go in the kitchen and have a drink," he says. There aren't even mixers for the gin, but you kind of get used to it. Mom comes in, "You, you're a disgrace, and you're corrupting my son," she says. "And you, you're my son, not his, you're meant to be on my side." Next morning Richard somehow manages to get the club bottle store opened, and comes back with a boot full of booze just in time for the morning visitors. But he's upset. He'd called into the tankhouse to check up on things and some of the black workers were drunk. He'd lost his temper and hit one. The thing is they have to walk along above the tanks of sulfuric acid to move anodes and cathodes, and if they fall in they're dead, so drinking is out. He says others get hit by overhead cranes and locos and there's about one death in the tankhouse every couple of weeks, out of about six hundred workers. He gets blamed but often it's because somebody's pissed.

Anne's pregnant from when she and Eddy went to Durban. Mom has her wounded look, "She absolutely promised she wouldn't sleep with him. How could she do this to me?" Richard misjudges, "I'm not having that bloody slut in my house!" Mom says all quiet, "If she goes I go! Get it?" Anyway Anne's getting married next month. Glen comes in. He's been talking to a friend about dogs. "Mom, what does mate mean?" "Er, it's a kind of dog," says Mom. He looks startled but says nothing. When he goes out Mom breathes out, "Whew, that was close!" I know better than to criticise her, she'd go mad, but it's strange, I feel easy sitting in the kitchen drinking tea, in a way I wouldn't with Catherine. It's cosy while it pours outside and Mom makes lunch. We chat and tease each other, comfortable. "I hear you were with Lucy on Christmas Eve, snogging her in a corner of the dance floor." "Ya and then I took her outside for a bit more." "Don't be disgusting, you'll end up like Eddy. But she's a pretty girl isn't she...." Maybe it's just that she's my own mom, familiar. But behind it all I watch her, separate.

Ndola 1964

January, back in Ndola for a few days before taking the train south. Kaunda's just won the election, even beating the ANC in Muf. Everyone's scared, specially jumpy because of the army mutiny, right now in East Africa, against its white officers. Tonight Kaunda's going to address the nation.

We're round at the Wolfs', friends of the Aunts, to watch his speech on TV. I'm hoping their twenty year old daughter will be there, I've only ever seen her from a distance but she has the most beautiful soft, angelic face, and what a body. Oh wow there she is, in shorts! The room's full and I position myself on the floor, just behind her chair, her wonderful bare leg a pillar almost blocking my view. I'm so close I can quietly examine every pore, every dimple of her soft brown skin. She raises a heel, tightening her calf muscle and I admire the new shape, from the point of the toe through the ankle, up to the dimpled knee. I feel a sweet but uncomfortable development in my shorts, and sneakily adjust them. Kaunda comes on with his strange high hairstyle. We've never heard him speak, we don't know what to expect, hatred, payback time, communism, blacks seizing our houses, which is what they're hoping for. Instead, with a gentle smile, he begins by saying let bygones be bygones, we are all one nation, whites are valued, nobody should have any fear, we must work together, my dear fellow citizens. I feel a warm glow. I want to cry, like when you think somebody hates you, and you feel all guilty and lost, then they put their arm around you and say it's OK. I can't read everyone's face but all must be feeling the same, it's going to be all right. Mr Kaunda ends with "One Zambia, One Nation!" "One Zambia, one bicycle," says Mr Wolf, but obviously he's joking. "I'm sure he's a sincere man," says Auntie Mary. Then the angel stands up, she speaks! Her voice is strangely harsh, like a parrot's. "Bloody baboooon!" she says, and walks out.

On the train down to Salisbury, my last hours of freedom. I wander the corridors and just four compartments down, there's Myra Duplessis with two other girls. One, her cousin Elise, is about seventeen, much bigger than me, in a short skirt, with a fantastic figure, the other her little sister about twelve. They're Afrikaansy, going down to Potgietersrus in South Africa where Myra's Dad's got a job as a security guard. Elise's Dad hasn't, but they're leaving anyway. Before I know it, Elise has her arm around me, her head about three inches above mine. "No man, but you're so cute," she says, getting me in a headlock, "Jiss jong a reely laak you," she turns to the others, "A ony smaak this ou, get out and go sit in his compartment." The little girl shouts, "You know Ma says you mustn't, I'm gonna tell on you, you ony gonna be in big trouble," but they leave. She puts the blind down and locks the door and we climb on to the top bunk. The next second she's taken off her blouse and bra, shit she's got the biggest tits I've ever seen, well I've only seen a few. "Not bad eh?" she says. "Unghh," I say because now she's lying on top of me, her tits in my face. For a second I feel slightly claustrophobic like when someone holds your head down in a fight, then I think, "Relax, go with the flow," and start kneading them and sucking her nipples. This seems the right thing because she starts making noises, then her hand moves down. I think, "If she touches me, I'll go mad, I'll come all over her hand." Then she does, it's such a thrill I start reciting the twelve times table backwards to distract myself. It helps because I've always had trouble from nine times onwards. I start to take off her pants when suddenly she stops me and I realise there's yelling at the door. "Let me in, I'm gonna tell Ma!" and then a man's voice, "What's going on in there?" She whips on her clothes, then a key in the lock, and the conductor comes in. "Go on, get back to your compartment," he tells me.

Salisbury 1964

Well, here we are, staying in a residential hotel, the Avalon, for white people who are poor or broke, plus a few immigrants, and one or two boys about my age whose parents are outside the country. In the evening everyone talks poor-white talk, about how things should be, the munts, how stupid they are, chasing cheques, and where you can open an account and get credit. But it's OK, I've got my own room and you get three proper meals a day with pudding and fruit and cheese. Dad's started his printing business and has upstairs offices in Manica road. He had no money but we're in what you call a depression, with the collapse of Federation nobody's confident about business, and half the offices are empty, so he's got it rent-free for three months. Everyone's talking politics, they're saying that while the Federation still exists (til the end of the month), they should make sure that all the main things, like the air force, army equipment, money and so on, are in SR so the blacks can't get their hands on them. They say my country's going to be ruined, but they're not going to let it happen here. No way. Dad's joined the Rhodesian Front which is a tough new party to protect the whites. He talks ruthless, all about military tactics and that kind of thing which sounds a bit odd because he's not actually like that.

Anyway, I'm helping him with his business and he says I can join him full time. I feel excited, free! No more school, real wages when the business takes off. Maybe we'll branch into other things and I'll become a big business man with a Jag and a blond girlfriend! But then I think, how will I meet anyone, working in a dusty printing office? Even when I'm thirty will I know anyone or will I just be living at home with Dad and Catherine, watching TV on a Saturday night, dinner on my lap? In Muf and Ndola everyone knows you, and whether they like you or not you're somebody. But here, I'm nobody, like I don't exist. It does strange things, you start living more inside your own head and it's amazing how quickly it happens. Every day I go to the Standard Bank for Dad, and sometimes I catch the eye of this girl who works there, she's nice. Now she looks back, but I don't smile like I would have a month ago, I just look away. I've become self-conscious, she might think I'm just a strange staring guy.

Last night we had a big family row. Catherine said, "George, it's not fair, this boy should be back in school," and I argued, but in the end agreed because I know there's some sense in it. So there's been a meeting at Prince Edward school over the road, and I'll be starting there in January to repeat the GCE year, what a drag. It's an all boys' school, ridiculous, and you can stay there til you're about nineteen to do those fancy English exams. Peter Atkins from Ndola is down here, at another boys' school, St Georges. He says they have to wear school uniform in town, even in the holidays. I get that sinking feeling.

Started school, new uniform from McCullough and Bothwells the old fashioned clothes shop in First Street, where they put your money in a cylinder that runs along wires to the cashier upstairs, then your change comes shooting down. Khaki shirt and shorts, a trilby hat, and red blazer, embarrassing, a good thing there's no girls to see me. I'm in 4M, one below the top, 4A. It means we're aiming for M level, like Matric, for hard working thick boys, to get into a South African university. But there's lots of lower streams down to G. The guys here are different, though some of the lower stream okes seem like my friends from Muf, like the apprentices, and so do a few in my class, relaxed, wanting a good time. But then there's another type, mainly A stream, also quite relaxed, some of them Jews, who I think have rich parents, and I don't understand them. I heard one calling the kaffirs "Africans" and saying things like Auntie Mary does, which I've never heard an oke do before. It feels a bit like how the English class system must be. Then there's a boy scout group, perfect mommy's boys, who love sport and obey all the rules, and want to be prefects, and don't have hairstyles, and don't seem to know any girls, and don't seem to mind. They're the biggest group because lots of them are boarders, farmers' sons from all over the country and they make the school feel like a big scout camp. And that's the other thing, we have to do army cadets on a Friday, imagine that, the start of the weekend, and these boy scout buggers just love it, and they're in charge.

This is all confusing and it's hard to know how to fit in, or who's who, but I've made friends with a few ou's, mainly a guy called Pricey. His hair's combed back in a ducktail style like mine, and he seems a bit like my friends from Muf. He came out from England a couple of years ago, and when he speaks to his mom his accent goes really soutie, though he doesn't realise it. Dad says he's "working class". Sometimes we go to his place for lunch, and he orders the houseboy round like an English lord, "Freddie, make tea and corned beef sandwiches, clean my cadet kit," etc, like we wouldn't do in my family. He and his friends don't seem to know any girls. There's no clear place you can go to meet them like the bioscope or the mine club. On Saturday mornings we go to the pool and sit there with a battery radio and cigarettes, trying to look cool, but it doesn't really work.

School's a complete drag, no girls, and much more serious than Ndola High. They expect you to work hard, they check your homework, your uniform, and have a squad of dead keen prefects who are allowed to whack you on the bum with a tackie or give you an essay for the smallest thing. What's the matter with these buggers? How can they suck up to the adults like that? Don't they feel embarrassed? We each belong to a "house" with names of SR heroes like "Jameson" and you're expected to be loyal to your house. To a house? The boarders seem to live in a world of school and sport and hunger, always begging "sambos", or trying to bum your tuck shop sweets, or throwing rugby balls around like ten year old kids. But the place where they really rule is cadets. "We'll sort you out in cadets, Hassall," said a prefect because I'd been breaking a few rules and talking back a bit. Cadets is on the school fields and there are maybe two hundred boys in platoons of thirty, each with a boy sergeant and second lieutenant, the whole thing commanded by a captain who's a teacher. But the real power lies with two little sergeants from the army. Last week four boys fainted in the sun, one by one, and the captain looked concerned and told them to go and sit in the shade. One of the sergeants marched up to him and in the politest way shouted something about "Rhodesians, tough, discipline, Sir!" Next thing the four fainters were running around the field like white faced ghosts holding their rifles above their heads, followed by a shouting army sergeant, pausing only to vomit and then carry on. My lieutenant, Colin Fowler, happens to be a prefect who doesn't like me so I'm on defaulters most weeks which means an extra session after cadets or even on Monday at school, where they try to break you down. "See that tree over there? Get me a leaf from it, on the double. Not that leaf you fool, you know I didn't mean that one, do twenty press ups. Now go and get me the right leaf. No, idiot, that's still the wrong one, up two three four, up two three four!"

Some boys mainly in the A stream are starting to grow their hair like this new band the Beatles. It's strange because it's the same non - style like all the squares and boy scouts and birds' egg collectors have, except a few are growing it a bit longer. The headmaster says, "I'm not having any effeminate British hairstyles here, you are Rhodesians and you will wear your hair short." If it touches your ears, you're in trouble.

The blacks are different here. They're not mad and political like in NR, they're quiet and friendly. I few nights ago Pricey and I were walking behind three near the show grounds and I shouted something cheeky like, "Eh uwe, muntu, kwacha!" Pricey looked at me, shocked. They stopped, turned round, and came towards us. I wasn't sure whether to stand or run. One, quite old, maybe twenty three, said, "Why you talk like that? That is not good, my friend," as if talking to a naughty younger brother. I felt embarrassed, and then apologised in a clumsy way. What else can you do?

The Wilson brothers are in Salisbury for a few days, their old man was a friend of Dad's in Ndola and he's got a job at the coal mine in Wankie. They're kind of mad, and were always in trouble in Ndola. They've just joined up to fight as mercenaries in the Congo. They say the money's fantastic. Would you believe it, Tshombe's Prime Minister of the whole Congo now, and they're fighting a new rebel group, the Simbas, under a guy called Gbenye. These are real savages who do ritual killings and rapes, and pour holy water over themselves and then believe they can't be killed by bullets. A mercenary told us their belief almost works, they just keep coming after you shoot them, until you hit them good and proper.

Ian Smith's taken over the RF, replacing Winston Field. He was on TV last night, seems a hard guy, with one funny eye, talks slow and doesn't say too much. He calls SR "Rhodesia". He's going to be **fair** to the blacks, the 1961 constitution gives them a chance to **move forward**, but this must be **evolution, not revolution**. Look at the mess where they've been given independence by **irresponsible** European governments infected with **defeatism and socialist ideology**. The **rot stops here**, and now Rhodesia will stay in **responsible hands**. There will be **no majority rule in my lifetime**. He says the British Government promised Rhodesia independence if we accepted the break up of the Federation and the 1961 constitution. We must have independence so the country can progress, and if the British go back on their word, we'll have to take matters into our own hands. People are talking about a unilateral declaration of independence, UDI, they say the British will never give independence to a white government so we'll have to take it.

Yesterday afternoon this old Portuguese guy at the Avalon invited me into his room to look at some photos. His English was bad and I couldn't get what it was all about so I went in out of politeness. I sat on the side of his bed and he handed me this pile of family pictures to go through, then he put his hand on my knee. I didn't think anything of it until he started to move his hand up my leg. I tried to move it off, but he said, "No, no, is alright!" as if I was being totally unreasonable, then he tried to force his hand up towards my balls. I stood up and raised my fist to punch him on the head, but he kind of cowered, and I couldn't do it. So I kicked over his bedside table and walked out. I felt quite shocked and my hands were shaking. I told George, one of the other boys there, who's eighteen. We decided not to do anything but we gave him the cold stare so he'd know who's boss. He left the next day.

Pricey's been done for pinching a bike. He's going to be caned by the police, not nice, the scars can last for life. He's also been given six by the school. I've started mixing with some other ou's in my class who know the A stream guys. They've all been friends since infant school, and most live around the Avenues in nice houses. Some of these big shot families have been here since their grandparents' days and are well known and run the big businesses in town. On Saturday night I went with Keith and John to a party in Avondale, which was full of these guys and lots of mooi girls, some dark Jewish looking with olive skins and big beautiful eyes. I tried to chat up a few but they didn't want to know. One of these blokes, tall and snooty was watching. He said slow and deliberate, "Jesus Hassall, where's your culture? You fucking Northern Rhodesia peasant. That's the shittest technique I've ever heard. You'll have to jack up your act if you want girls like these, and stop hanging around with yobs like George Price."

Our English teacher is Mr Bridle, known by everybody as Johny Bridle. He's great except he doesn't support the government. But even the boarders have to respect him because he's not soft, he takes rugby and other sports. He lets you argue in class. Politics come up a lot these days, and sometimes I say, "Let me put in a word for the Rhodesian Front." Some okes clap and cheer, others groan, but Mr Bridle says, "Come on boys, let Hassall have his say," then he kind of chairs a debate. Of course we try to keep it going to avoid rubbish like poetry. Yesterday we were discussing the fact that the government spends about the same in total on black education as on white education, but there are twelve times as many blacks in school, and the black population is eighteen times higher. That was news to me. "Well maybe it's because they're thick, it wouldn't get them anywhere," I said. "Are you saying every single black is thicker than every one of those peasants in the G stream?" asked a boy. "Maybe they should stop spending on a thicko like you Hassall, look who failed his GCE last year!"

I went home and told Dad about this, he loves an argument. I was surprised that he half agrees with Mr Bridle. "Everyone deserves the same chance," he said, "but it's not surprising. Because of the state of our culture, more white children go further, so it costs more." "Yes but Mr Bridle says ten times more is spent on each white child at every age, even in primary school." Catherine was getting upset "Your teacher shouldn't be talking politics in class, filling your heads with all that rubbish!"

Mr Bridle said, "On Wednesday night we're showing the film of Shakespeare's Richard III in the hall for the A level pupils, and you're all welcome." I said, "Shakespeare, sir, it's boring, I'm not going!" Mr Bridle continued, "And the GCE girls from Queen Elizabeth and Girls' High have also been invited." Well, that was different! I arranged with Keith and John to arrive early so we could scope out the chicks. We joined the tall snooty guy, Bob, who was in a group which included four girls, a couple really mooi. I couldn't believe it, they were discussing the play, all serious, in detail, like they knew it inside out! Bob was at the centre of things, you could see the girls were listening to him, trying to say things he would like. Shit man, in Ndola girls wouldn't go near the school swot D'Arcy. But Bob and his friends are different, they've got good hairstyles and clothes and know how to chat up girls. Bob had just turned to the prettiest one, who had been shy and quiet, and said, "And what do you think, you sweet young thing?" The film started. Lawrence Olivier as Richard III turns and looks straight at you. He says, "Now is the winter of our discontent." It seems ridiculous over-acting. Half the audience piss themselves, me too. Then I notice Bob and friends aren't laughing, one of the girls looks at me and whispers something to him, I feel embarrassed. But as the film goes on I forget everything and seem to be pulled more and more into the play. Some lines send cold shivers down my spine. At the end I feel happy, strange, like I want to laugh or cry, and would gladly watch it all over again.

Politics are hotting up, it gives me a sinking feeling, like a repeat of NR, I don't want to have to move again, and where would we go? Smith's pushing UDI, just like Sir Roy did at the end of Federation, and that got him nowhere. Now Sir Roy's changed his tune. He's the leader of the new Rhodesia Party campaigning for independence but against UDI. The RF doesn't like opposition. In the paper today Smith said, "If anyone stands in our way, we will deal with him. If it happens to be a rogue elephant coming out of the bush he will be dealt with accordingly." Sir Roy was a hero just two years ago. Now people are calling him traitor, communist, bloody Jew. His meetings are being shouted down. It's unpatriotic to oppose the RF. Sir Roy has just stood in a by-election in Arundel against Clifford Dupont and been badly defeated.

Smith's been in Britain negotiating with Sir Alec Douglas Home. Why's he called "Hume"? The British are so bloody complicated. Anyway, he's said we can have independence if we can prove the people want it, so Smith's held an indaba of all the African chiefs at Domboshawa, and every single one of them has said yes. But at the same time there's been trouble in Harare township and the Government's declared a state of emergency there. Now Smith's held a referendum of the electorate with the question, "Do you want independence under the 1961 Constitution?" The vote was nearly ten to one in favour, including black voters. But only about 12,000 blacks can vote. Smith's gone back to the British saying, "There you are!" but the new Prime Minister, a sneaky guy called Wilson isn't having it, and Smith's saying we've been betrayed.

All this stuff's being discussed in class. Mr Bridle says Sir Alec had warned Smith a long time ago that the British wouldn't accept a decision by the chiefs, who are paid flunkies of the government. When I tell Dad, he starts discussing it, but Catherine cuts in and says, "Are you calling our prime minister a liar?" "I don't know," I say. "That's ridiculous and disloyal," she says, "you should show some respect for your prime minister and government. They're doing the best they can under difficult circumstances. You should be ashamed of yourself." I reckon that about sums up the feelings of most white people.

Dad says one the reason they haven't yet declared UDI might be that they want to make sure that white police, army and officials will stay loyal. It's a big decision because they could be accused of treason if they obeyed a rebel government. On 24 October the head of the armed forces Major General Anderson, who's against UDI was retired though he's only fifty-one. Dad says that means they're serious. But then on 27 October he showed me this statement by Harold Wilson in the Herald:

'A declaration of independence would be an open act of defiance and rebellion and it would be treasonable to give effect to it.... An illegal declaration of independence in Southern Rhodesia would bring to an end relationships between her and Britain......inflict disastrous economic damage upon her;

and would leave her isolated and virtually friendless in a largely hostile continent....'

Can they hang you for treason? If we lose British protection could we be invaded by the Russians or Chinese through Zambia? Maybe they'll get cold feet now and not go ahead with it. That's what I hope.

David Wilson's back from the Congo. He's been discharged because he had a nervous breakdown. He was shitting his pants before they went on "ops" and was beaten up by guys in his own platoon. He says he saw terrible things, murder, rape, hangings, but won't talk much, he just starts crying, and jumps at every noise. His hands shake. His brother John's OK, but he's changed, hardened up, and won't speak to David.

Mufulira 1964

Back in Muf for Christmas, hitched all the way up with Nick Stavros who stays at the Avalon. He lives in Elizabethville in the Congo. Dad let me go with him because he's a year ahead of me in school and is more like a man than a boy. We parted in Ndola, Nick going through the border post at Sakania, he didn't seem to be worried.

Muf seems to have changed. In a way it's all the same, the mine club still all white, as are other places like the Flamingo bar, but most of my friends are gone, and there seem to be fewer whites around. It's like a car that's still running, but with some parts missing. I've teamed up with a guy called Alec Turner, who I've always known, but only vaguely. He also failed his GCEs and is at a cram college in Bulawayo. The headmaster is staying with him at his parents' house, I couldn't believe it, a sixty year old man staying with a seventeen year old boy, is he a queer? But Ian says no, he's a piss head alcoholic. In term time he visits a brothel once a week, and a bar all the other nights, and comes in so smashed that the boys have to get him to bed. But the next morning, he's up early, clear as a bell, sets them to work, no nonsense, and gets first class results. His wife left him years ago, so each holiday George lands himself on somebody, and parents put up with him because he's saving their child's future. In the week before Christmas I go round to Alec's house every morning, and the three of us drive to the Flamingo and start drinking. Then it's off to the golf club to join the regular boozers, then perhaps the little theatre bar, George paying for everything. I get dropped home for lunch so George can have his afternoon beauty sleep, and we start again at about four at the club and stay til midnight. Yesterday morning he dropped in at our house for mince pies and tea with Mom. "Ooh Mrs Moodie, this pie is divine, the best I've ever tasted," he says in his super posh Oxford accent." "Isn't he a lovely man!" says Mom. Alec's started "borrowing" George's car while he naps, a new Toyota Corona, and we drive it round town to show off, no licences.

Things have fallen apart since Christmas, and George's gone back to Bulawayo. On Christmas Eve at the club, as the band started up, George, who was already well away, pranced on to the empty, darkened dance floor, and started doing a strip under the revolving glass ball. He was down to his jockeys and removing them when Mr Turner and a couple of friends ran across to stop him. George resisted, and in the struggle Mr Turner got a surprisingly hard punch to the nose and was covered in blood. George then passed out. Alec had to drive them both home. On the way back he rolled the car where the road curves round the park. He's all right, but the car's a mess. Anyway, George's mad with Alec, and the family's sick of George, so he's buggered off.

Ndola 1965

In Ndola, staying with the Aunts for a few days. Like with Muf, most of my friends have left. Last night I was drinking in the Selbourne Hotel bar with Gerald Fourie when two blacks came in with two whites and sat at the corner table. Everyone stopped what they were doing or saying. I'd never seen a black in any white bar, and never blacks and whites together. One white and one black were middle aged, the others two in their twenties. Both the whites had longish untidy hair and the soft, soppy look you sometimes get with priests. The older white man smiled vaguely round the room as if blessing it, but without catching anyone's eye, and then went up to the counter to buy drinks. The men sitting along the bar moved away as if he had leprosy and gathered in one corner. He was served silently by the black barman who had the look of a frightened rabbit. Then as he went back to his table, two muscular guys in T shirts followed. One said, "You kaffirs, get out of our bar. And you, you dirty fucking kaffir lovers, you make me want to puke. I swear if you're not out in thirty seconds I'll kick your teeth in." The rest of the guys were coming over. The older white looked like he wanted to say something, but his black friend laid a hand on his arm, and they walked out.

Down with a bad dose of Flu, maybe too much booze over Christmas. I get up to shower, and then feel too buggered to brylcream my hair, so just get back into bed. When I wake up and look in the mirror, I'm staring at one of the Beatles! Well that's flattering myself but the hairstyle's the same, so I decide to leave it as it is. "Ian, you do look awful," says Auntie Beth. On the train back to Salisbury my fortunes seem to have improved, two elvises both over twenty, and one beatle are competing for this quite lekker babe, and it seems to me the beatle's winning! I spend the night in her compartment.

Salisbury 1965

I've passed my GCEs! Actually I've done quite well and I'm going to do A level English, French, and History, and also Latin to Matric level. Where would I be if we'd stayed in Muf? I've chosen Latin partly because we do it at Girls' High School. Girls from GHS and Queen Elizabeth come to our school to do French and Afrikaans. About a dozen of us do arts A level, and another twenty, sciences.

Winston Churchill's dead, I think of his great achievements and how long he lived, already in his twenties during the Boer war. Catherine says he jumped over her Granny's fence, on the run from a Boer prison camp, but I've heard that story before, seems like SA was one long row of back fences and Churchill a hurdles champion. Smith's been over at his funeral and is having talks with sneaky Wilson, who's warning him about the consequences of UDI.

I've started having discussions with Dad about politics, because I feed back what Johny Bridle or some boys have been saying in class. Not one of the arts boys supports the government and only a few of the science pupils do. The qualified franchise gives people the vote if they reach a certain level of education and earnings. But black earnings are less than ten percent of whites' and the way things are organised they'll never catch up to white levels. I find Dad's views quite sympathetic to blacks, or rather he wants to be fair. So why's he a member of the RF? "Self preservation," he says. "We need to slow things down. Look at Northern Rhodesia, most of your friends were born there, yet you're being pushed out of your own country as they "Zambianise" jobs, which means reserving them for blacks. Imagine if they did something similar in Britain, referring only to whites as "British" and throwing everyone else out of work, it would be Oswald Mosley stuff. Here it's positive discrimination." That does bother me, though it's funny how whites like my dad are suddenly critics of racism. But slowly my views are changing, maybe I'm just fitting in with my new friends.

School has a different feel now, I sit with roughly the same twelve to fifteen pupils in each lesson, and I'm getting to know them, along with some boys who do sciences. They don't seem to care about being tough or delinquent as in NR, with them it's about being clever, having correct politics, good clothes, liking the right kind of music, picking up girls. I'm still seen as a "peasant" but, as Bob says, improving. Fortunately an accepted sign of brains is to get a good essay mark without doing much work, "Oh I only started it at twelve last night when I got back from the party," so there's still some scope for loafing. Sport is treated with disdain because it's the religion of government supporters.

These guys are isolated, in a sea of almost hysterical support for the government, yet they're not bothered, they seem completely cool and confident, even arrogant. It's only as I get to know them and visit their homes, that I realise that their parents, most of whom are second or third generation Rhodesian, have exactly the same views. Most of these adults know members of the RF government, were brought up with them, sat together with them in the thirties, in these same old fashioned, red-bricked classrooms. Their political differences are like a family row, and they still greet each other in the street, all members of the same elite. But the adults I've always known are the "peasants" who blindly support the government, so I'm always sensitive and vulnerable to their views, even a glance can wound me.

The election results are in, Smith campaigning for independence. The RF have taken all fifty of the A roll (mainly white) seats wiping out the RP, along with their call for "partnership". The turnout for the mainly black B roll seats was about 14%, just over 2000 votes in a country of four million. Smith now has a two thirds majority, and can change the constitution. ZANU and ZAPU have been banned. Dad voted RF.

Two of us attend the girls' school for Latin. It's great, being the only boys there we get a lot of attention, and I've already heard that a couple of girls like me, can't wait to get my hands on them. In class, Miss Watts, a dry old stick, asks me to translate. She's astonished. "But this is wonderful Hassall, girls, listen to this, you'll have to raise your standards considerably, oh my, oh that's so apt, oh so well put, oh well done, well done!" Then, "But that phrase isn't in the text! What's going on? Hassall, you are not using a translation are you?" I decide to come clean, taking the crib from my lap and waving it in the air. "Yes miss, of course, doesn't everyone?" Now I've been banned from Latin for two weeks for corrupting her girls. Our deputy head told me off with a half grin on his face. Now all the girls have cribs, and my reputation is up.

Social life is improving. Bob and his friends know everyone, and we spend most Friday and Saturday nights driving from party to party, tanked up on half jacks of brandy or vodka, passed around in the car.

Some parties are just rumours, some run by complete strangers which we try to crash, and others full of our friends. Bob's in a rhythm and blues band, and I'm fast becoming chief amp carrier or mate, so we arrive with a certain arrogance and nobody tries to stop us when we change the record from the Beach Boys to the Stones. Usually we're looking for particular girls, and collect them one by one as we move between parties. Bob seems to have girls stashed all over town including Jane in Mabelreign who he screws regularly but never takes out. His father was upset to find a pack of twelve Durex in the car glove compartment. It wasn't that his boy was experimenting and doing what comes naturally, but that aged seventeen he was buying in bulk.

Around midnight we all end up at Nick's Café in Avondale, run by Mrs Nick an enormous Mediterranean lady who sits behind the till like a huge spider, and stands no nonsense. Last Saturday we arrived with Anne, a girl who Bob had taken out a few times. He went up to play pinball and a few minutes later this attractive blond girl came in. "Suzie!" called Anne, "Come sit here. How 're you getting on, who're you going out with these days?" "Oh a guy called Bob Thomas, he's in a band," said Suzie. "What? I'm going out with him, he's over there!" They looked like they were about to tear each others' eyes out, then a strange thing happened, they started hugging, then whispering, then both got up, went across to Bob, and smacked him hard across the face. Then arm in arm they marched out of the café. By now the morning papers were out, the headline taking up the top half the page saying, "UDI next week", then below the fold in smaller letters, "Unless British Government agrees to Smith's Demands."

Music's the thing, and being yourself. The Beatles, brilliant, setting the scene but fading, the poet Bob Dylan showing the mess we're in, Chuck Berry, father of R and B, Mick Jagger and Keith Richards, kings of Fuck You and Do What You Want, John Mayall *Live at Klooks Kleek*, The Graham Bond Organisation, Yardbirds, Davey Graham and *Anji*. In an electrical store in Gordon Avenue I discover a pile of unwanted LPs going cheap, six shillings each, and buy the lot, Muddy Waters, John Lee Hooker, Little Walter, Howlin Wolf, who would have expected these in Rhodesia? When I was a kid we used to look to America, Elvis, Little Richard, but now the British blues scene is where it's happening. We quiz the few people who've visited England but can't quite get a feel. We all have Levi jeans and know the few shops that sell the right clothes. We hang around with anyone interesting like Max from England who's "travelling through". He looks and dresses like Paul Jones in Manfred Mann, boots, jumbo chords and denim shirts and calls himself a "beat". He breaks all the Rhodesian rules on how to treat a girl, "Hello darling give us a kiss. No? Well fuck off then!"

My love life's improving, picking up girls most weekends, mainly snogging on the dance floor, or in the cinema, and a bit of groping in the car. There's this girl Marge who lives just around the corner in the Avenues. She's the most beautiful thing I've ever seen, a mixture of Kim Novak and Marilyn Monroe but softer. Every afternoon a crowd gathers at her flat, boys after her, girls after the boys, all wanting her attention. It's hard to tell who she's focussing on, one minute she seems to like you, then she acts all cold. But I've a feeling things are moving my way. On Friday night I arrived at this party with Pete who's in the Matric class. Betty came up and said, "You're in luck,

Marge is looking for you." Just the way she said it, I could hardly breathe! I went into the darkened lounge and there she was, soft and intense, pulling me towards her without a word, kissing me. We staggered round the dance floor, vaguely keeping time to the music, locked together for what seemed the whole evening, snogging more and more passionately. At the end her face and lips looked red and crushed. I didn't try much else on her, I've heard she doesn't give. They were playing that song by Herman's Hermits, "Something tells me I'm into something good" which seemed to fit. But when I went round on Sunday she was quite distant, until I said I was leaving, when she came up and gave me a big sexy kiss, saying, "Now you know where you stand!" That night I walked past her flat hoping to see her, with that Billy J Kramer song in my head, "So meet me tonight just where the light shines from a window", and it was enough just to be there, near her, alone. Back in school on Monday I'm in my school uniform, and a prefect boarder who's spent the whole weekend bumming sambos, playing kids games, and probably playing with himself says, "Hey Hassall, where's your hat?" Well fuck off!

Friday, down to Beira for the long weekend with Pete and some other guys. The old Studebaker rolls out of the east end of Jameson Avenue at about ten in the morning, through Marandellas and on to Umtali. We cross the Rhodesian border at two. The customs building, fresh and air conditioned, brilliant white walls relieved only by a picture each of the Queen and Smithy, the white customs officers in their tight white starched uniforms, seem to sum up white Rhodesia. We're stamped through quickly and drive the hundred yards to the Portuguese post, its whitewash cracking and mud stained. Inside the old fashioned building sits a single, fat, middle aged official, feet on the desk, half an inch of ash dangling from the cigarette in his mouth. Cockroaches cover the browning walls. He stares at us with dull, yellowed eyes and doesn't move. We line the desk and eye him out, but not too much, these guys have absolute power. Finally he shuffles to his feet and slowly stamps each passport.

As soon as you drive off you notice the holes in the road, everything looks run down. At Villa de Manica a few miles in we stop at a cafe for our first beer. The buildings are unlike anything I've seen, like films of Europe. Then it's a bar crawl down to the coast. As we descend towards the sea, the temperature and humidity rise and the vegetation becomes more tropical. I feel a growing euphoria, I haven't seen the sea for seven years. We arrive at Beira and drive out to the Estoril, a holiday area for Rhodesians. The sea! We run in with our clothes on. All we have for sleeping is a big tarpaulin which we put over a wall between some beach chalets. A guy comes out, "What the hell are you doing, this is my chalet, bugger off!" "Not your wall," says Chris. "Yes it is, would you like this in your face?" We inspect a large fist and retreat. After being moved on a few times a young couple lets us use theirs. The sand is soft and there's a latrine block nearby, what more could you want? It's high tide, big waves, so we body surf, you can only last about half an hour before you're exhausted, then it's in to Beira to do the bars. The grey-brown buildings, people drinking wine, give a feel like Paris or something back in the war. With every Manica beer we're given free tapas, anything they can't sell, small shell fish, curried tripe and baked beans, fried chicken feet, the skin hard and chewy but quite fleshy on the ball of the foot. No one else will eat theirs so I have four lots each round, and realise that if I stick with these guys I won't have to buy food, so my fiver will go a long way.

Back at the Estoril by nine and into the Pavilion, a bar and dance floor jutting on to the beach. My euphoria is still there, that warm sea breeze. Bob and his band are setting up, and I go and help, to make sure I'm seen with them. I persuade them to let me play the tambourine for a bit to establish my credentials, and this lasts three tunes before I'm thrown off for being out of time. Pissed, I watch the drummer to keep to his down beat, but I'm a millisecond out, thump-crash. Nevermind, now I'm on the dance floor and the band are up there so I have the advantage. One of the groupies comes up and we start dancing. "Ooh, it's just like dancing with the Beatles!" she says. After a while we go outside. There's a big moon and the sea crashing nearby, and it all feels good. We lie down behind a wrecked boat. She's Millie from Marandellas.

After a while we hear a commotion inside and go to investigate. They say some Rhodesians hit a black waiter, so the police came in and whacked the trouble makers with rubber truncheons. This was too much, shit, who do these porcs think they are? The Rhodesians threw the cops out of the building, and they buggered off. Now we're back to normal and the band's playing again. I'm at the counter buying drinks when everyone turns to look at the landside door, a truck has backed up to it. A cop jumps out and pulls aside a curtain to reveal a nervous looking black soldier sitting behind a big machine gun pointing straight at us. Everyone gets down, then a squad of police pour in, searching for the trouble makers, clubbing anyone in their way. They grab about six guys, and lead them off to a second lorry whacking them as they go.

We spend Saturday mainly on the beach. A few Portuguese blokes turn up, trying to pick up Rhodesian girls who they regard as easy. I hear if you take a Portuguese girl out, her mom and aunts come along too, though they say it's amazing what you can manage in a dark cinema with a jersey on your lap. These guys seem to think the way to pick up girls is to do hand stands and other strongman stunts, but our girls mainly just laugh at them. But what I notice is how mixed race they are, you might see a group of three guys, one nearly black, one clearly white, and one in between. I don't know how their system works, except that all the shop keepers seem to be completely white. Later we go into town. The place is full of drunk, barefoot, shirtless Rhodesians trailing Lagosta bottles, wandering in and out of shops, the local people, who are well dressed, seem almost not to notice them.

Sunday morning we're on the beach by 9am drinking Manica, trying to look hard. My shoulders are so burnt they're blistered and weeping, and Mandy says I should put cream on but I reckon the sun will burn them dry. Anger is high because the six guys haven't been released, perhaps they're being badly treated. There's a bull fight this afternoon and everyone's going along. It's a crummy wooden ring in a patch of open land, and we all turn up, maybe two hundred Rhodesians, mainly young men, in swimming costumes, the locals in family groups in their Sunday best. The proceedings start slowly and our lot soon start throwing bottles into the ring. Each one is carefully removed by the Portuguese. The bull-fight is a let down, the bulls either won't charge or if they do the matadors run away. The Rhodesians start shouting abuse, then, to a round of applause one stumbles into the ring, approaches the matador in a friendly drunk way, puts his arm round him and pretends to instruct him, demonstrating with his towel. Two stewards rush up to take him off. He struggles and then one hits him. It's like a signal, in minutes the ring is full of Rhodesians, bull fighting with their towels, trying to ride the bulls, releasing others, the afternoon collapses in chaos.

Dad's business is doing well and we've moved into a flat in North Avenue, just around the corner from the school. He's bought a blue Mark III Zephir six with a bonnet like an aircraft carrier, and because I've just passed my driving test I'm allowed to use the old MG Magnette. I've forgotten to say what a beautiful city Salisbury is, mauve jacarandas all the way down North Avenue, and, between us and town, the Avenues, old colonial houses with wide open verandas and tin roofs, then the park right on the edge of the city centre. Salisbury's older than Muf or Ndola, started in 1890 as Fort Salisbury, and you can feel the difference. In the book shops are pictures from the turn of the century showing a wild-west town, already with some brick buildings in Manica Road, and, even earlier a handwritten daily newspaper. Firms like Meikles, Dulys, Stuttafords, have been around for years. The place is humming with industries making sophisticated goods, there's energy and confidence, traffic jams in the morning and evening. The white population is over a quarter of a million, half of them in Salisbury, and they're not going to give in easily.

Went with Dad to a RF meeting at Harry Margolis Hall, to hear Smith speak. The audience, several hundred, was almost entirely white, just a few blacks in the back row. The atmosphere was charged, excited. Smith came on to a huge roar, everyone stood up clapping and cheering. He was much livelier than on TV, more of a rabble-rouser than I'd expected, easy with his own supporters. He went through all the arguments for UDI: the British government can **not be trusted**, they will use their reserve powers to **undermine us** and we must get out of their clutches. **Britain has lost its way**, the **long haired degenerate Labour** government is in the hands of the **unions and communists** and under the influence of **pan African terrorists**, betraying the **values** that have made **Britain great**. Look at the mess England is in, the **welfare state** that's **destroyed the British character**, **strikes**, a **collapsing economy**, they can't run their own affairs and yet are trying to dictate to us. The **empire** is slipping through their fingers. **Rhodesians**, who have fought and died alongside their **kith and kin** during **the war** are the **true holders** of the old values, and by declaring independence we will be a **rock for western democracy** until it comes to its senses, as it must. **God save the Queen**!

As the audience stood again and cheered a man came on to the stage and whispered in Smith's ear. Smith raised a hand and the crowd fell silent. "Ladies and gentlemen, I must interrupt these proceedings to bring you some news, which I hope you will agree should not deflect us from our purpose." There was a long pause, "India, India! has just threatened sanctions if we go ahead!" The place packed out with helpless laughter. A middle aged man near the front stood up and turned to face the hall. Swaying slightly he raised his hand for silence and said in a mock orator's voice, "Prime Minister, ladies and gentlemen, I say in all earnestness, do not take this matter lightly, in fact we're all ruined." He paused for effect, "No more poppadoms!" The audience pissed themselves again. "Let's sort the bastards out, send in the RLI!" yelled someone.

Smith started talking again and I became aware of some voices across the aisle to our left, and realised he was being heckled by a group of five or six young white men, probably students. They were led by a tall skinny bloke with bushy red hair and buck teeth, and now were chanting, "One man one vote!" Smith quickly gained control, saying quietly, as if thinking aloud, "I see our African friends at the back are showing exemplary behaviour." Everyone looked round. "Thank you. And most of our Africans, unless led astray by communist propaganda are only too happy to work with us." The heckling became more apparent and irritating as we struggled to hear what he was saying. He raised his voice a little, "But we're being let down by a few disgraceful troublemakers." Then he pointed at the hecklers and shouted, "And, they're all white!" The crowd went mad, rising to their feet, pointing and shouting "Out! Out! Out!" their fingers jabbing with each call. The chanting became more intense and I thought the hecklers would be attacked. I was surprised to see our doctor, a small, mild, middle – aged man, leading the shouting. Then some stewards arrived. The students sat refusing to move, so were carried out, shoulder high, the tall guy still struggling and yelling.

Feelings are running high. Hecklers and protesters have been beaten up at meetings, lighted cigarettes thrown into girls' hair. Last week three visiting British labour MPs were roughed up when they addressed a meeting in the same hall. They tried to reason with the white audience, saying that steady progress towards majority rule was in everyone's interest. "This would lead to a benign African government which will ensure a place for the white population into the future. But by taking the present course you risk civil war, and the eventual possibility a more extreme black regime." The crowd grew increasingly hostile, shouting things like "rubbish", "communist bastards", "long haired queers", "kaffir lovers", and eventually a few got on to the stage and snatched the speaker's notes. When he tried to grab them back he was punched in the face and had a jug of water thrown over him. The police smuggled the MPs out through a back window.

Radio Rhodesia and its announcer Harvey Ward warn of the forces of evil that have infiltrated the West, its institutions, even its churches, distorting its values, sapping its strength and resolve. Liberals are either communist fellow travellers or poor fools. The new pro RF paper the Citizen gives out similar propaganda. We are a bastion of civilisation and Christianity holding back the forces of barbarism.

And what do the blacks think? Who knows? I've heard there were mass protests a few years ago, led by the NDP under Joshua Nkomo, who's now head of ZANU. This pushed the British Government into insisting on a new constitution in 1961, widening the franchise for blacks in exchange for less right to interfere in Rhodesia's internal affairs. Now most African leaders like Nkomo, Ndabaningi Sithole, and Edgar Tekere, are in detention in Gonakudzingwa or out of the country and you don't hear a peep from African politicians. The RF claims most blacks are simple souls, happy with the situation unless intimidated or influenced by propaganda. But then why are they declaring all these local states of emergency, like the one in Harare township right now?

As the crisis builds, various British ministers like Arthur Bottomley and Lord Gardner are visiting Rhodesia to try to sort things out. Some guys in my class go round to Smith's house because they're friends with his son Alec and we pick up all sorts of rumours, for example that Rhodesian ministers can't stand Bottomley because he looks soft and pink and is about as far from a Rhodesian as you can get. They try to intimidate the visitors, telling them to get a haircut, involving them in heavy drinking sessions and silly bar games which they can't handle, and communal pissing around a particular rose bush. Some of the visitors are embarrassed, can't piss, and so are mocked, and their authority weakened.

But Dad says the British aren't just allowing Rhodesia to stay as it is, they are actively pushing six requirements including, "The principle and intention of unimpeded progress to majority rule", an "immediate improvement in the political status of the African population", and "progress towards ending racial discrimination". The British Government are under pressure from the Labour Party, the Commonwealth, the OAU, and others. So it seems Smith is under pressure to jump one way or the other. People are beginning to build up emergency stores of food and essentials. Everyone keeps their petrol tank full, and Dad checked our passports last night.

October, November, will he won't he? November 11, Armistice day, of course! We are sent home from school early to hear "an announcement" at midday, 11am British time and we all know what it will be. Bob and several others come back to my flat which has become a kind of coffee club between lessons because it's so close to school. A woman's voice comes on the radio, "There now follows an announcement by the Honourable Ian Smith MP, Prime Minister." Here's what he said:

Now I would like to say a few words to you. Today, now that the final stalemate in negotiations has become evident, the end of the road has been reached.

It has become abundantly clear that it is the policy of the British Government to play us along with no real intention of arriving at a solution which we could possibly accept. Indeed, in the latest verbal and confidential message delivered to me last night we find that on the main principle which is in dispute the two Governments have moved further apart.

I promised the people of this country that I would continue to negotiate to the bitter end and that I would leave no stone unturned in my endeavours to secure an honourable and mutually accepted settlement.

It now falls to me to tell you that negotiations have come to an end. No one could deny that we have striven with might and main and at times bent over backwards to bridge the gap which divides us from the British Government.

. . . Let no one believe that this action today marks a radical departure from the principles by which we have lived, or be under any misconception that now the Constitution will be torn up and that the protection of the rights of all peoples which are enshrined in that Constitution will be abrogated and disregarded.

Neither let it be thought that this event marks a diminution in the opportunities which our African people have to advance and prosper in Rhodesia. Far from this being the case, it is our intention, in consultation with the chiefs, to bring them into the Government and administration as the acknowledged leaders of the African people on a basis acceptable to them.

It is our firm intention to abide by the Constitution. Indeed, we have never asked for anything other than independence on the basis of the present Constitution, and only such amendments are included as are necessary to adapt it to that of an independent country.

With regard to the position of Members of Parliament, judges, civil servants, and members of the armed forces, as well as the police, provision has been made for all of them to carry on their duties, and all are deemed to have complied with the requirements of the New Constitution. They will continue to carry on their normal work. All present laws shall continue to operate and the courts will enforce them in the normal manner.

We are doing no more than assuming the right which various British Ministers have in the past indicated were ours. And in fact this Constitution was the one which would carry us to independence.

Let no one be persuaded that this action marks a change in our attitude towards our neighbours in Africa, to whom we have ceaselessly extended the hand of friendship and to whom we have nothing but goodwill and the best of intentions.

We have never sought, nor will we ever seek, to interfere or in any way attempt to influence their policy and their internal affairs. All we ask in return is their goodwill in permitting us to look after what are, after all, our own private and domestic matters.

There can be no solution to our racial problems while African nationalists believe that, provided they stirred up sufficient trouble, they will be able to blackmail the British Government into bringing about a miracle on their behalf by handing the country over to irresponsible rule.

There will be no happiness in this country while the absurd situation continues to exist where people such as ourselves, who have ruled ourselves with an impressive record for over 40 years, are denied what is freely granted to other countries, who have ruled themselves in some cases for no longer than a year.

There can never be long-term prosperity, which is so necessary for the nurturing of our endeavours to improve the standard of living and increase the happiness and better the lot of all our people, whilst the present uncertainty exists.

No businessman could ever seriously contemplate massive long-term investment in a country in which chaos and confusion will always be future possibilities.

Whatever the short-term economic disadvantages may be, in the long term steady economic progress could never be achieved unless we are masters in our own house.

That some economic retribution will be visited upon us there is no doubt. Those who seek to damage us do not have any great concern for the principles to which they endlessly pay lip service; for if they really believed in these principles, which they ceaselessly proclaim, then they could not possibly deny, the many disasters which have been brought about by the premature withdrawal of European influence from countries in Africa and Asia who where nowhere near ready for it.

There is no doubt that the talk of threats and sanctions is no more than appeasement to the United Nations, the Afro-Asian bloc, and certain members of the Commonwealth; and undoubtedly some action will be taken.

But I cannot conceive of a rational world uniting in an endeavour to destroy the economy of this country, knowing, as they undoubtedly do, that in many cases the hardest hit will be the very people on whose behalf they would like to believe they are invoking these sanctions. We for our part will never do anything in the nature of taking revenge on any neighbouring African State for what other countries may do to us.

We may be a small country, but we are a determined people who have been called upon to play a rôle of world-wide significance.

We Rhodesians have rejected the doctrinaire philosophy of appeasement and surrender. The decision which we have taken today is a refusal by Rhodesians to sell their birthright. And, even if we were to surrender, does anyone believe that Rhodesia would be the last target of the Communists in the Afro-Asian block?

We have struck a blow for the preservation of justice, civilization, and Christianity; and in the spirit of this belief we have this day assumed our sovereign independence. God bless you all.

Unilateral Declaration of Independence

Whereas in the course of human affairs history has shown that it may become necessary for a people to resolve the political affiliations which have connected them with another people and to assume among other nations the separate and equal status to which they are entitled

And whereas in such event a respect for the opinions of mankind requires them to declare to other nations the causes which impel them to assume full responsibility for their own affairs

Now Therefore, We, The Government of Rhodesia, Do Hereby Declare:

That it is an undisputed and accepted historical fact that since 1923 the Government of Rhodesia have exercised the powers of self-government and have been responsible for the progress, development and welfare of their people;

That the people of Rhodesia, having demonstrated their loyalty to the Crown and to their kith and kin in the United Kingdom and elsewhere through two world wars, and having been prepared to shed their blood and give of their substance in what they believed to be the mutual interests of freedom-loving people, now see all that they have cherished about to be shattered on the rocks of expediency;

That the people of Rhodesia have witnessed a process which is destructive of these very precepts upon which civilization in a primitive country has been built, they have seen the principles of Western democracy, responsible government, and moral standards crumble elsewhere, nevertheless they have remained steadfast;

That the people of Rhodesia fully support the requests of their Government for sovereign independence but have witnessed the consistent refusal of the Government of the United Kingdom to accede to their entreaties;

That the Government of the United Kingdom have thus demonstrated that they are not prepared to grant sovereign independence to Rhodesia on terms acceptable to the people of Rhodesia, thereby persisting in maintaining an unwarrantable jurisdiction over Rhodesia obstructing laws and treaties with other states and the conduct of affairs with other nations and refusing laws necessary to the public good, all this to the detriment of the future peace, prosperity and good government of Rhodesia;

That the Government of Rhodesia have for a long period patiently and in good faith negotiated with the Government of the United Kingdom for the removal of the remaining limitations placed upon them and for the grant of sovereign independence;

That in the belief that procrastination strike at and injure the very life of the nation, the Government of Rhodesia consider it essential that Rhodesia should attain, without delay, sovereign independence, the justice of which is beyond question;

Now, therefore, we the Government of Rhodesia, in humble submission to Almighty God who controls the destinies of nations, conscious that the people of Rhodesia have always shown unswerving loyalty and devotion to Her Majesty the Queen and earnestly praying that we and the people of Rhodesia will not be hindered in our determination to continue exercising our undoubted right to demonstrate the same loyalty and devotion, and seeking to promote the common good, so that the dignity and freedom of all men may be assured, *Do, by This Proclamation,* adopt, enact and give to the people of Rhodesia the Constitution annexed hereto.

God Save the Queen

"Pompous bastard," said Bob, "that's straight from the American Declaration, only without the bit about all men being created equal." "But I'm sure her majesty will be relieved we still want her," said Keith. "Maybe she'll move here when the British labour party abolishes her." "Shit this isn't funny," I said, "we could end up fighting the British. We'll all be called up!" "Yes," said Bob, "and weren't you born over there? They'll hang you for treason if they catch you, you nasty little traitor. And you'll need a proper haircut too."

Then they went off home as if nothing much had happened, so I went into town to see what was going on. I was half expecting black demonstrations, or at least an afternoon edition of the Herald, but nothing, even quieter than usual, strangely quiet. I went to Dad's work but he wasn't there, he'd gone off to the stamp shop in Colonial Mutual Buildings, Gordon Avenue, run by a friend of his also from Muf. The shop has become a kind of club at lunchtimes. Ten to twenty men turn up and sit in the back room at tables, going through stock books or even bulk boxes looking for postmarks or nice copies. Then they price the stamps themselves at one third Stanley Gibbons catalogue and hand the man or his wife the money or just leave it by the till. Nobody checks because dishonesty is out of the question. These men are the backbone of white Rhodesia and genuinely pride themselves on their standards, their efficiency and honesty, the lack of corruption in government. "Ya, they can afford to be, that's because we've ripped off the blacks big time in the first place," I said one night. Dad and Catherine were shocked. "How can you say that, they're always helping their Africans. Free healthcare, education, we have the highest level of black literacy in Africa. Where would they be without us? Back in the bush fighting each other. Take Mr Marshall, he's a member of the RF and he's spent thousands on a school for his farm workers and is even funding one of them to go to university. He doesn't have to do that. How many of your English immigrants would do that, or your friends' liberal parents? With them it's just talk." Anyway, they're all discussing the declaration. About half are expecting a British invasion, the others say Wilson would never dare because the British Army wouldn't support a socialist like him against chaps like us, they'd refuse to fight. If they did, our forces would clean them up on our own ground and there would be an outcry in Britain once casualties mounted. "Anyway, where would they base them, Lusaka? We could cut off their fuel supplies and bomb their airport no problem." An English guy asked about the possibility of a black uprising, but everyone pooh poohed that, no chance. Meanwhile Rosie and Carolyn, the two senior black girls were handing out tea with their usual smiles, "I think no milk Mr Englebrecht?" "Ya thet's right Carolyn, thenks, you got a good memory heh?" "Thenk you sa."

The British and United Nations have set up sanctions against us and seized our assets overseas. But nobody's bothered, they say it'll just stop us importing all sorts of rubbish, and help us build up our own industry. Dad read an article in the Financial Gazette which says Rhodesia will retaliate by not paying debt and dividends to Britain and Zambia, and we'll actually make a profit. The Government's introduced exchange controls which will reduce imports of luxury goods, and Dad's full of plans to extend his range, moving into children's books, package labels and all sorts of things. New local goods are coming out, tomato sauce that tastes like strawberry jam, Rosemary Creams to substitute for Romany Creams, and chocolate that tastes like soft cardboard. It'll all improve in time says Dad. The Government have declared a state of emergency, it's a matter of survival now the deed is done, and basically you're a traitor if you're not on side. They've imposed press censorship and are jamming broadcasts by the BBC and Zambia radio. The Herald comes out with blank spaces headed by the word "censored", sometimes nearly a whole page. But then how does it make a profit when most readers are so pro government? Oops what a slip, I'm thinking of the white population, of course, lots of blacks probably also buy the paper, and looking at my entry a few weeks ago about full petrol tanks, I meant mainly whites. In truth the term "Rhodesian" seems to apply to whites only, "Rhodesians, and our Africans" just as, in cowboy films, the term "American" doesn't seem to apply to red indians. At the moment, I don't know what I am, anti government but pro country, pro Rhodesia. Whatever that means. But who cares? As Eddie Cochrane says, come on everybody, let's have a party. The sun is still shining, and everything's fine.

Mufulira 1965

Up to Muf by train for Christmas. Surprisingly I get through customs easily, but then I've a British rather than Rhodesian passport, chosen for security and self preservation. Despite Kaunda's rhetoric about sanctions, Zambia is still trading with Rhodesia, except for oil. Just about all Zambia's oil arrives through Rhodesia, who now won't give it passage because Zambia supports the international embargo. Now the British are committed to flying in all Zambia's requirements. They also have to supply aviation fuel to a squadron of British jets based in Lusaka to protect Zambia against the Rhodesians. They say more fuel is used flying in the fuel than the fuel itself. The arriving British jets required the help of Salisbury air traffic control, which handles all traffic south of the Sahara and north of South Africa. British troops and airmen are drinking and fraternising with the Rhodesian military at the Falls and other border points. From time to time RRAF Canberras fly straight at the border to force the British to scramble, so wasting their precious fuel. The stamp shop which Dad frequents is now a hotbed of information and rumour, because some customers are the newly arrived correspondents of British newspapers, like Chris Munnion of the Telegraph, while others are senior government, military or business people. But also, everyone knows everyone else, for example you sometimes see cabinet ministers around town or at the bioscope. Last week I saw Ian Mclean buying avocados in the small shop on 2nd Street extension, and sometimes, driving home, you see Smith in the back of his car going up 2nd Street, just him and his black chauffeur. A couple of weeks ago he smiled at me and waved, and I waved back, why not? It's only polite.

Anyway Muf is not really that different, but it's lost something, older people seem less confident, talking about difficulties and getting out, young people are wilder and act like they don't care. It's still only whites in the club. UDI has caused a petrol shortage, much worse than in Salisbury, and some people are going across to Mokambo to buy it in 44 gallon drums at a high price. But it's dangerous and chancy, some have been sold a drum of water with a layer of petrol on top. Richard wanted to go, and to take me with him, but Mom kicked up a big fuss and in the end he promised not to. "They'll kill you Richard, they'll kill you, then where will I be?" Never mind about me! But she's right, a few weeks ago Koos Labuschagne and Dannie Armstrong went across and were "invited" for a drink with five black Congolese squaddies hanging around the border post. They went to the local hotel, and every time they tried to leave it was, "No no, my friend, one more drink." Finally they stood up and said they must go, and the squaddies pulled guns and robbed them of everything. The translator who had seemed all friendly stuck a gun in Dannie's face, "Now we kill you anyway, fucking white bastards!" Fortunately, at that moment the petrol vendor and two officers came in and saved them. The officers started whacking the squaddies round the head. Apparently everyone gets a cut from the trade and they didn't want it wrecked.

This guy's arrived in Muf from Bulawayo to do some research on the mine. He has an MSc which is higher than a degree and he's studying for an even higher degree called a PHD. He's the son of a RF MP but he's got long hair and acts a bit soft, so everyone's saying he's a queer, or a kaffir lover or a communist or something. Lenny Englebrecht at the garage wouldn't service his car until he'd fumigated it in case he caught something. Some guy in the bar says, "Look at your hair, you'd better watch it or people will start talking about you too. You've changed you know." Maybe I have and maybe I don't fit in here any more.

Christmas eve, I'm out with a group of guys from the old days. We go to the club, til about ten, then to the Congo Border Hall where there's a dance. Only about forty people are there, and most of the girls or women are taken, except for one really pretty dark haired girl about eighteen, who everybody's chatting up, but who's not dancing with anyone in particular. I get two or three dances so I'm beginning to think I'm in luck when Richard arrives with a couple of old guys. When a slow tune comes on he asks her to dance and I can't believe it, she sticks with him when the music stops, her head on his shoulder, his arm around her. They dance two more slow numbers and snuggle up all cosy. Then a fast Elvis number and Richard looks embarrassed, he doesn't jive, says something and goes over to the bar. She comes across, grabs my hand and leads me to the dance floor. After the dance she holds my hand, Christ, I'm competing with my stepdad! I make an excuse, and go across to Richard at the bar. She watches, puzzled. "Let's go, I'll give you a lift." In the car he says, "Don't mention that to your mother, heh?" "Of course not." Why should I?

On Boxing Day the boys persuade Richard to bring out his coins. They're in an old tin box, crowns from Britain, South Africa and Southern Rhodesia, a few Krugerrands, Congolese and Kantangese notes, and a large ring. I pick it up, it has a large swastika. Everyone stops to stare. "Jesus Richard, what's this for?" I ask. He's embarrassed, "Just some thing I picked up before the war," he says. "Were you a Nazi?" I ask. "Of course not!" he says, "all that European bullshit and fancy uniforms." Then he wouldn't talk about it, but afterwards Mom told me she thought he'd been a member of Ossewa Brandwag. A section of them, the Stormjaers were involved in sabotage and beating up troops.

Muf High school's going downhill. Glen's been sent off to some technical college in Pretoria, and Grant to

Falcon College near Bulawayo. Glen hates it, he's bullied there, and he's due to go back tomorrow. Today he started crying and yelling and saying he wouldn't go, he'd kill himself. Mom was comforting but Richard just lost his temper and told him not to be so soft. It occurred to me that Richard has always been hard on Glen.

Richard's taking me back to Salisbury. We left yesterday morning at five, quite cold in shorts and shirt, with a bottle of brandy between us, sped past Ndola in darkness towards Kapiri Mposhi, plenty of game on the road. Dawn came suddenly, flickering through the trees, everything in black and grey, except for the yellow ball of sun. We stopped on a rise, in full light, for breakfast, the bush below still in shadow, chicken, boerwors, buttered bread from a big old biscuit tin, and sweet thermos coffee. I watched Richard chewing a chicken leg, something unconscious about his enjoyment giving a sense of his ease out here, his world, old Africa, stretching from Muldersdrift to the Congo border, from the Boer war til now, and at this moment it seemed real. By mid morning our bottle was empty and we were stopping at roadside hotel bars, arriving at Kariba just after midday. We parked the car and walked on to the massive, bulging wall. The hills towered above, two curves of water joined the sluice gates to the river over four hundred feet below. Behind us stretched the largest man-made lake in the world, over two hundred miles long, and up to twenty miles wide. Dazed by the heat, light and booze, I watched a fish eagle circling in the white sky, and felt this is the place to be.

We booked in to the local motel and slept until six. Then Richard announced he was going out and would drop me at the Kariba Hotel for the evening. Where could he go? There's hardly a village here. I assumed he was off to look for women, but how does he know where to go, does he have contacts here? It's as if there are levels at which you can know a place, as if even a small town has a secret sub frame that experienced people like Richard can tap into, but I can't see. It's a comfort really, similar to how, at my age, everything's somehow arranged for you, train tickets, fees, by the hidden world of adults. Anyway, Richard and I had one beer at the hotel until I'd got in with some national service troopies, then he disappeared and came back at about midnight.

Today the trip back was uneventful, except for a great herd of elephants as we climbed from the Zambezi valley. Before leaving we had visited the Kariba snake park. There were fluffy yellow chicks in some cages, walking all over the snakes which only notice them when they get hungry, and then pounce. I thought, why don't they cut up the snakes for the chickens, who's to say which are more important? We arrived in Salisbury at about six and as the sun set, my heart sank. Richard invited Dad out for a drink, they're quite affable these days. At the George Hotel Richard was giving Dad all the news from Muf. He said, "I'm going to drain my lizard, Ian, order us some more beers." As soon as he was out of earshot Dad asked, all urgent, "Are you all right on two beers?" Yes, I'm home.

Salisbury 1966

Last Wednesday afternoon Dennis and I were walking down Moffat Street into town and passed these three girls outside QE School. One was Mandy, Janet's friend, and next to her this beautiful girl I've seen once before, about my height, black hair, wonderful long brown legs, slim but not at all thin, in fact quite full, and everything just right. Her nose doesn't dip much at the bridge, giving her a Latin, Roman look with her dark eyes. I stopped to say a few words to Mandy, but when I caught this girl's eye, it was as if we knew each other. I could hardly speak and we soon shoved off. The next day Janet came home from school and said "I've some news, Marion Jameson was asking Mandy all sorts of questions about you, what music you like, your politics, but she's going out with David Levitt at the moment." "Tell her blues, Spencer Davis, shit, Levitt?"

Over the last few days she's become an obsession. Levitt is in my year doing sciences, a perfectly nice guy, but as I look at him I feel increasingly hostile. I realise I'd do almost anything to get her off him, I've just got to have her. Anyway, the school dance is next week, and hallelujah, Marion asked Mandy if she knows if I'm going! Even her name makes me shiver! But I could have it all wrong, what if she's there with Levitt?

It's the night of the dance. The sky is deep blue and black as a storm develops, lightning hanging for seconds towards the east, then thunder straight overhead. A warm, soft breeze is quickening, bringing the dusty smell of new rain. There's a tropical feel, the world coming alive, that excitement and anticipation. In the school hall a boarders' group is murdering the Byrds' massacre of Bob Dylan's Mr Tambourine Man. Then I see her with the same two girls, my hypersensitive stereoscopic vision having spotted Levitt at least ten yards away, in a group of guys. Looking good! I take a few deep breaths to calm myself, then go over, all by myself, can they hear my heart thumping? "Hi Marion," my voice comes out thin, maybe she'll be put off by my school uniform, despite my unbuttoned tie and a few other modifications. When I meet her eyes, she holds my gaze, I have to do something, and I hear myself saying words like, "Dance?" and the next moment we're all alone, or so it seems, on the darkened dance floor. "Crap band," I say, "what kind of music do you like?" "Blues, Spencer Davis," she says, home and dry. Then we start snogging, ah the smell of her, the softness, we slow dance, nevermind the pace of the music, and time seems to stand still. Vaguely I notice some of the boarders giving us hard stares, but who cares! Then we go out to the car and into the back seat, half soaked by the warm rain. I'm tempted to suggest she take her dress off to dry, and imagine her brown body, in just white bra and pants, but I know it's a bad move, so I decide to play it cool and not touch her at all. But it's enough just to hold her sweet face in my hand and kiss her forehead and the top of her nose and down to her mouth and ears and throat and then her arms, until I think she's as frustrated as I am, and I know she's the girl for me.

Back in school on Monday the head gives this talk about a few boys spoiling the tone of Saturday night by unseemly behaviour on the dance floor. Straight after assembly I'm called by the housemaster who says he was referring particularly to me, and that right through the evening they were in two minds whether to throw us out, but didn't want an incident with the girls' school. Then he goes on about my general demeanor and says that I and my friends are disloyal to the school, undermining the prefects' authority, and if this continues there'll be serious consequences. The thing is, some of the little kids are terrified of the prefects and their arbitrary power to whack them. The number of whacks depends on the prefects' judgement or prejudice, and some go right over the top. Of course some prefects are in our class, and the more liberal ones seem uneasy about the whole thing but feel they have to maintain the system. "Justice" is administered mainly before morning assembly, or at break time, and a few of us have taken to sitting outside the prefects' study by the main hall, making comments like, "Hey Jones, why don't you take on someone your own size, you stupid bastard." Some of the kids have noticed this and now come to us for help, and sometimes we'll raise the case on their behalf with the more reasonable prefects. Of course it's easy to get sucked into the system as proxy prefects, "You've done what? Jesus man, I don't think I can get you off that one!"

But what can I say about my love? No dirty detail, someone might read this, I'll just say things are going like a dream, surely no one else could have what we have? We've passed the usual stages. Having treated her like a madonna the first night, how do you move on? At first it was fine, George let us use his room in the Avalon, and the first opportune Saturday we spent three hours on his bed, just snogging, which was wonderful, except for the most horrible case of lover's balls. But the following Thursday, after about half an hour I suddenly rolled off her panting, "Oh god, shit!" She sat up, startled, "What's the matter?" "I'm so sorry," I said, "I nearly touched you!" "Oh," she said, and paused, "it's fine, you can do what you like." Wow! I took it very easy that day, just to emphasise my reverence, but a couple of Friday nights later we lay in my bedroom, my parents away, the wonderful novel feeling of her body totally naked under mine, head to head, toe to toe, in the dark, while the rain fell gently on the roof. Now it's not always head to head, or in the dark, but the opportunities are rare enough that they're all taken urgently, as the lift door closes, behind hedges, and mostly, in snatched moments in the car.

All this makes me feel a bit of a heel as they say in the films. Marion's family are like the Kennedys of Rhodesia, social leaders but on the liberal side. Her dad's an important surgeon, and a big wheel on the Constitutional Council, and in their lounge are pictures of him with Wilson and Bottomley. They're personal friends of Sir Humphrey Gibbs, and often visit him now his staff and official car have been removed by Smithy, his salary stopped, and his phone cut off. They have dinner parties with black leaders as part of his Council role. And we all know who her uncle is. I love going to their house, so cultured, huge African stone sculptures in the garden, persian carpets, afghan rugs, real paintings. And I'm learning new things: at lunch they had these French wines called claret and burgundy, like in novels, and Marion showed me pictures by these guys called impressionists. She's one of the country's leading junior artists, and her parents' pride and joy. And here she is being screwed by a skate from Muf! When her mother discovered a love bite on her neck she was shocked and asked, "Who did that?" Marion said, "Ian," but assured her nothing else was going on. "Well tell Dracula to lay off," said Mom, and got even stricter with her movements. But her parents seem to like me and if I'm there at about six her Dad will offer me a beer. I find it hard to talk, I'm so in awe of them, but I feel good, why? Because they're the only adults I know, other than Auntie Mary, who accept my political questions, accept who I am, and don't make me feel immature or worse, a traitor.

Through Marion's parents I've met a couple of lecturers at the university, out from England, who've lent me some books and papers which show how Rhodesia developed. Most people know little about this because we only learn a simplified outline at school.

White liberals tend to look at voting rights, freedom of speech and things like that, but it seems that for the blacks, the real issues are land, jobs and wages. When whites first arrived in force in 1890, black agriculture was doing fine. Of course let's not ignore the Ndebele invasion of 1836 and subsequent continual raids on the Shona, which the whites eventually stopped. However, from the turn of the century, partly because of peace, and the needs of the white community, black agriculture flourished, maize production by blacks rising 25% from 1904 to 1921, but this was the high water mark. As white agriculture developed, measures were taken to increase land available to whites and reduce black competition. The Land Apportionment Act of 1931 divided the country into six categories, including African Reserves, (renamed Tribal Trust land in 1965), Native Purchase areas, European, and unassigned land. The best land with the best infrastructure went to whites, so that today we hold over 95% of land suitable for forestry, fruit and intensive beef, and over 80% suitable for intensive arable farming. Other early measures included the 1934 Maize Control Act, giving preference to local white farmers in the domestic and international maize Market because "the native" could out compete "with their low standard of living and methods of farming". Similarly Africans were prohibited from selling their beef directly to the Cold Storage Commission, they had to sell it through European farmers, their competitors! The Native Land Husbandry Act 1951 provided for individuals to hold title to land in the African Reserves, where hitherto land was held communally, resulting in dispossession of existing communities who consequently were forced on to the labour Market. Whatever the original motives for the creation of the Reserves, they are now overpopulated and unproductive, and their subsistence farmers are the real losers in the system, creating a vast pool of potential labour. Crudely dividing populations into designated land areas you get about 230 acres per white and 16 per black.

On the employment front, the BSA Company first imposed a 10/- annual hut tax then in 1904 amended it to a £1 poll tax. Taxes on blacks formed 41% of government revenue in 1904-5, while whites on lower incomes paid nothing. The chief aim of the poll tax apart from revenue was to force blacks on to the labour market. The 1901 Master Servant Act provided legal penalties for blacks who failed to perform to satisfaction, and use of the sjambok was widespread. From 1926 every African over 14 had to carry a registration certificate and the 1936 Native Registration Act tightened the movement of blacks in urban areas. The 1934 Industrial Conciliation Act, introduced industrial boards, from which blacks were excluded, which developed agreements between industry and labour, in effect laying the delineation between white and black jobs. Rhodesian competitiveness was underpinned by black labour. Prime Minister Godfrey Huggins said in 1944,

"We cannot exist for five minutes without the native today. He is absolutely essential to our wage structure if nothing else....if we went on a purely European basis with the same conditions of living and pay....the country would be sub-economic and down and out in five minutes."

An interesting divergence of interest was developing between big business which favoured a stable contented skilled black workforce, and white labour which saw potential competition in this. In 1946 the Native Accommodation Act allowed for the provision of decent permanent accommodation for employed urban blacks, with emphasis on married quarters, and in 1948 the Native Labour Board set a minimum monthly wage equivalent to Rhodesian $3 (still below the datum poverty line). In 1949 black trade unions were allowed on the railways and gradually in other industries. For Government the old dilemma Dad once raised in Muf is ever-present: whilst it is strongly in the interests of big business to allow blacks to do white jobs at lower rates, or to redefine them to allow blacks in, white workers cry, "Equal pay for the job and no fragmentation." The government stands uneasily in between, seeking national efficiency but wishing to protect its electoral constituency. Average wages, (discounting subsistence workers) are $300 for blacks and $3100 for whites. Whilst the absolute gap between white and black salaries has increased over the years, proportionately they have narrowed, from about 13 to one in 1954 to 10 to one in 1967.

Enough of all this! How come I'm prepared to spend so long reading and writing all this shit when I'm two essays behind in History? Gibbon Wakefield and the development of Australia, New Zealand and Canada, their constitutions in detail, god it's boring! But I'm beginning to see why we don't study our own country, it's too controversial. No wonder my fellow whites don't know any real facts, and deal in childish myths and half truths. And conversations are so cheerfully bluff and superficial, sport, cars, and jokes about blacks, "Ja man our cook produces real hout cuisine. Ha ha!"

But on reflection, I did feel a little uneasy with those university lecturers, I mean the ones out from England because I wonder what makes them tick. If they're so opposed to the whole Rhodesian setup, why are they here? After all, as Sir Godfrey Huggins made clear, their wages, standard of living, cost of food, the very buildings they stand in, all benefit from exploited black labour. Is the whole thing a meal ticket, a career move, studies in racism, publications?

Or do they really feel impelled to come out here and solve the problem? Fat chance! Sometimes I even wonder how Auntie Mary squares everything. The original white arrivals invaded somebody else's country, but for most there was a coherent view, a belief in their racial superiority! Those who arrive challenging that position need a different argument. Of course I believe that we who were born or brought up here have nothing to answer for, but we have to try to put things right, or get out

Yesterday gave a lift to a black guy about my age, on the Bulawayo road. He was shaking, with bruising on his face and bloody wheels on his back. He said he had been tied up and whipped on a well known white farm for being a "Cheeky kaffir" after he had tried to organise some of them to demand more wages. He'd been sacked. I dropped him in town and gave him all the money I had on me. He looked surprised and started crying, "Jesus man! Thank you, thank you!" and continued his tale. I'm ashamed I felt relieved when he got out of the car, it wouldn't be good to be seen fraternising with a black in that way. It's strange, you can be cordial with a black, you can even share a beer in certain circumstances, you can stand on a street corner talking him, but it must be clear that ultimately it's part of a boss-subordinate, or professional situation. A white and black chatting in public, on equal terms, as real friends, is not on, as I saw one morning in Gordon Avenue, when two young guys rapidly went their separate ways after receiving first stares then comments from white passers by. Things are different at the university, but it's viewed with suspicion. On Saturday, I was working at the counter in Dad's shop when an African messenger came in and asked for Dad. I went into the back office and said, "Dad, there's a man to see you in the shop." Dad walked out, looked around and asked, "Where?" He literally didn't notice the black. Afterwards, he was annoyed and told me not to do it again. He and I clash on issues where there's potential social stigma or pressure. For example, if you're driving your black maid you put her in the back seat to show you're not having an affair, or just that you recognise the convention that she's not someone with whom you have a full social relationship. Dad goes mad when I refuse, saying what would people think? But in his business he and Catherine are good on African salaries, concerned about the staff, and happy to give them more challenging opportunities. Similarly at home the maid's little daughter runs around the house, and Catherine pats her on the head like any other kid, though does her hand actually touch?

How do you break through these social barriers? Last Saturday night Mandy and I went to dinner with her brother John and Sarah his wife, who live at Christon Bank, about eighteen miles out of Salisbury. John works in his Dad's factory, and, in a crude attempt to address the problem, had invited along the firm's two African women supervisors. Just getting the women there and back was an operation, picking them up at the outskirts of the African township, dropping them back close enough to their house to be safe, but balancing this against the danger and illegality of entering the township at night. Anyway the evening was jovial and enjoyable, although the two black women, Betty and Rosy wouldn't be drawn on politics and kept calling us "sir" and "madam". All was fine until after dinner when we moved to the open veranda for drinks. John, in a fit of expansiveness went and invited the garden boy to join us, an old Malawi man of about fifty called Ingezi. As soon as he appeared from the dark at one end of the veranda the two black women stood up, shrieked and retreated to the other. Some social taboo had been broken! Ingezi was completely impassive, as if he had expected this. John was pissed off. He and I spent the rest of the evening sitting on the steps of the veranda with Ingezi, talking in Chilapalapa and drinking beer, while the four women huddled inside the house.

But Mandy was telling us that even liberals like John make compromises. About a year ago, on his way home from work, he picked up a young black man on the road, and dropped him at the turning to a village near Christon Bank. This guy worked as a garden boy in Malborough, and daily walked about fifteen miles each way, getting home after ten, and then leaving for work at three am, almost unbelievable. He was overwhelmingly grateful for the lift, which transformed his day, but gradually others began to hear of John's benevolence and wave the car down. Similarly in the morning he and Sarah once stopped to pick up four black children, saving them a five mile walk to school, and this again became an obligation, the group of sweaty kids growing each day, fighting to get into the car, inevitably some being left behind. Now the journeys have become psychological torture for them, and sometimes they just snap and pick nobody up, causing resentment all round. The local whites have spotted this and are full of sage told you so advice.

Anne and Eddy have arrived in Salisbury and are living in a small house in Malborough. Eddy's job in Kitwe was Zambianised. He's a fully qualified fitter and turner and has found a job on a low wage with a Salisbury engineering company, but was lucky because hundreds of whites from the Copperbelt are in a similar position. His eyes are permanently inflamed because of the chemicals at work and the long hours.

They're always going on about being broke and how they miss life on the Copperbelt. Anne's taking drugs for depression. We had a little talk, she and Eddy are fine, but for some reason she always feels anxious and insecure, and it's a lot worse since they've moved. She says things like, "But what would happen to me if Eddy dies?" She has no qualifications, can't get a job and doesn't know anyone down here besides Eddy's family. She keeps away from Dad and Catherine. Sometimes I feel sad when I think how things have turned out for my clever sister.

Brian was talking about this strange dream he has. He can't get it out of his head. Some people, civilians and military, have taken over these big, bright modern buildings, busily organising everything, but as you watch they begin to fade and slowly disappear. Some reappear in grey England in tiny tenements and you realise that life in the buildings is a projection of themselves, but others do not, there's no base. Then Brian realises he's one of those people, will he end up in Russia where his parents are from, or nowhere? Then he wakes up.

Bob's parents have moved to Malawi so he's staying at the YMCA while he finishes school. On Friday afternoon I dropped by, he wasn't there but there was this guy Hank who I've met before, just back from a mercenary tour in the Congo. He's about twenty four, super friendly, smarmy with a cultured style, but something about him makes you uneasy. He invited me in to his room to look at some Congo pictures and I went, partly out of curiosity, but also because I was a bit scared not to. The first few pictures were typical squaddie mates subjects, then a few showing the Congo River and towns and villages, then white troops kicking down hut doors, cigarettes in mouth, holding guns. He was doing a running commentary saying something about clearing things out, the superstition, witchcraft, smell and disgusting practices. The next picture I clearly remember showed a group of black teenage boys standing by a river, hands tied behind their backs, three white soldiers on a bridge above, and a couple at the water's edge. Each picture was neatly labelled at the base in black ink, and this one said, "Prisoners being prepared for execution." Then a series of pictures showed several executions by hanging, from a tree, the victim standing on a chair which was pulled away. What struck me was the strange impassive look on the victims' faces as they waited. "Don't they care?" I asked. "No that's terror," he said. "They know there's no way out and just shut down." The final one I remember showed a man hanging dead or dying, with three white soldiers posing, smiling, holding the tensioned rope leading up to the hanging-branch, and a forth leaning against the victim, head against his hip, holding his leg. There was something obscene, almost sexual in this pose. Then he showed me his knife, still covered in dried blood. I made an excuse by suddenly looking at my watch and saying, "Shit, I'm late," and left before he could think. That very night, Bob was chatting up a girl at a party, and Hank had him against a wall with a knife at his throat, threatening to kill him if he didn't leave her alone. The following morning Hank was back to his usual friendly self.

We have full scale petrol rationing these days. Dad finds it hard to manage but even though I get a tiny allocation I have no problems because it's easy to make a deal with any garage attendant. They have to take a full coupon for each gallon or "part thereof", and whilst most sensible people part fill their cars to an exact gallon, a few fill right up, leaving part of a coupon free. These add up, and the attendant will fill your car, charging about sixpence for each coupon you don't have. Of course he wouldn't dare do this with a proper self-righteous bwana, but he knows a young skate when he sees one. It's the same with the car parks, I pay the guy half the fee which he pockets and he doesn't give me a ticket, so we're both happy but the Council isn't. Dad was shocked when I told him. "You'll come a cropper some day. Corruption undermines a society."

That doesn't bother me but I'm consumed with guilt about Marion. It's the school holidays and we'd arranged to go for a picnic in the hills near Lake Mac before dawn, huddle in a blanket and watch the sun come up, romantic. I was up at four thirty, then started thinking how good it would be to screw her on a blanket right out there in the bush, with the rising sun on my arse! But then I realised I didn't have a frikkie. So I drove all the way from The Chase to a garage in town, no Durex, sanctions, only this new local one called Alpha, yow, I'd heard some bad stories about their reliability, "Wilson babies". By the time I got back to Marion's in Avondale the sun was up and she was in tears. What a shit I am. Anyway, we still went out and boiled our tea, but it wasn't the same, and even so I couldn't resist carrying out my plan, so all in all I think I ruined it for her. Now things are much, much worse. The Alpha broke on me and she's three days late! Christ just imagine if she's pregnant, her parents, their pure darling little girl, oh no. I ask Jackson the houseboy, who asks his wife, she says yes probably. Day four Dad comes into my room just before dinner and makes it plain he's guessed. "Bingo," I say. That night I eat much better, but Dad's off his food. Day five and six, every time I see Dad he raises an eyebrow and I shake my head, he looks pale like me. Does Catherine know? No idea. At night I dream of a desert, dry yellow sand with a dead tree like a broken stick, then blessed relief, it rains. I wake rapturous, all's well, and then fear grips me as I realise nothing's changed. At school we're doing Blake, "Oh rose though art sick! The invisible worm," that's me. Then day nine, she's come on, oh! I say to Dad, "Blood everywhere!" "All right, all right!" he says, and tries weakly to moralise. I rebuff him sternly, declaring legitimacy, true love, but feel close to him, good old Dad.

Saturday night, the band are playing at a typical Rhodesian engagement party, in a first floor function room in Manica Road. I'm chief amp carrier along with a guy called Rodrigues from Mozambique who's staying at the YMCA, and speaks almost no English. The Portuguese are our mates now because they're helping us break the oil blockade, and cars are plastered with stickers saying, "Obrigado Mozambique". A clash is developing between the dad and band because the guests don't like the R&B numbers, and the band can't or won't play the square tunes they're requesting. "Why'd you hire us then?" asks Bob. "We were unable to get the Drifters, and for some strange reason my daughter likes your music, if you can call it that," says the dad. To make matters worse, the band clatters to a halt with a floor full of dancers as Brian puts down his guitar in mid tune and wanders over to get a sandwich, his head on one side in his usual pensive way. The dad rushes up. "Hungry," says Brian. As they thunder out *Route 66* and *My Babe*, a crowd of blacks has gathered in the street below and are whooping and dancing to the music. I go on to the balcony and give a regal wave, the crowd cheer, then I start conducting them, clapping in time to the music as they clap back. Someone shuts the glass doors behind me but the music is still loud. Then I glance round and see the dad striding across the room to sort us out, his finger pointing in an angry just a minute gesture. There's a huge bang as he walks smack into the glass door, and collapses, stunned. The band packs in as the guys sit on the floor pissing themselves, so unprofessional.

Later, for the toast, the black waiter delivers champagne to the band stand, and then, with a wink, doubles up for each band member at our table. I hoover it all and suddenly reach that happy dizzy stage where I wander around trying to dance with various unlikely girls, polishing off half full glasses on empty tables, till I end up cuddling a toilet bowl, sick. Rodrigues says to Bob, "You know Ian?" "Yes, yes, I know Ian!" "He pissed as judge." "You mean fart." I find myself being driven home by Sid the drummer, at great speed, must be a band break. The world seems different, you ignore red lights, my block of flats looks right, but not quite, like in a dream. We get to my door, but as I lean on it, struggling with the key, it flies open and I stumble inside, scattering milk bottles, and clutching at Dad's shoulders, slide down him, ending up holding his ankles. Only it's not Dad, what a nightmare, Catherine is having an affair, no impossible! "Who're you?" I ask. "No, more to the point who are you?" says the man, all calm. Anyway it turns out to be the next block of flats which is identical to ours. The man was quite decent about it. At home I piss out of my second floor window as usual, to avoid disturbing the household.

Back from a couple of weeks in Mozambique. I went down to with Dennis to Beira, and we took a boat to Sofala where Marion was camping with her family. This served as the ancient trading outlet for the Great Zimbabwe and Monomatapa empires from the

11th century onwards. Taken over by the Portuguese in 1505, it was for Milton the land of Ophir in Paradise lost. Now there's not much except ruins and huts. The boat was perhaps forty five foot long, open except for a small shelter in the middle above the engine, crammed with people, goats and chickens, those great African smells! We were the only whites. I swopped my Lucky Strikes for thin Murusi cigarettes, sweet black paper, dark tobacco, dirt cheap but delicious, and my sandwiches for some of their mealie meal and kuku, but only after they had offered me the food in the first place, so kind and generous. Of course Dennis, stuck up bastard, wouldn't touch it. We arrived at Sofala after a few hours but the boat can't dock because of the sandbar, so were taken in by dugout canoe. You really know you're in Africa here, blue sky, calm turquoise sea, fish drying in the sun, sandy road through palm trees, thatch hut bakery in the forest, and wonderful blinding heat. That night I lay with Marion on the beach, stars above, the sea gently lapping the shore, Dennis a discrete five yards off staring out to sea. Tenderly I kissed her lips, then bzzz, she slapped her face, then her leg, then we were in a cloud of mosquitoes and had to retreat to the family tent. Funny how the early Portuguese settlement was nearly wiped out by malaria, yet we take no pills and are fine. No go, we sleep in the boys' tent.

Returned to Salisbury with the Aunts who had arrived for a few days in Beira, an eighteen year old with two old ladies, but I love it. Somehow they bring back old Africa. We stop on the roadside at eleven and four to make a fire for tea, and stay at country hotels dating back to the early years. Arriving at Melsetter in the Chimanimani Mountains, Auntie Beth says the cool air and pine trees remind her of Austria before the war. I feel all romantic and dream of Marion. In the mountain hotel they're playing the Beatles

And I Love Her, which seems just right. I taste French dressing for the first time and play pool with a troopie on leave from the army. His mom asks if I'm going to join the RLI when I leave school, as if that's what everyone does, and I feel strangely complimented.

Then we cut across country to Fort Victoria, back into the heat, to stay at the Great Zimbabwe ruins, one of the largest ancient structures south of Egypt, built by the local Shona people around the eleventh century. At that time it was capital of a kingdom stretching hundreds of miles, there are similar ruins all over the country, some as far as Bulawayo, but off the main roads. The kingdom, associated by some with King Soloman's Mines, traded gold with the outside world through Sofala. Late afternoon we leave the shade of the thirty foot high main walls to climb to the Acropolis, built into the hills above. Some way up we come suddenly upon a very old man, seated in an alcove by the path. He seems to have appeared from nowhere, almost camouflaged against the brown bush. He claps humbly but his gaze is firm as he says, "Eh mambo, mzungu, ini endaba wena quela lapa kia ka lo baaba ktina?" The hilltop, he says, is the home of his ancestors and soon he will join them. Some black cultures believe that as death approaches, old people can enter and leave the spirit world with increasing ease, until finally they step over permanently. He says white tourists trample the site without care and should approach with due reverence, particularly so late in the afternoon. I offer him a cigarette which I light for him, and he gives us his blessing to proceed. The defensive walls are built intricately into the contours of the hill, so that attackers would have to approach in single file. Emerging at the top into a natural amphitheatre we find ourselves back in the light of the setting sun. The place is silent except for the occasional scrabble of dassies. On the plain below, the ruins of the main settlement are in darkness, and beyond, the great hill tops are lit in gold, but moving into shadow. I feel uneasy, perhaps my usual evening melancholy, but more, a sense of facile trespass against great antiquity.

After dinner at the hotel, Auntie Mary and I go for a walk. The gate to the ruins is now locked against wild animals. I have this urge to climb over and melt into the bush, permanently. That night I have a strange dream. I climb the gate, and ascend towards the Acropolis, my heart thudding with fear. I pass a seated leopard which stares at me with glowing yellow eyes, but makes no move to attack. At the top I look into the ampitheatre from behind a rock, and there assembled is a great host in traditional costume facing a figure enthroned at the far end. An orange moon casts its glow and illuminates a sky streaked with white cloud, but strangely the figures below are bathed in dull blue. They sway slightly as if stirred by an undetectable breeze, and I realise that most, but not all, are spirits. Closer to me are guards in full regalia, holding spears at attention, and I notice they are baboons. Some other animals sit around the periphery. Our old man sits near the central figure, the great nkos, who then begins to address the assembly. Although his lips move I can hear nothing, but feel I would, if I could just tune in. His gaze, like a blinding blue light begins to move from figure to figure, towards me, and I stand transfixed, in terror, knowing that if it meets mine I will die of shock. At the last moment I wake, sweating.

Enough of this bullshit! Back at school things aren't going so well. Here's my second term report from the form master:

"A record of very limited application. He seems to be gaining little and giving less to the school – a pity as I'm sure he has it in him to provide a very copious two-way flow. At least he should exert himself enough next term to gain the material goal of his two sixth form years."

Dad says, "I've given up all hope of you passing your A Levels, what are we going to do with you?" Then last week just before assembly I'm sitting chatting to Levitt when up comes Baker, one of the boarder prefects. "Shut up Hassall!" he says. I say, "Can't you see I'm having a conversation? Stop interrupting!" "I said shut up Hassall!" he shouts. "Hey keep your voice down, you're causing a disturbance, run along now we're nearly finished." And so on. As I leave the hall after assembly I'm summoned to the prefects' study by a small posse, almost an ambush. Most of the prefects are there, including those in my class, who seem embarrassed. "OK," says Baker looking triumphant, "Dooks or essay?" "Neither thanks," I say and walk out. At break a prefect in my year comes up, "I'm sorry Ian, you've got to report to the head's office right away. Better not mess around this time, it's serious." A surge of anxiety runs though me, Owen the head is a disciplinarian, and I'm likely to get six, or if I refuse, expulsion. To my relief, he's not there, and I'm shown in to see Mr Brown, the new deputy head from England. "Hassall, Hassall, he says, this is no good, do you really want to ruin your future so late in the day?" He seems sympathetic. I explain I find it difficult to take orders from Baker, and might have stopped my conversation if asked politely by someone I respect. "Yes, yes," he says, "the system is rather problematic, but you put me in a difficult position. Mr Owen is concerned about what he sees as a subversive element in your class and will want to know what action I've taken. I don't suppose you'd accept caning?" "No sir." "Could I suggest a compromise, a token caning which will maintain my credibility, and hopefully yours?" I agree. Mr Brown holds the cane nine inches from the end and touches my backside twice with it. Then he says, "Now if Baker asks, please say you've been caned, and for heaven's sake try to stay out of trouble for the next few weeks."

Anyway, felt boosted by a small incident the following Monday. Marion and another girl who take A level French at our school were sitting on a wall at break, helpless with laughter as Potgieter drilled some cadet defaulters. He was giving these young kids a really hard time, playing to the audience. Finally, tanned, muscular, six foot three, he swaggered across to the girls and said flirtatiously, "Ladies, ladies, please, it's not fair to laugh at these boys just because they can't march properly." Marion said, "We're not laughing at them, you ridiculous tit, we're laughing at you." Potgieter, stunned, now bright red, stumbled off and soon dismissed his troop. Marion said, "You can imagine him and his friends in the SS."

We spend a lot of time at Columbo's in Angwa Street, an Italian café, just two tables wide, where moustachioed Columbo at the far end facing the shop presides proudly over his cadillac of a coffee machine. He kind of looks after us, gives us spaghetti with just a little sauce, and a coffee all for one and six, about half the real price. Sometimes I come in with Dad and he tells him, "They good boys." Anyway that's where Dad came to find me with a grin on his face when the A level results came out. I'd done almost no swotting, but I've passed, not well, but good enough for university. You can get into a South African university with virtually any A levels, even a couple of Es. They're regarded as a kind of gold standard compared with the South African Matric. It's not so easy to get into the local varsity, which is a college of one of the British universities, and I don't know if I could. But for some reason I've chosen to go away to SA, even though it means not being with Marion? Why? Novelty, adventure.

South Africa 1967

On the train to Rhodes University in Grahamstown the sadness of leaving Marion is trumped by excitement. The train is packed with students and already a hierarchy is developing. First year students count for nothing, and the older guys are establishing their credentials. I'm beginning to realise with a shock that the top dogs are not the most intelligent or academic students, just the opposite, the largest rugby players, in fact the boarders and prefects rule the roost. Duncan Jones makes his way down the crowded corridor, head slightly on one side, fists at chest level, punching anyone smaller who's vaguely in his way. Spud recounts his success with women last year after he made the first rugby team. Beautiful girls are chatting them up, I'm simply not noticed, it's a new world. The following morning we're stopped on the track, in the middle of nowhere; two white men are working along the train, tapping the wheels. One of the manne leans out the window, "Have we got a puncture?" The tapper explains straight faced and in some detail how trains don't have tires, they're listening for cracks in the wheels. "Shouldn't that be an African job?" asks another manne. "No man, I mustn't make a mistake eh, or you all die! It's chudjment. The bleck, he got no chudjment for this job." Despite the racist remarks I feel more repelled by the manne's arrogant put down, cruel within white culture. It's the first time I've really seen this intra – white hierarchy. I actually feel sorry for the tapper. South African Railways reserves most jobs for whites, and is a lifeline to those of low ability, who are threatened by black competition, and naturally they try to rationalise their position.

Grahamstown, jewel of South Africa, is said to be architecturally the most British of Commonwealth cities, founded by the 1820 English settlers. The high street is dominated at one end by the cathedral and the other by the Old Drostdy, formerly a nineteenth century British barracks. These are the oldest buildings I've seen, tall flat fronted houses, painted pink, white or pastel blue, like iced cakes, with an 18th century look. There's an academic feel to the place, bookshops with old mullioned windows, philosophy students in tweeds and cords, pipe in hand, peering into infinity at an angle of forty five degrees, ignoring the manne. Many are theology students who become atheists by second year, but reach an accommodation by third year and go on to be ministers.

On the first day of term I attend a kind of fair in the main hall. Professors and staff of each department sit at tables and try to recruit you. I've only a vague idea, and end up doing English, Psychology, French and Economics. Next year we have to choose two majors from these.

The settling in period is frenetic. Inks and inkettes are required to wear big name plaques. Bob and I don't comply and are constantly hounded by blots and third years, other boys submit to arbitrary orders. Girls turn up obediently to cattle parades in boys' residences, scantily dressed as ordered, running the gauntlet of insulting or salacious remarks. In wet short skirts, showing their knickers, they clean senior boys' cars watched by an appreciative audience. But girls' residences are strictly controlled, you can't get beyond the waiting room unless you're an expert drain pipe climber. In Smuts, the inky residence, friendships are formed and hierachies established. At the bottom there's a group of untough men called "the girls", one, Jewish, is in tears because a swastika has been daubed on his door. The perpetrator is genuinely perplexed, "Shit man, where's your sense of humour?" One of the manne, pleased to have his cake and eat it says, "Fuck that's not good, we're not Nazis."

I feel lost in this maelstrom, used to a clear identity and easy acceptance, but somehow in the current setup my particular social type is unrecognised. Acutely aware of this conservative prism, my self image is becoming distorted and I'm losing confidence. I turn to rationalisation, how else could the white elite maintain cohesion without a rigid social hierarchy, a tightly defined set of values and conformity? How would Mick Jagger fare here? Badly I'm sure, so there. But day to day I feel like a second rate mongrel that's been kicked, losing even the will to fight. Like a lonely child I return from lectures, tense and anxious, to scan the letter board for Marion's familiar envelope, that I can spot, with thumping heart, at five yards. Then off to my room with my prize. If it's not there I'm dejected for the rest of the day.

But life's not all bad, my analysis above was a little stark, I have plenty of friends within a middle group of guys. There's also the novelty of being away from home, and the mystique of a university that considers itself the Oxford of South Africa, its main buildings incorporating the old barracks, steeped in a dreamy sense of the last century. We are a liberal university, unlike say, Stellenbosch where the Afrikaans students aren't even allowed to wear denims, and wouldn't want to anyway. Andre Brink treads our corridors, and the English lecturers are gentle souls who love to indulge enthusiastic students in long discussions on Paradise Lost over cups of tea and cigarettes. Or on my Middlemarch essay, "A very interesting and original analysis, but somewhat lacking in detail: have you read the whole book? Please come and see me." Yes I have! Indignant, having spent whole mornings in my room reading the thing, with a pot of tea and pipe, aping a nineteenth, no, eighteenth century academic. Or an overcast Englishy afternoon, tea in the ancient Ramona cafe, then to the tobacconist to ogle the pipes and buy a pouch of black cavendish, then to the mullioned bookshop with its treasury of shiny new books. Dad has an account here, so I buy one on Confucious, off the syllabus, but good for my mind, must read it some time. Then to dinner in the refectory, jackets, ties and gowns, padding in like so many bats. "Benedictus benedicat," says the prof at high table and we all sit, ten per table. "Heh, Hendriks pass the meat," I say. Hendrik, conservative Afrikaans, straight from the plaas, says, "You know my name's Hendrik." Then as if delivering a coup, "How would you like it if I called you Ians?" "Fine, go ahead," I say. Bob says, "Heh Hendriks, you can't take three potatoes, it's two each." "Ya but look, you took three," says Hendrik. "Yes, but that's irrelevant, you can't base a moral proposition on someone else's misdemeanor." "Eh? Stop tocking kak man!" and takes three. Of course the conversation's pointless, the waiter simply brings more, you can't let white boys go hungry. But the argument, with our petty bullying is really a proxy for a row about apartheid the previous night. Gradually we settle down and get on. At least, unlike the main manne, we're discussing politics. I'm sure that if they're still alive after the revolution they'll claim to have been appalled by apartheid and to have discussed little else, certainly not sport exclusively in a time of crisis and oppression. Still, that's all we do, discuss.

Such discussions, about the nature of things, go on late into the night, even to dawn over yet more tea. Sometimes at three or four am we drive down to Port Alfred to watch the sun rise over Cowie beach. Then back in to breakfast, exhilarated, feeling apart and superior. We discover dagga, from the garage boys, ten cents a finger, one rand an arm, wrapped in newspaper. You start to notice plenty of blacks smoking it. A friend has a huge room in town, one night we prepare spliffs or pipes in a ceremonial way under the expert lead of Smoky Jones and play *Sergeant Pepper* with the lights low. We're discovering non debutant girls, socially parallel to us, outside the hierarchy, and three have joined us. I'm feeling strange, a little dizzy, I put my arm round the nearest one, no resistance, feel her breasts, quite plump, no resistance, put my hand on her thigh, then I realise she's not responding at all. A figure two foot high appears near the ceiling, it's Jesus! He's staring into the middle distance, beatific, when suddenly, completely autonomous, he notices me, focuses, and comes alive, waggling an admonitory finger. I remember Marion and take my hand off the girl. Slowly he fades.

One of our new friends is an out and out queer, called Paul Elliott, tall, thin and pale, eyes close together, dracula - like. He's about twenty four, a professional actor for a few years, and regards himself as probably the most intelligent person on the campus. Contrary to my image of a queer he's ebullient and quite aggressive, preying on "the girls", some of whom he says are not clear about their sexual identity and others, virgins. He says that in his Johannesburg clique the queers are grouped into "boys" and "girls". The boys play golf together, with no mutual sexual interest and discuss the girls. Maybe all this is bullshit, but anyway he's always cheerful and a good laugh. Last night four of us went to the Vic at eleven, just as the barman was closing up. "Four beers," I said, and after a hesitation he served me. "Four beers," said Alan. The barman, surprised, protested, but finally served him and then John as well. "Sixteen gins," said Paul. "What?" said the barman. "Oh please please please" Paul begged, seizing the barman's hand, who pulled it away as if bitten by a snake. He got them, eight doubles lined up, and downed the lot. All the way back he quoted non stop from Henry V.

It's the night before rag, and I start off in a group of about six. We have Rosanne wine 35cents a bottle mixed with beer, the cheapest way to get pissed when you're on R7.50 per month. The campus is full of drinkers and people finishing off floats. At the end of the evening I'm somehow alone and take a short cut through the gardens of a women's res, when a girl calls me over to her window. It's barred, and a little high, her waist level with my head. The lights are off and I can't see her too well but she soon indicates what she wants and I accomplish it to her satisfaction through the bars. She says her name's JayJay and invites me to her room at three the next day, which absurdly is permitted, for one hour on rag day, despite all the usual restrictions. Back at the res I tell the guys, "Shit, JayJay, that fat whore, how could you touch her?" Who cares, I enjoyed it but maybe I won't go tomorrow. There's a commotion in the corridor, one of the main manne is parading around with a filled frikkie on the end of an umbrella, shouting, "I've done it, I've done it!" his friends patting him on the back. Bob's nonchalant voice drifts down the corridor, "Better late than never." The next night is rag ball in the main hall, the guys in penguin suits, main manne, girls in nice frocks, not our style, out of our league. Bob and I wander past the main hall on the way to kaif and there's this lovely girl standing in the vestibule, looking upset. "What's the matter, you beautiful young thing?" asks Bob. "The bloke I'm with is a complete bore, I'm sick of the whole thing." Her name's Veronica. "Well come along with us Veronique." "I can't just leave!" "Course you can, we'll bring you back in a bit." So we wander off and settle on a grassy bank. Bob starts snogging her. After a while she says "I want your friend now," so I have a go, just kissing and a little fraying. Then she says "I want Bob now," and so on, til it's too late for the ball and we walk her back to her res.

Four of us were drinking in the lounge of the Graham Hotel, at about five in the afternoon, discussing politics. We were having a heated argument about how the apartheid regime might eventually fall, will there be an uprising of the proletariat, are the seeds of its destruction in white South Africa's insatiable need for black labour, the townships ringing white towns?. Or will the real threat come from guerilla war, through Umkhonto we Sizwe? Roy was arguing that the progressive introduction of democracy through a qualified franchise would help to forestall such events, and transform the problem into a class struggle. Suddenly this voice cuts in, a man about fifty, sitting alone at the next table says, "You boys are complete extremists, how can you talk like that?" "Why? We're we're only talking about how to promote democracy," says Roy, "that's quite moderate." "Ya, I heard what you were saying, or rather shouting, but in the South African context, to support democracy is extremist." "Well," I said, "then in any western country you'd be an extremist, you can't have two sets of standards." "That's exactly the point," says the man, "you can, and must. We have to fit the political system to our own situation. Democracy doesn't work when you have several racial or religious groups like we do here, one side can gain power and then do what they like to the others. Look what happened in Nazi Germany, they got in democratically and then killed off the Jews. The reason I call you extremist is that you don't really care, you haven't thought about the consequences for individuals. You just talk theory. How does a man feel knowing his wife and daughter might get raped or his son won't get a job? You university types can just bugger off if things get bad, but the average person can't. Where do we go if we get it wrong? England? Five million of us? My family's been here since the eighteenth century. I know nothing about England and I don't want to." "Yes, OK," I say, "but what about the blacks, don't you accept there's injustice? You say we talk theory, but what about black poverty, unemployment, people dumped miles from anywhere? That's real isn't it? " "Ya I accept that and I don't agree with everything this government does, but there's one big difference. The blacks know where they stand, they're the big majority, as a race they're safe. We've had our wars, last century they nearly wiped us out in the Eastern Cape. But we've never tried to exterminate them like the Americans and Australians did to their natives. And now these people who murdered their way to power boycott our goods and treat us like pariahs. It's not that we're right, it's just the hypocrisy. Ok I'm ranting, but the basic point is that South African whites must be the largest and oldest population who, in the eyes of the world, don't have a legitimate country, or basic security. For us, one false move and we're finished. What we do is basically defensive." Just then a woman came in dressed as in her Sunday best, with a flowery hat. "This is my wife Hettie," he said. We stood up. "We farm near Bathhurst and it's our day in town. Now we're going home. Go easy boys, hamba gashle," he said and patted Roy, who was nearest to him, on the shoulder.

I feel a warm glow, a child accepted by a father, we've argued our cases and parted as friends. I can see his point of view. I sometimes feel irritated by American films, or books by writers like Mark Twain or Harper Lee, so proud of their "indigenous" white idiom and culture, their weak struggles with slavery, so settled and smug. And cowboy and indian films, genocide as entertainment. Even British books with their parlour dramas, are usually indifferent to the snarling power politics that defend their borders and way of life. Then I realise we've both been accommodating, perhaps he needs his views sanctified by "liberals". What would he really be saying to his pals on the plaas? How would he react if we laid it on thick about the horrors of modern apartheid, forced movement of populations, torture, murder, Sharpeville, and the evil and hatred at the regime's centre, the government, BOSS, the police?

A few days later, we attended a speech by our local United Party MP. He said he did not approve of apartheid, really it was totally abhorrent and excessive. For one thing the coloureds, who had always supported the Party should have a vote, and perhaps even the Indians. Of course the party did not support social or residential integration but they did propose a legislative body comprising representatives from each racial group, naturally with whites in control. He did tentatively go so far as to say the party might support a relaxation of segregation in sports such as cricket, and this should ease international boycotts of South Africa. However, he drew the line at body contact sports such as rugby, as obviously we would appreciate. On the international sporting boycott he said, "Keep politics out of sport," virtually a South

African axiom, it's unfair on our young players who are not interested in politics. Most in the hall clapped. "Young white players don't you mean?" someone yelled, "Keep sport out of politics!" The heckler was shouted down. The MP felt it most unfair when a member of the audience suggested the UP's differences with the Nats were trivial, who cares about sport anyway? And that they were hiding behind the Nats, letting them do the dirty work while his party claimed the moral high ground. But maybe we're all guilty of that. That's our white parliamentary opposition apart from the great, brave Helen Suzman.

The latest scandal, Professor Oosthuizen, our wonderful courageous Afrikaans philosophy prof, has commented that probably about twenty five percent of Afrikaaners have some African blood. This has created a national furore, the Prime Minister condemning this slur on our people and demanding its withdrawal. What slur? replies the prof, and how can you withdraw an empirical point? Let's debate the evidence. Similarly an unpleasant debate arose in one of our psychology lectures when some of the main manne challenged the lecturer's statement that the human race is pretty homogenous on most measures. "No, but blacks are thicker than whites," says one. "All right," says the lecturer after a heated debate, "let's assume the average African IQ is 90, which I don't accept for a moment." He draws a bell shaped curve on the board. "In that case around 20% of black people you happen to come across, barefoot, in menial jobs, unemployed on street corners, with no vote, are brighter than the average white person, and assuming you personally have an IQ of 110," (the class titters), "about 5 -10% are brighter than you."

Salisbury 1967

Got a lift to Salisbury in the back of a VW 1300, driven by two guys intent on proving their virility by doing the fourteen hundred mile trip non stop, just a pause for a piss or pie as they swop driver. But I pass the time well enough in a sleepy gooey haze, imagining, slow and patient, hour after hour, what I'm going to do with Marion. We arrive at about 11am after 26 hours and I'm dropped at the office to say hello, phone Marion, and borrow Dad's car. It's a bright sunny day. She's waiting for me at the end of her drive, god, her beauty, such a shock, her soft face, her body, so full, in a short tube dress. "Hello, hello!" running alongside the car as I stop. Well, no need for details, but soon we're in my room, and I'm actualizing each of the images, so poor against the wonderful reality. Suddenly there's a crunch outside, I dive to the window, it's Catherine parking her car! Shit! Clothes on and out the french windows, across the lawn, through the pine hedge, across the storm ditch and on to the road, barefoot, Marion no pants. We wander down to The Chase shops, spend half an hour and then come back, squatting in the road to peer up the drive, when Catherine's car stops behind us. She doesn't say much, just hello in a cold voice, I think she's just anxious to protect Marion from her wicked stepson. The houseboy's compromised having covered for me by saying I was asleep on my own. But I realise how I rely on Marion to get me through Rhodes, how her unconditional love boosts my security and ego. When we make love in the bright morning sunshine I feel great, but sometimes after love in the afternoon, as the shadows lengthen, my heart sinks when I kiss her lips, and I know this can't last.

Grahamstown 1967

Can you believe it? The 1820 Settler's Society, that bastion of the English speaking establishment, purported champion of British values of democracy and free speech, has invited Prime Minister Vorster to lay the foundation stone for some new monument! Despite his protestations against apartheid, Professor Guy Butler, one of the Society's bigwigs seems to see no inconsistency. We students discuss this over lunch as the crowd of dignitaries assembles on Gunfire Hill. Bob and I cobble together an impromptu banner comprising a broomstick with squares of cardboard hanging from each end, one saying, "Bring back British rule", the other, "Hou links". Stelio Stamatis was tempted to join us but has chickened out, and follows us up the hill three yards behind. Within minutes our path is blocked by two huge guys. "Would you come with us please?" says one, the rise of his voice at the sentence end typical of Afrikaans officialese, as if talking politely to a naughty child. "Er, I don't want to be rude, but could we see some identification?" asks Bob. "You'll see it at the station," says the guy, his voice hardening and dropping. For some reason they also arrest Stelio, despite his protestations. At the police station, we're lined up along the wall facing a counter manned by a sergeant, then asked to come forward individually to give our names, all very polite. "You first please," to Stelio, who goes forward and leans on the desk. "Er, Ste," whack! The sergeant's fist slams on the counter. "Stand straight! What's your name!" "Er, er," whack! "Don't say er to me you little shit what's your fucking name? Look at him, constable, chust like a fucking goffle. Look at his dozy eyes, he must be on trucks, are you on trucks?" Stelio manages to get his name out and protests he never takes drugs which I'm sure is true, then denies he has anything to do with us. This just makes things worse. "You fucking Greek coward, letting down your friends eh?" Stelio has deflected a lot of their hatred and surprisingly we are treated a little better. After leaving us standing for three hours without a piss, Bob and I are led into a room. Sergeant Sweetman says, "Bring back British rule, is that what you want?" "It's kind of humour," I say. "Humour?" he yells six inches from my face, "Humour? To insult our Prime Minister? You call that humour?" Bob says, "Well not exactly humour, more by nature of a satirical comment." This really sets him off. "Don't be fucking highfalutin with me!" I'm vaguely surprised he knows the word. He turns to me, "And this hou links, that's communism you know, that was a mistake my boy, you're in big trouble, we can get you under the Suppression of Communism Act and detain you indefinitely. Who do you think you are, coming to this country as our guest, and causing trouble? We've already contacted the Rhodesian police to check you out, and we've asked them also to pull your parents in for questioning." So far I've just felt numb, like in a dream, but this sends a surge of fear through me at some fundamental level, the idea of one's Dad being mistreated, powerless. Then a tough looking plain clothes guy throws open the door and punches his palm. "Can we have them now sergeant?" "Not yet, not yet, I'll send them when I'm finished." "Now who are you working for, who's in your organisation?" In the end nothing really happened, being white and basically harmless we were released after about six hours and told to bring in our passports the following day. The university organised a lawyer to go with us. Phoned Dad without mentioning the arrest, obviously nothing's happened to them up there. But it raised for me pictures and stories of African homes raided by the police, in the early hours, children crying, wife wailing, the man, perhaps being slapped around, stony faced, trying to maintain his dignity. Before today this hadn't quite penetrated, the full horror of it.

Strange how every day my gonk, a present from Marion, moves around my room, and sports a different, more ridiculous hairstyle. Is it a poltergeist? I respond by moving it myself, in rough synchrony with the latest position, inverting if upright, facing left if right. In the bright sunlight I imagine it dancing round the room, its daily movements accelerated, syncopated to kwela .The first time I bunk my ten o'clock lecture I find the poltergeist is Nomsi the cleaner, a middle aged woman with a big bum and wonderful warm sense of humour. We quickly become friendly, and I start pinching meat for her from dinner. Now after lunch on Saturdays I drive her back to the African location on the edge of town. I always feel nervous in the compound on the way back, partly in case I'm picked up by police but mainly the fear of being attacked. What a sick society where one section of the population fears the other, and feels so separate from it, or is it just me? No, my friends warn me not to go and won't come with me. Or do we have the same in all countries, slums, ghettos? There's a severe drought, and we're told to bath in no more than three inches of water, or preferably take very quick showers, but Nomsi tells me they've turned off one of the two standpipes in the location, and there are permanent queues at the other. Strange how, having seen African townships since early childhood you hardly notice the squalor, usually a core of single or double room brick buildings, dirt roads, open sewer ditches, no electricity, and an efflorescence of illegal corrugated iron and cardboard shelters. And yet somehow its inhabitants turn up for work in white establishments, clean, in severely ironed clothes, cheerful and smiling. What do they really think of us?

My exam marks are average to poor. I'm astonished I passed Economics, there are so many students that the lecturer stands on the stage of the Great Hall, handouts on tables below, and if you don't turn up early you usually get about half of them. Once you miss a few lectures you're buggered, swotting for the exam I had about twenty pages of notes and handouts while everyone else has a bulging lever arch file. Got two percent for Saxon, I think for knowing the word Konig.

Had a drink with a British student, who's reading for an English degree and is on a month's exchange visit. She intimidated me, so cool and sophisticated, so disparaging of the whole set up here. She's attended some of our lectures and was scathing about their naiveté, their focus on the author's intentions, relationships between characters, symbolism and meaning. Her course follows a structuralist approach, the book or even poem a construction in a cultural medium, an unwitting product of social influences, analysed with godlike objectivity through lenses such as Marxism, psychoanalysis, and feminism. Leavis, Jung, Lacan, Sartre, Bakhtin roll from her tongue. She plans to be a journalist, disdainful of my feckless lack of ambition. And politics! I argue my position weakly. The same structural analysis, we liberals are part of the system, beneficiaries, our opposition mere theatre, shambling, disheveled, undisciplined self deception. Who can trust a liberal, someone who fights for others? He'll desert you when the chips are down. "You've no analysis, it's all just sentiment. Now in England we fight for ourselves, whatever our cause, be it the trade unions, or personal politics such as feminism, our rights, our bodies, what we eat. We are the people, the proletariat so at least we can be straight forward and honest in our demands." She tells how they held a prolonged boycott of their student union because the quality of the meat was poor, and were vindicated when an audit found that the manager had been swindling. She sips her South African wine through nicely sculpted lips, quite kissable, in retaliation I appraise her. "To be frank, South Africa appalls me. I've been taking notes since I've been here and I'm going to get an article published. You might even be in it!"

In Salisbury for Christmas, I'm not going up to Muf, partly because of Marion, but few people are allowed into Zambia from Rhodesia these days, the countries are virtually at war. Mail seldom gets through, Rhodesian stamps are invalid. I haven't been in touch with Mom and Richard for nearly a year. Last year I felt I was drifting away from my Muf friends. It's not that I don't want to see them, it's more fear of rejection, people easily sense a difference in attitude, the first racist joke I don't respond to, even the fact that I attend university. I wonder what I would be like if we hadn't moved away. That's also why I don't stay in touch with Chris and the Gearys, fear of rejection. Dad's still in touch. He says they moved to Germiston after Uncle Oscar's job was Zambianised. He couldn't take to the new life and is hitting the bottle hard.

Anyway it's all fine, I'm working in Dad's shop and enjoy the Christmas rush and the money. He's bought a new offset litho printing machine and is filling gaps caused by sanctions. Trade is booming, good ole Smithy! The Aunts are down here permanently, their jobs in Ndola having dried up, and Auntie Beth helps Dad with his accounts. Even Anne helps Saturday mornings, and some days during term time, but she's not much use because of her anxiety problems. Auntie Mary drops in for a cup of tea, there's a cluster of nice new cups and she picks one up. "Er, Auntie, those are the Africans' cups," says Anne. "They won't mind will they?" asks Auntie Mary, and goes ahead. Anne stands there open mouthed. Have bought Marion a huge book on Picasso, just line drawings of bull fights, from the smart bookshop at the bottom of Colonial Mutual Buildings in Gordon Avenue. When I went in to browse, the owner ignored me, but as I started looking through the art books his face lit up, and he came across to chat, as if we were old friends. He asked if I knew so and so or so and so, and of course he knows Marion's parents. He reminded me of a guy who gets the New Statesman from Kingston's every Friday, and waits around in the hope of meeting the other two subscribers, thirst for compatible company in an arid world. Catherine is appalled "You paid fifteen pounds for that rubbish? I could draw like that!" "No you couldn't!" "Well I wouldn't want to anyway!"

Dad and Catherine have bought me a car! It's a 1960 Mercedes 180 which has already done over a hundred thousand miles. It was three hundred and thirty pounds. They think a larger car is safer for travelling the route to varsity. I love it! Before I go to bed I stand at the back door just to admire its beauty. Marion and I also like its big back seat.

South Africa 1968

Off to university in the Merc. I leave late morning with Brian and two other guys. We have a kitty for petrol and hamburgers. Past Fort Victoria, it's stifling hot and dry, we stop at the Lundi River hotel for a beer, and dive into the pool fully clothed. Half an hour later we're totally dry, down to our underpants.

The car runs sweet and smooth, and everyone anticipates their turn to drive. We cross the Beit Bridge border at about five. On the South African side the middle aged customs man looks us up and down and says to his colleague, "Jiss man, look what the cat's just brought in! Students! Where's your shoes my boys, you're not a bunch of bloody blecks eh? Shit but this one needs a haircut! Heh Franz, I think we better look this lot over, you, drive your car up to the front there and bring your suitcases in, better not have any dagga heh!" He watches us from the door. He picks up a brightly coloured paperback. "What's this, pornography?" "No," I say, "it's a play by a man called William Shakespeare. He lived in England about five hundred years ago." "Don't be funny with me son, I know who Shakespeare is." After a token search he says, "Ok, that's it. Now, I want you boys to behave yourselves in South Africa eh? John Vorster doesn't want any trouble from you students." I'd love to say, "I'd be happy to discuss politics outside your working hours," but of course wouldn't dare, he could rip the car open pretending to look for drugs, and keep us there for days. These petty officials are almost unaccountable, the glue of apartheid, reinforcing the power and structure of white society in every community. People like us are nothing, and blacks less than nothing, and this everyday powerlessness begins to wear you down, into compliance or defiance or both. Most of the time you just feel intimidated, diminished. Anyway, enough of that, there's a great café at the petrol station just outside Messina where we stop for coffee, boerwors, eggs, bacon and chips.

We arrive in Johannesburg, seven hundred miles from Salisbury, at about midnight, stay at the Victoria Hotel in the city centre, and go out drinking in Brixton. Leave at nine the next morning with hangovers. But there's something about being on the road, the big sky of the flat Transvaal, open fields, bright sunlight, brown baking little towns like Pietersburg and Nylstroom, and in the car, koeksisters, biltong, and a family size bottle of Coke. There's only one road so you form acquaintances as you pass cars and then meet them later at petrol stations or cafés. Mid afternoon in the Free State a farm truck's ahead of us, in the back a load of nartjies, a little boy and a pretty girl of about eighteen, barefoot with fantastic fleshy brown legs. We slow down to enjoy the view, smiling and blowing kisses. When we stop for some road works she jumps down and runs up to our car, pushing a bag of nartjies through the window. She smiles, "Totsiens," and then back on to the truck. Ooh!

Suddenly, there's a turnoff. "Who wants to go to Durban? Quick!" I shout. A hesitant OK from the back, and I swing left, adding four or five hundred miles to the journey. But it's great to drive through the Marine Parade, with a quick stop for a swim and an eskimo pie, then along the south coast through Amanzimtoti, Illovo, great sugar plantations on our right, Scotsborough, a beer at the Cutty Sark, and then off into the night across the Transkei. We stop at some remote bar and buy two whisky bottles full of sweet tea. Everyone sleeps while I drive. I'm happy, alone, Marion in my head, crackly music on the radio, a clear sky, the bright milky way, sharp mountain bends, and sheep to avoid. Then at four am a cow stands up on its hind legs, looks at me, and quickly runs across the road, front feet waving. I break violently, just a hallucination, time to sleep, and someone else takes the wheel. We arrive in Grahamstown mid morning.

I'm in a senior house, Struben, not a bad lot of guys, about sixty of us. It was once for tough guys, its moto FOF, fuck (girls) or fight (other boys), but it's become a bit of an oddball house, and includes some guys who aspire to be main manne but don't quite make it. It's hard to tell whether that's because they lack the requisite manliness or whether perhaps in their case these qualities are leavened by a little too much intelligence or imagination. The house has an interesting history, Ian Smith occupied the room next to mine just after the war. He and some of his first year colleagues were hardened military veterans and much older than the second or third year colleagues who had come straight from school, and according to legend, they terrorised the youngsters, blowing things up, and riding motor bikes up and down the stairs and along the top floor. There's a two week initiation period when the established residents ignore you, or order you to come and play bridge. You need to learn fast, if you go four light you're thrown fully clothed into a cold bath, which happened to me twice in two days. At the end of the initiation period we have a booze-up in a sampling room hired from the Graham Hotel. The smallish wood floored room is completely empty except for a shelf all the way round at shoulder height for your beer, and a trestle table in one corner for a bar which you buy in from the hotel. Everyone puts in ten rand and then the drinks are free. Each new guy has to stand on the table, say who he is and do a turn. Mine was press ups, I carried on until beer was poured over my head and then I could stop, I'm now the house press up champion, probably because nobody can be bothered to compete. I feel comfortable here, the common room has a homely feel, and we play chess or hands of bridge between lectures and before and after meals. If you're working at night and want a break, you wander down and there's always someone to talk to. It's like a big family, obviously there's some back biting but also plenty of pranks, tolerance and loyalty.

A couple of weeks ago, just to prove a point, Craig and I went down to meet the train full of new students. I had been arguing that the conservatism of young white South Africans and Rhodesians, and their failure to challenge the older generation must be part of a culture of general conformism, Adorno's authoritarian personality, isn't first year psychology wonderful. Others argued that they were simply acting in their racist self interest and intrinsically were as rebellious as any other group of young people, say, the British. I think that's true of the youth in NR where the cultural conservatism of South Africa hasn't penetrated, but not here. Or maybe my argument holds just for the elite, the main manne, a type I didn't come across in Muf or Ndola, we were all skates there. Anyway to win a rand's bet, Craig and diminutive little me swaggered on to the platform full of students and yelled, "First year students here!" About thirty gathered around us expectantly. Reasonable, we might have been reps with information. "Line up in threes, on the double! Threes I said, can't you count? You! Yes you! Stop talking! Now, by the left quick march! You, idiot, get into step!" and so on. They complied with all our ridiculous orders, encumbered as they were by suitcases and other luggage. We marched them to Fort England, the mental hospital, over a mile away, plenty of time to question or rebel, and left them outside the door. No doubt there'll be repercussions some night, once they've settled in, but I'm a rand up.

Sometimes we go to the Saturday night rock session in town, and a few times I've danced with this blond girl called Elise. She's a shop assistant in town, and quite Afrikaans, and we don't have so much to say, but she's pretty and I like her. I feel easy with her. On Saturday night she was dancing with this other guy, but when I arrived she finished the dance and then came over to me. We drove up Gunfire Hill, and stopped where you can look down on the town. When you see its lights twinkling below, and the darkness beyond, you almost feel you're back in its early days, the nine Frontier Wars with the Xhosa. I told her about the fifth war, when Grahamstown was nearly wiped out, probably not a good chat up line, but she indulged me, her university boy. "You're different from the other boys," she said. Then we had a snog and a bit of a grope, but she said she had a rule about "above the waist" so that's as far as it went. But I had a hell of a guilt thing about Marion, and really was missing her, which took the edge off it. Then as it was late I dropped her home, and went back to the dance to find my friends. The hall was quite dark, but I spotted the guy she'd been dancing with, staring at me and talking to his friends. About five minutes later he suddenly loomed into my right field and I moved my head just enough for his punch to catch my ear rather than my face. A couple more punches hit my head, and I went down thinking, "Keep punching, keep punching," and by luck landed one full on his nose. He stepped back stunned, blood all over the place, and then, luckily for me, the fight was stopped. I felt bad about it, he's a town guy a bit like some of my Muf friends. I know how we'd have felt if a load of smart arses had descended on the town and tried to take our girls.

One of my new friends is called Mark, a gentle intellectual soul, loves reading, but always on the edge of mental breakdown, because he's never fitted in and has been bullied all his life. He's treated fine in Struben, but was given a rough time last year in Smuts by the main manne who he calls "gods of mediocrity", and had a psychotic breakdown. He imagined the

Special Branch were after him and finally began to believe the pigeons outside his window were wired to spy on him, their cooing a kind of morse code. In the end he had ECT which he said knocked him back to reality, but damaged his memory and made him rather disorganised. Now he seems impervious to the original pressures on him, living in a parallel world of literature, Jane Austen, and afternoon teas. If pressed, his politics are anti government but it seems more because of the regime's boorishness, than real concern for the plight of blacks. One wonders how many liberals have arrived by a similar route, incompatible with the society generally. That might be splitting hairs, but perhaps explains why many whites with the strongest political views are uninvolved in politics. They're on the fringes of this society and only just surviving psychologically, so have no energy or means to influence politics. Nobody would listen to them anyway. Paradoxically, some of the student liberal leaders don't appear so different personally from the main manne, confident and assertive, and it's hard to decide how sincere their political position really is, or whether they've just found a useful social niche. I'd like to see where they are in ten years' time.

A few students have become so alienated they're virtually nihilist. Some weeks ago four of them were discussing the possibility of putting cyanide in the town's water supply. "Why?" I asked. "Why not?" said Lankey Davis. "But it'll kill us all!" "So?" I didn't really take them seriously, they did have cyanide, which they gave to another acquaintance who used it to kill himself. I won't to go into that except to say he was the brother of a friend, a fine looking young man who, with the fatal flaw of intelligence and sensitivity, had his sense of manhood systematically undermined by the main manne. Temporarily buoyed by his first romantic relationship, he became over - dependent, and killed himself when he thought the girl had dropped him.

But these nihilist guys are cheerful, mentally dis-associated from this society, always up to something, a bad influence, and never get caught. One night they arrived at my room with a load of dagga. We started smoking then drove down to East London. The next thing I remember we were at the docks on a South Korean ship, and after being shown around by the proud crew pinched their girlie calendars. As we were getting into the car, some police came towards us so, and as if in slow motion, we stashed the dope under the seat, and somehow weren't searched. Then we had a huge meal in a restaurant and walked out without paying, all natural. Towards dawn we went and swam in the sea. By now it was eight am on May Day, so we walked into a department store and bought a square of red cloth. The woman in the fabrics department seemed bemused but had no idea of its significance, neither had I for a while. On the way back home they waved it out of the car window. It was amazing how many blacks, sitting on the backs of lorries perked up, cheered and gave clenched fist salutes. I hadn't realised they were so clued up.

Paul Elliott seems less stable this year. Last year's group has drifted apart now that we've moved to different houses, and Bob, bored with Rhodes, has gone off to Capetown varsity. Paul's started taking anti depression pills and occasionally over-doing it and getting drunk at the same time. A few weeks ago he barged into my room at about three and collapsed on the floor and ended up in hospital being stomach pumped. This over-dosing happens about once a month, but between times he's still ebullient and mad. However, he's just told me he's going into a mental hospital for a few weeks to be cured of his homosexuality.

Protests are going on all over the place. Recently I joined one in Capetown where the government has rescinded the appointment of a black academic. Exciting, great atmosphere, and some beautiful girls. OK, superficial, but that's how it seemed, privileged kids salving their conscience and expressing their individuality safely. Now there's big trouble at Fort Hare, the University for blacks at Alice. Under the 1959 Extension of University Education Act it had its links with UNISA cut, and was placed under the Department of Bantu Education. Non white universities were now designated for particular racial groups, Fort Hare for Xhosas: blacks refer to them as bush colleges. They're staffed by Government place men and police spies, and Fort Hare's new Vice Chancellor Prof de Wet is said to be a member of the Broederbond. Recently he refused to recognise their new representative body, the University Christian Movement, or to meet them. When most of the 550 students protested he invited police and dogs on to the campus, and then said all protestors had to re-apply for admission. Some have been arrested or expelled. We've had some meetings and decided to go along to Fort Hare to show solidarity. The government's set up road blocks around Grahamstown to deter other white students from joining us and Vorster's made a statement warning that he's not going to be so soft on white students in future and we'd better watch it. At a meeting one of the student bigwigs stood up and said portentiously, "John Vorster has promised trouble, and John Vorster does not lie. I say do not go!" Somehow his speech carried weight, and most of the subsequent speeches were in favour of pulling out. By the end of the meeting, all the enthusiasm had drained, people were scared, and almost nobody was going. "That guy's right, the government might use it as an excuse to teach us a lesson once and for all, we could even get shot, that would deter whites for a decade." "Rubbish!" said Lankey Davis, "He's probably a special branch stooge, you won't get shot, they wouldn't want to upset your mummy and daddy." On Saturday afternoon Athol Fugard turned up and addressed us outside Kaif. With his strong accent, hairy face, and arm waving he seemed like a small Afrikaans leprechaun. He urged us to go, to leave at five minute intervals so we could not be stopped as a convoy. We left at about two pm, four in my car, white – faced, hearts pounding. We were stopped at a road block just outside Grahamstown, the police impersonal, unfriendly, but correct. We said we were out for a drive. They took our names and allowed us to proceed. There was another road block near Alice. But the whole thing was an anti climax, when we arrived, expecting armoured cars and god knows what, there was no police presence, no one to protest to. Like Napoleon's entry into a deserted Moscow, no one to surrender to him, or a naughty kid left to its own devices! We joined a small group of black protesters who someone said might be police informers anyway, and made our way home as night fell.

We felt ashamed of our impotence, dilettantes, inconsequential, inadequate, illegitimate, nothing. Even the Afrikaaners, in their certainty and with their history have some integrity. We liberals do nothing but talk. I think that's how African nationalists see us. Last year a NUSAS conference was held at Rhodes. Although it was the winter holidays black delegates were not allowed to stay in the empty white residences and had to find accommodation in the African location. A guy called Stephen Biko moved that the conference be adjourned until a non racial venue could be found, but this was defeated by the white majority. Apparently, the blacks were saying that NUSAS was not vocal enough on the bread and butter issues which really concerned them. Fundamentally most white students are not prepared to put themselves in harm's way, and however radical individual NUSAS leaders might be, the body of the organisation restrains them. Some Africans are now considering forming their own black consciousness movement.

Our own struggle is really within the white community, probably irrelevant to the overall balance of power, perhaps more about our own personal dignity. On a day of protest to mark the anniversary of the 1967 Terrorism Act, a group of us march into the Mayor's office, where he's holding a meeting, and harangue him and his officials. "So you like terrorism?" he says, "What if somebody comes to kill you?" "The Terrorism Act has nothing to do with terrorism." I sagely reply, "It's a catch-all to prevent protest." "Ya then Mr professor, so why's it called the Terrorism Act?" he asks triumphantly as if scoring an irrefutable point. That evening I'm enjoying a delicious pepper steak in the Vic restaurant with Mark, who's paying, when the manager comes in to chat up the customers. "Good evening sir, how is your steak?" but it's one of the officials from this morning. It takes him about twenty seconds to make the awkward transition from obsequious caterer to indignant owner and town leader, and a minute later I'm on the street without another bite. I can still taste it. What a sacrifice!

But at a recent party I was chatting to a lecturer who has an illegal copy of the ANC's Freedom Charter 1955. He says it's not anti white, it asserts that South Africa belongs to all, calling us brothers, but demanding equality. The party is linked to the Congress of South African Trade Unions, and the South African Communist Party. This seems comforting, cutting through the liberal "sacrifice" argument, giving whites a place if we join, or accept the legitimacy of the struggle. This seems different from the "settler" rhetoric of ZANU in Rhodesia which can look like reverse racism.

Salisbury 1968

Back in Salisbury for Christmas, I had a drink with Atkins from Ndola, who's been on holiday in England. He reckons it's a real toilet, dirty, dull with miserable looking people. At thirty thousand feet you approach London in bright sunlight, then descend through solid grey cloud, the light fading progressively until you wonder that any human can live down there. Under this cloud is a dark overcrowded world, people living in houses joined in rows with virtually no garden. The accents that you thought were a joke, exaggerated in the *Carry On* films, are real. You talk to a big guy who looks like a main manne and expect him to talk slow and deliberate, and instead he gabbles something in a comedy accent and waves his arms around. So many accents, they fill your dreams at night. They bath three times a week. They seem to have no dignity or authority, you even see white men sweeping out the fronts of their shops or working on the roads. Of course that's logical but still a shock, you do a double take. It rains every day, it's bloody freezing and gets dark at four o'clock! And weirdly, the nights are totally silent apart from traffic, no crickets, no animals, no insects, you notice it straight away. "Yes but it's their winter," I say. "Maybe it's different in summer." "No, no, they reckon it still rains all the time, you can't even plan a braai more than a day ahead. I got a cold as soon as I arrived and it carried on the whole holiday. It cleared up the day after I got home. And they all drink this weird beer called bidda, dark brown, you can even get black beer!" "Christ!" I say. "And even if the queue for beer is three deep the barman spends ages pouring it out through this bloody slow tap, standing there with a vacant look like a bloody cow. Shit why don't they just use bottles? They've got no get up and go. Our kaffir barmen could teach them a thing or two about slick service. It's strange, you expect to feel at home there, because they speak English, the mother country and all that crap, but it feels more foreign than any other country I know, even Mozambique or the Congo. And these people, they're different, like I didn't know how to chat up the chicks, they're helluva unfriendly. Like on the tube in London I would go and stand next to the nicest bird and give her the spiel, but she'd just bloody ignore me, or even move away." "That's because you're so ugly." "Ha, ha, but also they're bloody miserable. One evening we visited this place called Beaumaris in Wales, helluva old fashioned, with these tiny houses from back in history, and my dad leans against a door that only comes up to his shoulder so my ma can take a snap. Suddenly the door gives way, and he falls in backwards, across this little lounge and ends up on his arse against their TV. They went bloody mad, yelling and screaming, specially cause me and my dad were pissing ourselves, shit man these English have no sense of humour." "Welsh." "What? Well what's the fucking difference, English Welsh, Scotch, Irish, same thing. No seriously, I know we always crap on about the blacks here, but you won't believe this, I actually started missing them. We forget how well we know them, at least they've got a sense of humour. I even missed talking Chilapalapa.

"So, we stayed with my mom's sister at this place called Southend on Sea in one of their provinces called Ussuks, what a dump. The people sound like cockneys but think they're better because they got semi detached houses, like two joined together, then a space, and fancy little gardens. We stayed in this part called Westcliff, up above the Thames estuary, which is just a shit hole really, mud and slime, no wildlife like on the Zambezi, and they all say what a wonderful view! And Jesus, they're just as anti black as us, but won't admit it. 'I'm not racialistic you understand, though I wouldn't like one of them darkies living next door to me. I've nothing against them, it's just that we're different.' My old man reckons that if you took the population of Southend and dumped it in Rhodesia, before you know it they'd be treating them just like we do, maybe worse.

"Anyway, we visited my mom's cousin in this suburb called Shoeburyness, and I went to the pub with their kids, an ou about our age, and his sister about eighteen, quite mooi. We were trying to find something to talk about, not so easy, when this ou, about twenty five comes up and says, 'Hoe gaan dit? Jislaaik, where you from man, I heard your accent!' He was from Kitwe! Can you believe it? The poor bugger's job was Africanised so he went over there thinking the streets were paved with gold and ended up driving heavy goods vehicles. Now the work's dried up, his wife also from Kitwe has this English sickness called ME, and his kid's got some learning problem. He was so excited to see me, all he wanted was to talk about NR, hear the news, and go over the good old days and the wonderful tastes of things like mangoes and biltong. 'Ya, we had this place out at the edge of Garneton, just a rough place, four acres. I used to get home from work on Saturday at about one. I'd stop at the butcher on the way for some boerries and lekker steak, maybe some T bones. The garden boy already had the braai going. Ya I used to sprinkle Knorr braai seasoning on the meat, I can still smell it. Jiss man it was good to sit there in the sun with a couple of Castles, looking out across the vlei at the hills. Still leopards in those hills. Then afterwards, I'd put a big piece of boerries in some bread for the kaffir, give him a beer or two and we'd go round the garden checking the veg and fowls and talking about next week's jobs. Heaven! My wife used to complain I was more interested in talking to the kaffir than her!' Although the guy was dirt poor, he insisted on buying us a round. This was their Saturday night out, they knew almost nobody. He kept on grinning but you could see the tension beneath. Then he left saying I had made his day, his week, maybe his year. But I felt shit sorry for him, stuck in the middle of nowhere, thousands of miles from home, like a bad dream. When he left I said, 'Poor guy, he'll never see his country again.' But that started a moerova row with my cousins. The girl, Alice said, 'It's not his country,' and started crapping on about us being settlers. The guy Paul is at a London uni called the Elesee and it came out they didn't want to drink with me, they were just pleasing their mom. They said Rhodesians had no right to be here at all, shit man I was born here. So I got pissed off and said how long do you have to go back, what if the voortrekkers had come up to Rhodesia in the 1830s would they still be settlers? So they said yes of course. So I said does that mean the Ndeble are settlers? They came from South Africa in 1837 and fucked up the local Shona, why not Shonarise their jobs and send them all back to SA? That killed the conversation, they told me not to be ridiculous and we left the pub straight after, in total silence."

The snooty self righteousness of Atkins' cousins is interesting, when from a broader perspective they themselves might be seen as part of a repressive British or Western colonial system. Free, in one bound, at his expense, from generations of guilt.

Dad tells me Auntie Elsie has divorced Uncle Oscar because of his drinking. I'm shocked, they seemed the perfect family, warm, easy going, a safe haven, how could this happen? After they left Luanshya he couldn't settle, getting odd jobs, nothing regular, too many refugees from the north in the same position. He's always been a drinker and it just deteriorated. Apparently now he's begging on Durban beach. Dad's had two telegrams saying things like, "Big business opportunity, need £50, will repay with 200% interest in three weeks." "I've sent him money twice, because of what he did for you, and perhaps I'll do it once more, but then that's it." What he and Auntie Elsie did for me, everything, beyond kindness, one of the family.

Glen's turned up in Salisbury for a couple of days on his way home from school. Dad was keen to invite him round. When he left I asked Dad why he was so interested. "I just wanted to make absolutely sure he isn't mine, there was just a possibility. But one glance and it's clear he's Richard's."

Today I drove Glen round to see the main sights, and buy him a few ice creams. When he's in Pretoria he gets taken out some weekends by Richard's cousin Johannes, and occasionally they visit a friend, Gert aged about forty-five, who runs a huge vegetable farm near Krugersdorp employing about three hundred blacks. Gert had been in the South African special forces, and Johannes had various stories about his fighting prowess and the ruthless way he defends his farm from blacks who have tried to pinch his vegetables or rob him personally. Most of these stories, including knocking a gunman's eye out with a key protruding from his fist, and peppering an intruder's bakkie with a shot gun, fall within local white acceptable self defence, but even Johannes felt uneasy when it emerged recently that Gert had seized a trespasser and broken each of his knuckles with a pair of pliers. The law's never been anywhere in sight. Unusually, he's not married though he speaks of his "girlfriend" who no one's seen, and has a formidable black woman as his top overseer. Well there are several possibilities, maybe he's screwing her or half the female workforce, maybe not. When Johannes and Glen last visited him he was sitting in his office reading the bible and underlining passages, no doubt finding the right words for his actions, a practice well established by the Dutch Reformed Church...

The day after Glen left for Zambia, Mom phoned me, frantic because he'd just disappeared. We established that he'd crossed the Rhodesian border. Richard went down to Lusaka to hire an investigating lawyer, and after five days searching, found that Glen had been arrested as a possible Rhodesian or South African spy. They've released him, Mom phoned me, "Sixteen years old and they didn't even tell us, we thought he'd been murdered. Glen! He couldn't spy his way out of a paper bag!" Things are getting tough up there. Richard hangs on to his job as head of the world's second largest copper refinery only because they can't replace him, but his job is becoming impossible because he can't impose discipline as before. Mom says Muf, meaning the white town, is beginning to empty and things don't feel the same any more. The good old days are gone. Richard once vowed he'd never live in South Africa again, but it looks like they'll have no choice.

Went out for a meal last night with Anne and Eddy. Marion and I were going on to the Coq D'or, so we went in separate cars. It was raining hard and we picked up a couple of people who waved us down on Second Street Extension and dropped them in town. Anne and Eddy were already at the restaurant, Eddy with a face like thunder. "Ya we passed you picking up those kaffirs, shit man what's the matter with you these days?" "It was pissing down, they were getting soaked!" "So?" Anyway the subject was soon changed, and the atmosphere became congenial. How does he view me and my actions? Adolescent, irresponsible, sentimental, a soft touch for cynical grasping or undeserving blacks, in that sense effeminate, like the do gooder who befriends criminals and can't see through them, while he, the true Rhodesian is upright, fair but unsentimental. But all that's predicated on black people being separate, different, not compatriots. I think Eddy's view of me mirrors mine of him, we're fond of each other within the family confines, actually get on well, but otherwise recognise an unbridgeable chasm, have totally separate social lives. I've had the same reaction to him, blind fury, when he wouldn't help a black guy whose car had broken down at Lake Mac. It must be how things work when families break apart in civil wars.

Our two day drives to university are odd, you learn a lot about people. I can't help dividing them into relaxed and authoritarian. Some regard the trip as a military, exercise requiring precision and efficiency. Others are easy going, living for the moment, happy to make a small detour to look at an interesting site, and if you get lost in Johannesburg, so what, let's stop at that café there while we work it out. There's always too much luggage, and the hard men battle for supremacy when packing the boot, "No man, not like that, you must put this in first then you can get those on top." Last time, just to provoke them I said, "Let's leave it to Janet, it's a girl thing," and for a minute they were speechless. In general I find rightwing sporty types more authoritarian and rigid than liberals, but this time was different. One passenger was a flamboyant beatnik type called Tom with long red hair, sandals and a beatific and comradely manner. He and his pals grow dagga at the bottom of Struben garden. We left at about ten pm, quite pissed, and the night went well, as he described how last time he hitched home he was stuck for the evening in a small Free State town. The police didn't like his appearance, pushed him around a bit, and told him to be out of the town in ten minutes or they'd "fuck him up good". Ten minutes later, on the road out of town, they came cruising past, while he hid under a culvert, and then mercifully a car picked him up a few minutes later. Anyway, back to my story, by dawn, Tom was a changed personality. When I stopped for petrol and was chatting to the attendant he leaned out all aggressive and asked, "What're you talking about, what's going on? Hurry up, we're losing time!" He and the other guy teamed up against Janet and myself and the situation deteriorated rapidly by mid morning when we wanted to stop at a nice little roadside café. The tea room was constructed entirely of wire netting covered by climbing plants, and the sun came through in spears of light. Tea and wonderful creamy melktert. "Christ man, why we stopping for tea, Jesus man Hassall you bloody woman what's the matter with you? Shit, what if someone sees us?" It was the last straw when I wanted to look round the little menagerie. In the end we were scarcely talking to each other, but recently things have looked up for Tom. During the holidays he found god, had a severe hair cut, gave up his sandals and dagga, and is becoming a good Rhodesian and potential heir to his father's farm.

But trips can be great in the right company. Brian has a Rover 90, and sometimes our two bumbling old cars travel in convoy. We take our time, stopping where we like, swopping passengers and drivers. We sing, tell jokes, play word games, and listen to the radio. "Mineral." "Is it decorative?" "Yes." "Big-end bearing," says Brian, gently lampooning Chris's preoccupation with a defective car part which would be better as a lamp stand. "Correct." In the flat Transvaal the road is straight for miles. Late at night you feel alone in this great expanse, as if at sea, but secure in your warm cockpit. You dip your lights for an approaching car, but it doesn't arrive, it disappears only to reappear, and you realise it's still five miles away. You almost form a relationship with it, your fellow traveller. We have strange experiences, at three a.m, on our second night without sleep we stop at a large brightly lit hotel and wander through its corridors and humming kitchens, unable to find anybody. We leave playing with the idea that the whole thing was a hallucination, or an alien space ship which would transmogrify and take off as soon as we left. An hour later god appears to our left in a pool of flashing red light, his face aglow, then we realise it's a train cab running parallel. At three am we stop for the night at a little country hotel, let in by a dozy night porter. We wake to a hot bright day and that fresh morning feeling, the sun at forty five degrees then, unexpectedly, it begins to set.

South Africa 1969

Maybe should have pushed harder to leave this place at the end of first year, it's becoming oppressive and I need to break out. Ma Oosthuizen my English tutor takes me aside for a gentle chat, too many smart arse comments and not enough work. Am I OK? The corrosive pressure of this conservative goldfish bowl gradually saps your self concept, you begin to see yourself as they see you, and your ego collapses. Last week on the East London road I stopped to pick up a black hitch hiker near a farm gate. The white farmer sitting in his bakkie gave me a level stare, that's all, I supplied the rest, feeling embarrassed and ashamed. Ashamed!

Elliott's dead, suicide by overdose, a note left for his parents. He wasn't the same after his return from mental hospital, lost his spark, his eyes dull, hung around with "the girls" who mollycoddled him. We, his friends wander around in shock.

July, the coldest month, there's the odd speck of snow in the rain but it never lands. We Rhodesians, who've never seen snow, phone the Hogsback Hotel in the mountains and they confirm it's on the ground there. We book for the night and head up in a convoy of three cars. Here's a different world. Arid semi desert gives way to soft deciduous forest, then pine as we wind up the precipitous dirt road. Black men on horseback, in blankets and conical hats are outlined against the sky as in a surreal western. It's overcast as we turn a corner and there, pristine and perfect lies a small pool of snow. We stop our cars and stand round it reverently. What will it feel like, soft, or hard like the frost in the freezer? Then we all dip in and destroy it. But round the corner the world's blanketed, a winter wonderland. The huge log fire at the hotel gives an Alpine feel, conjures film clichés like the prewar mountain scene in *The Young Lions* or *White Christmas*. Minutes later this is reinforced by a perfect vision of a young girl, seventeen, perhaps eighteen, beautiful, who comes in with her father. At times through the evening I catch her eye and hold it. Later when most of the public rooms have emptied, there she is, alone in a side lounge, reading. My heart thumping I sit beside her as if expected. All is going well when her Dad comes in and says roughly, "Isn't it time you were in bed?" I think, "Thanks, that would be nice," but anyway by the end of the weekend I've had a few romantic kisses and her address in Port Elizabeth.

Marion's off to Rome in September to study art. Perhaps it's a good thing. She found her mother crying because she feels Marion, in her devotion to me, is losing out on the simple pleasures of youth, different boys, an open future. Objectively I can see it. But I feel cold panic as I picture her, naïve and beautiful, the potential victim of every casual sophisticate. I've fielded various temptations, each confirming for me my devotion to her. But she, ardent, blindly sincere, will resist desperately, at first mere interest, then temptation, but finally will succumb one night to a skilled operator. The shock and guilt will convince her she no longer loves me, and I will lose her. Ironically, despite playing around, I'm the more vulnerable. At our last meeting we parked in Bots, made love, and clung together on the back seat of the Merc while she sobbed uncontrollably. I felt she knew.

Exams are over, I think I've bullshitted my way through, but not well. Graham comes out starry eyed, "I think my Chaucer paper's publishable," he says, "I've never written anything so good!" "Great! What about the other three questions?" "Oh, I didn't bother with those, no time." How will he survive without a degree? He has some idea about teaching English in Luanda, in melancholy exile with his books.

One night last week a few of us were in a café on the road out of Grahamstown, it does wonderful big homemade hamburgers. The window seat gives a good view of the road, and we watched as this car with no silencer weaved downhill towards us headed north. It struck a parked car just outside the café, bounced off, then continued on its way with an almighty scraping noise. A couple of guys jumped into their cars to give chase, and after a few seconds we heard a thud. Minutes later the driver was brought into the café, a middle aged man, blind drunk, just as a young policemen arrived, not much older than us. The man was saying, "No my boy, you must just let me go, chrys man I got kids older than you." Several police cars had now arrived, and an older policeman said, "We're not playing here, you just hit a black male up the road, he's in a serious condition. You're under arrest." Just then a black man burst in and said, "My brother is dying, we need help, who is the man who did this?" To my surprise the policeman put his arm round him. "Ne my kaffre, you can't come in here, you know that, the ambulance is coming now - now. Lets go outside and talk eh?"

Later, I was relating this in Struben, and James Anderson said, "I ran over a black child, a girl, about two years ago." "What, killed?" "Yes." "Shit, that must haunt you," I said. "No, it doesn't." "Why not?" "Because I can't stand kaffirs." "Why?" "I just can't." What shocked me was James. You'd never have expected it. He's the nicest, most considerate, caring, self effacing, polite person you can imagine. He'd do anything for you. You can understand the usual bullies having these prejudices, but why people like James?

Salisbury 1969

Back in Salisbury for Christmas, working for Dad who's offered me a permanent job. "We can really expand now, maybe even start exporting to South Africa," he says, excited. But things are flat without Marion, and I realise that few of my friends are still in the country, in fact only one or two remain from my A level cohort of about thirty. God knows where they've gone but no future for us here. It seems white Rhodesia has been inherited mainly by people from the lower streams at school, plus devotees to the cause, led on by the older generation. To quote a phrase they have it all now, but for how long? I just hope their arrogance and selfishness won't lead to the country's ruin. Ron Hughes one of my Struben friends arrives from Gwelo, he's been called up and is intent on skipping the country. He's no right of residence in Britain and is going to South America, though he can't speak the lingo. He has little money. You can say he's taking the "chicken run" but that implies some original solidarity or social contract with the cause. He says he doesn't want to kill fellow Rhodesians just because they're black and opposing minority rule, but similarly it's not right to depend for his safety on fellow white Rhodesians who are risking their lives. So, his country's lost to him and he must leave. On the morning of his departure we go in to town to buy him some supplies and he's poeping himself, seeing special branch agents everywhere. That afternoon at Salisbury airport I watch until the plane is in the air, just in case he's hauled off at the last minute, I'll probably never see him again.

Marion's letters are declining in frequency, and I'm edgy all day if I don't get one. I'm becoming ridiculous, looking under the fridge with a torch, in case a stray letter has impossibly skidded right across the kitchen from the letter box. Dad says, "You can't go on like this." Jack his mustachioed friend, ex RAF, takes me aside and says kindly, "Chaps mustn't get too stuck on one gal, chin up, plenty more." Then I got the letter saying, "There's something I have to tell you, I got off with a guy last night, it didn't mean anything, I was just feeling deprived after all this time." Like a stab to the heart, how could she, my Marion. "I got off with," the visual image, a dark nightclub? Her face, what did they do? Did she let him touch her? "Of course not!" said Janet, "She probably just kissed him, feeling lonely." Stunned, cold, shivering, I nearly had an accident sailing through a red light. After a few days I wrote back saying perhaps I could come to terms with it and didn't want to break up, but this was crossed by another letter proving Janet wrong, and "could happen again", as if outside her control. I've lost her.

South Africa 1970

Janet's gone back to varsity, she's been my friend and support in all this, almost nobody else around, and I feel I'm falling apart. Dad says I'm no good to him in this state, what do I want to do? Finally I pile into my old Merc with no real plan and drive south. When tired I pull off the road and sleep a few hours, the car and its surrounds my home. Driving off again I look back as if I've left myself behind. And so I travel stop, start, for three or four days, detouring through Durban, sometimes sitting for hours by the side of the road, with a little fire and some tea. Finally I pull into Struben car park. The guys are fantastic, there's a spare room, or someone's floor if it gets taken, and I go up to the refec for dinner as if nothing's changed.

So I settle in, reading in the morning, trying to find afternoon drinking partners, and dating girls. Yes I don't know what's happened, but somehow, being Janet's big brother, I've acquired senior status, at least at her residence, and so can benefit from the submissiveness of the latest inkettes. "Ooh, your big brother's lovely! Can I wash his car?" "By all means if she wears a short skirt and lets me splash her!" Or perhaps it's because, as one of the female liberal coterie says, "Somehow you seem more available."

After about two months the head student of Struben comes to see me. "Sorry Ian, the Prof's been happy to help for a while, but this can't go on forever, and I'm afraid you need to start making other arrangements. You can kip here a bit longer, but you need to stop eating in the refec in the next week or so." What to do? There's something bitter-sweet about this period, the blocked out past, no future, just living for the moment. Now I've taken a room behind the high street, ten Rand per month, with a tiny scruffy bathroom. I buy my food in the market and spend hours making a stew, which lasts a week or until it goes off. Janet and some of the girls sneak me food from their refec. I've started a UNISA BSc honours course in psychology and spend days needlessly reading original 19th century sources, Festinger, Titchner, Wundt, William James, Freud, good marks for my essays but already I'm two behind. I've taken up with an Afrikaans girl, Suzanne, nothing in common except my appreciation of her body, long hot afternoons on the bed, or lounging in the new "*Underground*" café, which endlessly plays the "*Bridge Over Troubled Water*" LP. Brian's become a good friend and sometimes we talk late into the night, take a midnight stroll in the dark, dreaming back streets, welcomed by a bright-eyed cat preening itself in a pool of lamplight. I play the new Beatles LP

"Let it be", and the songs feel right, end of era, sweet self pity. Enough of this, Suzanne's gone home for the holidays and my money's running out.

In Salisbury, I spent a whole morning begging Anne not to have ECT. But she's so anxious and depressed she won't listen. And I know it's not immediate causes, something deeper.

Uncle Oscar's died, another tramp on Durban beach. But not for me, I grieve as I would for a father.

Just before coming up, went to Lorenco Marques with Mark and Martin, north to Joburg then turn right through the Eastern Transvaal. As always, that euphoria as we descend to the tropical coast in sweltering heat and begin to meet lorries with loads of sugar cane or pineapples. Book in to our hotel, and then straight out to the red light district. Brightly lit and glass fronted café-bars, yellow neon street lamps, uniformed sailors, feels like a stage set from an American musical. I'm surprised to see how mixed race it is, then realise there are no black men other than waiters and barmen, just black women. I'm sitting on a bar stool with a beer when this black woman, maybe twenty, comes up and says, "Bymeandre." "Andre?" I look her up and down, usually I just don't look at black women. I think, if she had a white skin she'd be average attractive, maybe a bit skinny. She keeps pestering me, "Plis bymeandrii!" so in the end I buy her one. She sits on the stool next to me. "You wanna vuggy vuggy?" I look at her, she's improving as I drink, and I've been deprived for several weeks. She puts her hand high on my thigh and I get a jolt of arousal. The black barman says, "Good girl, is OK." The next thing we're in a taxi to her place and stop outside a dingy block of flats. She opens a door on the third floor and switches on the light, there's an unpleasant smell like stale clothes mixed with cooking. A little girl, about seven sits up in bed startled, rubbing her eyes. She protests, half crying as the woman pulls her by the arm from the bed, an older woman's voice comes from another room, and the child disappears in there. I feel like leaving, but, well here we are so I pull the woman towards me. She pushes me away and goes across to a bucket, removes her dress and pants and starts washing her fanny. She's skinnier than I thought, not a nice figure. Fine, now we're ready, I go up to her again, but again she pushes me away and starts squirting something up, then hands me a durex. There's a hard look in her eyes, not like in the bar. Her bra's still on so I try to take it off but she won't let me, pushes me away. Then she lies down on the bed in her bra and nothing else and motions me over. With rising panic I realise I've lost it, what's going on, this has never happened before, this is ridiculous! When she understands the situation she shows no surprise and fiddles with me until it comes back, but it doesn't feel right, as if there's a cushion between me and my thing and I can't feel much. Anyway, I accomplish the deed, just, and we go back in the taxi. Back in the bar it's late, old pissed Afrikaaners sitting holding hands with young black girls, recounting their misfortunes, what would mevrou think? That night I can't sleep, the whole thing going through my head. The next night we're back in the bars, joined by two black women, one big and fat, the other full figured with a pretty face. The fat one teases Martin, grabbing him and trying to kiss him. The other asks if I want to sleep with her. "No money," I say, which is true. "Do for love, you have nice face." But I'm demoralised, worried the same thing will happen, though wishing she'd been the one I met last night. We leave. But I realise how seldom I've spoken to black women, except in a functional way, and I've begun to look at them and see how attractive many are, as if a veil's been lifted.

Back in Salisbury my prick begins to hurt and I go to the doctor, the old guy I saw at Smithy's meeting, and tell him everything. He asks, "Have you got a sore or anything unusual on your penis, or anywhere else? No? Then it's not syphilis. Does it feel like you're pissing bits of glass or barbed wire? No? Then it's not gonorrhea. I suspect it's a severe case of cultural shock and imagination. As for the semi impotence, given your history, I'm sure you'll be fine next time you're with a nice girl."

Dad's ebullient, keen to get going, outlining development plans. But the place seems empty, deserted, everyone's gone, as far as I know there's not a single person from my A level class in the country. I spend Saturday nights alone with my parents, at odds with their quiet self containment. Contemplating the future I feel rising panic, claustrophobia, a stranger in my own town, well my third town, how will I meet women, will I marry? Uncertainty's better than this, I'd rather take a risk, plunge myself into something real. Finally Dad says, "All right, I'll buy you a one way ticket to England, and give you the maximum holiday allowance, £250, then you're on your own." I feel a thrill of fear and excitement.

London 1970

Here I am in London on a warm, sunny September evening, sharing a taxi from the airport with the middle aged man who sat next to me on the plane. We sweep past Buckingham Palace at my request, smaller than I expected, then Trafalgar Square where Granddad took me to see the pigeons, then up the Strand. Swinging London, a girl walks past barefoot, in a diaphanous dress, good brown legs. We stop at the

Strand Palace where Dad has booked me for two nights. I say to the man, "Give me your address and I'll send you a postcard," and he looks surprised, as if I've broken some rule, maybe I'm just trying to hold on to some contact. Up in my room, I phone Jim. Mike from Struben had said, "Don't worry, my bro Jim will put you up and you'll be OK in London," but bro's off hand, and soon makes it clear he doesn't want to be lumbered with yet another refugee from Africa "Ya, well have a good time in England, must go, bye." The same happens with all my little list, and suddenly I realise I'm totally on my own. I feel lonely, panicky, almost tearful, I'm too young for this, I want my mom. By now it's dark and I'm going outside. What will it be like, Dickensian, Second World War, swinging London? I step out and head right, towards Trafalgar Square, then Picadilly Circus with its half familiar images, then into Soho, wow those nude pictures, nothing like that in censored Rhodesia. I buy a coke, my first transaction, what a place, it's overwhelming, I'm euphoric. Unexpectedly I love the anonymity, the freedom. At first I'm self conscious, then realise no one can tell I'm foreign, I look just like them, part of the ethnic majority, one of the people, and that feels good, removing years of unnoticed pressure. But I feel unreal, an observer, a ghost.

The next morning, Sunday, is quiet and overcast. As I step out of the hotel a guy comes up and says in one of those cockney accents, "You a visitor here? Where you from? Oh Rhodesia, that's in Africa ain it? Near Nigeria? Let me take a picture for your family back home. That's a quid." I hand over a note. "And another one." "You said one quid." "Oh all right then." "Don't you want their address?" "Of course, write it here." I feel some disquiet, but surely a white man wouldn't do me on such a petty thing? But I'd better watch my cash. They say you can get a room in Earls Court for about six pounds a week, that's sixes into two fifty equals forty weeks, nearly a year, if I didn't eat, so lets say twenty weeks. They say that in Earl's Court you can meet Rhodesians on the street, I'll look for pub or waiter jobs. A guy comes up me, "Can you spare the price of a meal gov?" I give him two bob. Must stop doing that. Gov? Heard that on films, I wonder if I'm going to end up like him, they say Frank's in Marseilles living off discarded food from the markets, or will I be working class or maybe middle class? Must stop talking to myself, stop counting steps. Don't know, funny to think I was born somewhere round here.

By Ian Hassall

Glossary

The majority of words listed below are from either Afrikaans (labelled A), South African English (labelled SAE), Fanigalo (labelled F), or slang (labelled sl). Fanigalo, a pidgin based on Zulu, developed probably in 19th century Natal (South Africa) as a means of communication between whites and their servants, and then spread to the mines in the Transvaal, where it was taught as a means of communication between the various races and tribes. It spread informally across Southern and Central Africa and developed variants influenced by local African languages. The Zambia form is sometimes referred to as Chikabanga, and the Zimbabwe form as Chilapalapa. It is also sometimes referred to as Mine Zulu or Kitchen Kaffir. Today, Fanigalo is in disrepute with many Africans because of its association with colonialism and Apartheid.

The three dictionaries listed have informed the glossary, but have not been adhered to strictly where local usage seems to differ.

A

ANC African National Congress. Pro independence parties in Northern Rhodesia and South Africa

asi (F) will, as in "I will"

B

baaba (F) father

bakkie (SAE) van or light truck with open back

Bemba African language spoken on Copperbelt and into Katanga

bietchan (F) a little (quantity)

bioscope (SAE) cinema

black mamba (?) species of large poisonous snake

bliksem (A) scoundrel, bastard

blot (sl) Rhodes University second year student

blueskop (sl) large blue headed lizard

boerries (sl) short for boerwors

boerwors (SAE) farmer's sausage; now commercially produced

boma (SAE) administrative centre

boomslang (A, SAE) species of poisonous green tree snake

bopa (F) tie (knot)

BOSS Bureau for State Security (South Africa)

braai (SAE) barbecue

Broederbond Brotherhood. Secret Afrikaaner society established in 1920

buisha (F) bring

bulaala (F) kill, sometimes colloquially "beat up"

buya (F) come. **Buya lapa** come here or come to (a place)

bwana (F) white boss

C

catty (sl) catapult

chaiya (F) hit or slap, not as strong as "bulaala" or "donner", see below

Castle Castle Lager, beer popular throughout Southern Africa

Chaub (sl) pimple

checha (F) quickly

cheesa (chisa) stick (F, SAE) used to light dynamite fuses, sparks like a firework when lit

chocabloc (sl) absolutely full

choler box (F?) lunch, sandwich box

chongo (F) be quiet, shut up!

chongololo (F) large millepede

cluma (F) speak

colour bar informal or legal racial discrimination

coloured (SAE) South African of mixed descent, usually including black and white, whose first language is English or Afrikaans

coolie (SAE) Indian (derogatory)

cooldrink (SAE) soft drink

Constitutional Council A multiracial watchdog council, set up in Rhodesia to ensure the provisions of the 1961 constitution were upheld

cozzy (sl) swimming costume

Cutty Sark hotel on the sea front at Scottburg, south of Durban

D

dagga (SAE) marijuana

dassie (A, SAE) rock rabbit, hyrax

derms (A) intestines (pronounced "derrems")

dinky, dink Dinky Toy

DK (sl) double kia. A rudimentary house formed from two rondavels set apart, serving as bedrooms, joined by walls, the space providing a lounge, with an additional lean-to as a kitchen.

dooks (sl) corporal punishment with cane or plimsoll

dona (F) white woman, polite title

donner (sl), donder (SAE) beat up, thrash

dooze (F) near

donsa (F) pull

E

eina (SAE) ow, as in "Ow it's sore!"

ena (F) he, she

Engels (A) English

Eskimo Pie chocolate coated ice cream block (commercial name)

ewe (F) "Hey you" usually disrespectful

eksclaim (sl) Something like "Hey!" Literally "I exclaim", play on Afrikaans **ek** meaning I

F

Falls Victoria Falls

Fanigalo Southern African pidgin, see introduction to glossary

Federation Federation of Rhodesia and Nyasaland, 1953-1963

fray (sl) play with woman's breasts

frikkie (sl) condom

funa (F) want. **Wena funa?** would you like?

funica (F), like, similar to. **Funica so** like this

futi (F) more, again

G

ghoen (A) shooting marble, usually a metal ball bearing

ghut (sl) arse (expletive)

goffle (sl) mixed race "coloured" person. Derogatory

gonk (sl) doll-like figure, all face, made of cloth

H

hamba gashle (F) go carefully, slowly; take it easy. Also a chameleon, because of its slow, measured pace

hou links (A) keep left (traffic sign)

hout (SAE) African (derogatory). Short for **houtkop (A)** wooden head.

I

ini (F) what**. Ini ena kuna lapa pakate?** what's in it?

Indaba (F) meeting, event. **Makulu indaba** big event, trouble**; ini indaba?** why?

ink, inkette (sl) Rhodes University first year student

isa kuna (F) come here

J

jaapie (SAE) bumpkin.**(sl)** Afrikaaner (derogatory)

JD (sl) juvenile delinquent

jislaaik (SAE) exclamation of surprise or emotion

jiss (SAE) short for jislaaik

jong (A) form of address like "mate, pal"

jou (A) you

jukskei (A) game played by throwing the yoke pins of oxwaggons, said to originate in voortrekker days. Now played with wooden bottle shaped pegs.

K

ka (F) of

kaffir (SAE) black African (derogatory). Originally Muslim name for non believers

kaffir boetie (SAE) white person who likes black Africans (derogatory).

kafupi (F) short person, shorty

Kaif cafeteria at Rhodes University

kak (A) shit. **Some okes only praat kak (SAI, sl)** some guys really talk rubbish

kamina (F) my, mine

kapenta (F) very small fish, like whitebait

katina (F) ours

kia (F) house

KK Kenneth Kaunda, leader of UNIP

Knorr firm making barbecue seasoning

koeksister (SAE) twisted syrupy doughnut

kraal (A) African village

kuku (F) chicken

kuna (F) have

kwacha (Bemba) freedom, independence, literally " new dawn"

kwela (SAE, F) African pennywhistle street music

L

Lagosta a wine of that name, in a bottle shaped like a lobster

lapa (F) there, to

lekker (A) nice, good

lo (F) the, these, those

Lunar Park funfair that travelled around Southern Africa

M

maalie (F) money

ma boere (F) Afrikaaner, boer (usually derogatory)

macaque (F) monkey

makasa (F) cold

makulu (F) big

mampara (F) crook, delinquent

mambo (F) great ruler

manne (SAE) main man (men)

manze (F) water

matabele ants huge marching ants

mdala (F) old man

mealie meal (SAE) maize meal

melktert (A) creamy tart with cinnamon

mena (F) I, me

mevrou (A) married woman, madam, Mrs (polite)

mfazi (F) woman, wife

moerin (SAE) hell in, upset, (obscene origin)

moer of a (SAE) hell of a

moffie (SAE) homosexual

Mokambo small town in Congo just across the border from Mufulira

Moise Tshombe President of Katanga province which seceded from Congo in 1960. Overthrown by United Nations in 1963 but served as Congo Prime Minister 1964-5

mooi (A) pretty

munga (F) lies

munt (SAE) black African (derogatory)

mush (SAE) nice, good

mushi (F) nice, good

muti (F) medicine

muti mark (F, sl) tribal marks carved on face or chest

Mzilikazi leader of the Ndebele a Zulu breakaway group which invaded and settled in Zimbabwe in 1837

mzungu (F) white person

N

nagapie (SAE) bush baby, nocturnal lemur

nartjie (A) tangerine

Nats Nationalist Party: white supremacist, introduced apartheid. Mainly Afrikaans supported

Ndebele see Mzilikaze

njinga (F) bicycle

nkos (F) lord, god

now-now (SAE) immediately, very soon

NR Northern Rhodesia

NUSAS National Union of South African Students

nyoka (F) snake

O

one scaat (F, SAE) in one go

only (SAE) really (emphasis)

ony (SAE) really

oke (SAE) bloke, chap

okie, outjie (SAE) bloke, chap

Ossewa Brandwag Oxwagon Sentinal. Afrikaans nationalist organisation. Anti British, against South African participation in World War 2

ou (SAE) bloke, chap

ouma (A) grandmother

oupa (A) grandfather

P

pakate (F) inside. **Lapa pakate** in it

panga (F, SAE) machete

pasop (SAE) watch out, be careful

patch-patch (sl) table tennis bat-shaped wooden object used for corporal punishment. Corruption of "paddle"?

peepi joller (sl) pipsqueek, small player

pemba (F) to smoke

picannin(F) child, small

PK (F) toilet. Short for **picannin kia**, little house

Plaas (A) farm, place

poep scared (SAE) really scared, shitting yourself, literally fart scared

ponono (F) beat somebody up

porc Portuguese (derogatory)

praat (A) talk

puza (F) eat, drink

Q

quela (F) climb, ascend, sit

R

RF Rhodesian Front. White supremacist party led by Ian Smith

RLI Rhodesian Light Infantry

RP Rhodesia Party. In favour of white control, leadership, but open to "partnership" with blacks. Lead by Sir Roy Welensky

rondaval (SAE) house shaped like a round hut, usually constructed of modern materials

RRAF Royal Rhodesian Air Force

S

sambo (sl) sandwich

Sir Humphrey Gibbs Governor General of Rhodesia, 1959-1970.

Sir Roy Sir Roy Welensky, Prime Minister of the Federation of Rhodesia and Nyasaland, 1956-1963

sis (SAE) expression of disgust

situpa (F) pass book

sjambok (SAE) rhinoceros hide whip

skaap (SAE) crude person, literally sheep

skate (sl) low life, yob, chaav, (perhaps derived from cheapskate)

skop die blik (SAE) kick the tin, a form of hide and seek

skrik (A) fright

smaak (A) to like. **(SAE)** to fancy someone

sommer (SAE) just, suddenly, for no reason

soutie (SAE) Englishman. Abbreviation of **soutpiel,** salty penis, because one foot in England the other in Africa and penis in the sea

seer (A) sore, painful

SR Southern Rhodesia

sterek (F) a lot, very

Stephen Biko Steve Biko. Founded Black Consciousness Movement. Murdered in police custody in 1977

stompie (SAE) cigarette butt

Stormjaers storm troopers. Para military wing of Ossewa Brandwag

sucker (SAE) flat lollipop

susu (sl) sixpence

T

tackie (SAE) plimsoll

tata (F) take

tickey (SAE) threepence

tic toc (sl) game of knocking on doors and running away

tokolosh (F) evil spirit

totsiens (A) see you soon, good bye

touchers (sl) game of tag

U

Umkhonto we Sizwe Spear of the Nation. Armed wing of the African National Congress (ANC)

UNIP United National Independence Party. Pro independence party, Northern Rhodesia

UNISA University of South Africa

United party somewhat more moderate than Nats, but still supporting white supremacy. Supported mainly by English speakers

V

velskoens (SAE) suede ankle length shoe

vlei (A) low land, valley

voetsek (SAE) get lost! Go away (disrespectful)

vrou (A) woman, wife

W

wena (F) you

Z

ZANU Zimbabwe African National Union founded by Ndabaningi Sithole, Edgar Tekere and others in 1963, later led by Robert Mugabe

ZAPU Zimbabwe African People's Union founded by Joshua Nkoma in 1961

zonke scaat (F) always

References

Branford, J. 1980. A Dictionary of South African English. Oxford University Press, Capetown.

Kromhout, J. 1997. Klein Woordeboek. Little Dictionary. Pharos, Capetown.

Morkel, T. Dictionary. Fanigalo/Chilapalapa/Chikiwa English/Maboona. Sable Publishing House, Ilminster.

About the Author

Ian Hassall was born in England and went to Northern Rhodesia in 1951 aged four. His father's sister had arrived in 1946 to recover from TB in the African sun. Post-war work opportunities being poor in Britain, Ian's parents decided to emigrate to this land of milk and honey (for whites). His father's first job was with Costains, a construction firm in Chingola near the Congo border, literally carving a town out of the bush. The family lived in a hut and Ian can still remember being excited by the primitive conditions and wildlife. Then his father gained employment on Mufulira Copper Mine as a fitter and turner. He pretended to be qualified, saying his certificates had been destroyed when the family home was bombed during the war. He had some engineering experience and just learned the trade as he went along.

The story of the rest of Ian Hassall's youth, in Mufulira, Ndola, Harare and Grahamstown is told in the book. He came to England in the early 1970s as a foreigner. Now he lives a lazy retired life in the north of England with his second wife, growing some forlorn banana trees in a difficult climate, and still dreaming of Africa.

Lightning Source UK Ltd.
Milton Keynes UK
UKHW011021200820
368550UK00002B/698

9 781456 614454